Advance Praise For *Sting*

"Next time I get in trouble, I'm calling Cash
McCahill. There's nothing he can't handle.
Do yourself a favor and grab a copy of Paul
Coggins's page-turning thriller *Sting Like a
Butterfly*. Money and drugs, cartel honchos,
courtroom drama—this book has it all. I can't
wait for the next one."

—Harry Hunsicker, Former Executive
Vice President of the Mystery Writers of
America and Author of *Texas Sicario*

"Paul Coggins's electrifying, whip-smart *Sting
Like a Butterfly* is an adrenaline-soaked thrill
ride (in a cherry-red Carrera, no less) through
the twisted underworld of the drug cartel. If
you ever find yourself on the wrong side of
the law, make sure you've got Cash McCahill's
number handy."

— Will Clarke, *Rolling Stone*'s
"Hot Pop Prophet" and author of
*The New York Times* Editors' Choice,
*Lord Vishnu's Love Handles*

"Attorney Cash McCahill is trash-talking,
conniving, and quick with a quip—the
kind of lawyer you love to hate until he's all
that's standing between you and prison. Paul

Coggins's *Sting Like a Butterfly* takes readers on a thrilling roller coaster ride through the underbelly of the cartel world, with twists you don't see coming. Buy a copy and fasten your seatbelt!"

—Glenna Whitley, investigative reporter and author of *Stolen Valor*

"Cash McCahill is money in the bank for this Paul Coggins thriller, *Sting Like a Butterfly*. It's hard to put this one down!"

—Johnathan Brownlee, Filmmaker/ Director/Writer, *Three Days in August* and the upcoming true crime thriller, *The Eyes of Jefferson*

# STING LIKE A
# BUTTERFLY

# STING LIKE A
# BUTTERFLY
## PAUL COGGINS

A SAVIO REPUBLIC BOOK
An Imprint of Post Hill Press
ISBN: 978-1-64293-379-6
ISBN (eBook): 978-1-64293-378-9

Sting Like a Butterfly
© 2020 by Paul Coggins
All Rights Reserved

Cover Design by Jomel Cequina

posthillpress.com
New York • Nashville
Published in the United States of America

*To Becky, Gina and Jess–*
*Three Generations of Brilliant, Beautiful, and Bold Women*

I dreamt I was a butterfly,
fluttering around in the sky;
then I awoke. Now I wonder:
Am I a man who dreamt of
being a butterfly, or am I a
butterfly dreaming that I am a man?
Zhuangzi

# CHAPTER ONE

Cash McCahill stared into the broken mirror in the cell he shared with the psycho of Seagoville Federal Correctional Institution and the newbie on suicide watch.

Both cellmates made the long list of Cash's clients on the inside. Despite the loss of his law license, he had never been busier, filing appeals, habeas petitions, divorce papers, and the like. A tried and true jailhouse lawyer.

Actually, a tried and convicted jailhouse lawyer.

Muted sobbing wafted from the bottom bunk belonging to Big Black. Not from the behemoth himself, but from Martin Biddle, who should know better than to risk rousing the slumbering beast. Biddle hadn't yet come to accept his place in the pecking order without whimpering.

Cash couldn't see Biddle, who was wedged between Big Black and the wall. During his first month inside, the young husband and father of twin girls had been rechristened Marti and starved to a present weight of a buck-thirty. A blonde wig, heavy makeup, and lingerie completed the transformation from the chief financial officer of a high-flying investment firm to a prison punk.

Cash turned back to his split-level reflection in the mirror. He didn't have time to comfort Biddle. Not this morning anyway.

Two years in the joint had hardened Cash, but not to the point he could completely shut out the sobbing. He dished out a healthy dose of tough love. "What are you moaning about?"

"I miss my wife." Biddle's lament led to more crying.

Cash took a shot at humor. "Yeah, I miss your wife too. Now go to sleep."

"You asshole." Pent-up anger sparked a flicker of fight in Biddle.

Mission accomplished.

"Keep your voice down," Cash said. "You wake him, and it's your ass on the line, literally."

"You promised to get me out of here." The fight drained from Biddle's voice, replaced by resentment.

Cash sighed. If he had a dollar for every warning to a client that there were no guarantees in criminal law.... "I'm working on your appeal as fast as I can."

Biddle sat up in the bunk. "What are my chances?" He clutched something to his chest.

Cash didn't have to see the treasured object to know what Biddle held. A picture of his wife and daughters. The last link to a past life that was slipping away.

"Like I told you yesterday and the day before and like I'll tell you again tomorrow, you've got a good shot, which is more than ninety-nine percent of your fellow inmates have."

True enough. Biddle's trial lawyer was the poster boy for ineffective assistance of counsel. A hack who couldn't spell acquittal, much less score one. Cash had read the trial transcript twice and still couldn't decide whether the defense lawyer had been incompetent, lazy, crooked, or all of the above.

"Get some shut-eye," Cash said, "and we'll talk tomorrow."

"I can't sleep."

Cash knew the feeling, though Big Black certainly didn't. The beast chugged along like an outboard motor stuck in low gear, misfiring every few beats. Drool slicks spread across his pillow. Most nights he could sleep through a riot. On the few he couldn't, pity the poor fool who woke him.

Cash turned back to the mirror and the deadly serious business at hand. Nearly four a.m. Only five hours to show time.

Stripped to his shorts and socks, he launched into his pre-trial ritual. A quick run-through of his opening argument. Hurl the remains of what could be his last meal into the shit-stained toilet. Another rehearsal, slower this time and with more feeling. Followed by the dry heaves. Shave, shower, and slip on a power suit.

The hurling and dry heaves weren't actually part of his outside world ritual. Not since his first trial twenty years ago, anyway. Then again, today would be the first hearing with *his* life on the line.

Hence, the dicey gut.

The bedsprings groaned. Cash glanced nervously at the bunk. BB's massive arm dangled over the side of the bed. Misshapen fingers brushed the concrete floor. A single letter tattooed in white on each digit. B-E-A-R.

A tatt of a grizzly on its hind legs stretched from BB's elbow to his shoulder. Teeth bared. Claws out. Eyes wild with bloodlust. A triple-decker bicep bulged the bear's belly, as if it had swallowed someone whole.

A terrifying tatt so garish and badly drawn that it had to be a prison job. Minimal production values, maximum pain.

If only BB would hibernate for a few months. Or years. Anything to put off today's hearing on his most recent write-up.

The tatt reminded Cash to keep his voice down during the rehearsal of his opening argument. Let sleeping bears lie. As much as BB had riding on the outcome, Cash had even more.

For BB, the accused, a loss meant the hole for anywhere from three to six months. Having been shot once, stabbed twice, and clubbed more times than he could count, he wouldn't blink at the threat of another beating.

Bring on the billy clubs.

But the prospect of a stretch in solitary shook BB to the core. Prisoners didn't come back from the hole, not with all their marbles anyway. The longer the isolation, the more scrambled the brain.

Next stop after the hole: the looney bin.

For Cash, the stakes were higher. He had a legion of enemies inside the cold, gray walls, and not all of them were guards. A handful of former clients doing time at Seagoville blamed him for allowing a grave carriage of justice to be done. Even non-clients saw in him the same species of predatory scum who had bled them dry, then let them down.

Guilt by Bar Association.

And where were the worthless wretches who had been spared their just desserts by the grace of Cash's fast tongue and fancy footwork in the courtroom? On the outside, of course, and of no help.

Destined to suffer for the sins of the system, Cash had found refuge under the wings of a guardian devil. From day one at Seagoville, BB had made him a protected species: a jailhouse lawyer with real skills. The word had gone out not to mess with the mouthpiece.

The catch is, BB could lift the protection at any time and for any or no reason. For example, if today's hearing went badly.

Cash stopped kidding himself. How could the shit-show not go south? A kangaroo court behind bars before a hanging judge, who hated the counsel even more than the accused.

"May it please the warden." Cash's breath fogged the mirror. "Marcus Allen DuPree stands before you on charges of insubordination and assaulting a correctional officer. If convicted, he faces—"

A loud fart interrupted the dry run and echoed down the cellblock, sparking a chain reaction among the inmates. Happened every time the mess served rice and beans for dinner, heavy on the beans.

BB grinned from ear-to-ear. The sleep of the not so innocent.

Cash lifted his lucky jumpsuit up to the mirror. "McCahill, not everyone can pull off this color, but you look damn good in orange."

Biddle lapsed into a fresh round of sobbing.

"I'll get your brief filed," Cash whispered, "even if it's the last thing I do."

# CHAPTER TWO

*Two years, five months, and three days ago*

The gavel came down hard.

Federal Judge Anna Tapia, face red and lips white, sprang to her feet. "I want the lawyers in my chambers. Now."

Though pushing fifty and barely five-feet-one, *Her Honor* towered from the bench over the mere mortals quaking below. No doubt who ran her courtroom.

Donning the black robe had a nasty side effect of inflaming a person's ego. Lawyers had a name for the incurable disease. Called it judgeitis. Fatal to all but the carrier.

Tapia had a raging case of it. Even back in her days as a federal prosecutor, she could reduce hostile witnesses to rubble and opposing counsel to mush. Lifetime tenure turned her into a holy terror.

Cash stood his ground. "Your honor, before we adjourn to chambers, may I get an answer from the witness to my pending question?"

"What part of *now* do you not understand, Mister McCahill?" the judge said.

*Shit.* Cash's cross-examination had set a trap for the weasel-faced witness on the stand. IRS Agent Marty Shafer looked as if he had swallowed a toad. His Adam's apple bobbed, and his beady eyes ballooned. Even his forced smile had faded.

The break gave the prick a chance to huddle with the prosecutors and cook up a better answer to the out-of-the-blue question of whether his supervisor had disciplined him last month.

Based on the judge's tone, Cash had bigger problems than an aborted cross. After turning away from the lawyers and toward the jury box, Tapia shifted from sarcastic to solicitous. "Jurors, we'll take our afternoon break a little early today. Please be back and ready to resume the trial by 3:15."

Smooth as silk. Almost as if she were running for office.

As the jurors filed from the courtroom, Cash flashed a this-is-all-part-of-the-game smile. Jurors numbers seven and ten smiled back. The grandmotherly seven had a *Wheel of Fortune* fixation, and ten was the looker of the group.

Good sign.

Once the jurors were gone, the judge practically flew off the bench, robe flapping like bat wings. Twice before during the trial, she had lowered the boom on Cash. The first infraction had drawn a warning. The second, a five hundred dollar fine.

Seated at the government table, the one nearer the jury box, the prosecutor Jenna Powell let out a long exhale, the heat having shifted from her witness to Cash. Her gray eyes saw the world in black and white, and long ago he had shed the white hat. She gave him a serves-you-right shrug.

"You're in deep shit now," she whispered from five feet away. "Three strikes in this court, and you're out."

"No sweat. Got an airtight defense." His banter failed to slow his racing heart. "How can I be expected to remember the rules of evidence when I'm litigating against a woman I used to sleep with?"

Jenna's expression hardened into full-blown anger. "I can see how that would be a big problem for you. During our brief time together, a period I call *the year I lost my fricking mind,* you tried to nail every woman between seventeen and seventy who had the misfortune of crossing your path."

"For the record, there were no seventeen-year-olds."

She slammed shut her portfolio and tucked it under her arm. "Can't wait to hear you try to talk your way out of this jam."

"I should sell tickets."

"Good idea," she said, "since you're about to lose your meal ticket."

Jenna's heels clicked on the hardwood floor as she hurried toward chambers. He watched her walk and ached for what he had thrown away. Not just his best girl and his best job, but also his best life.

He could watch her all day. Just not today. Not with a contempt charge hanging over his head, and breathing down his neck a mob defendant facing twenty years behind bars.

As Cash rose, the defendant, Larry Benanti, grabbed his arm and pulled him back to his seat. The five-feet-five-inch Benanti had a history of dragging people down to his level. His padded shoes and sweeping pompadour signaled a desperate attempt to create the illusion of height.

"Do I go back there with you?" Benanti said.

"Lawyers only this time. Sit tight, stay out of the line of fire, and keep your mouth shut. I'll be back in five."

*With my shield or on it.*

Benanti's lips turned as white as his knuckles. "You're killing me, man. That judge fucking hates you, and she's going to take it out on me."

"She hates all defense lawyers. Besides, I'm not playing to her. I'm working on them." He nodded toward the empty jury box.

On the way to chambers, Cash passed by the witness on the stand. Shafer leaned forward in the hot seat. With the judge and jury gone, he defaulted to his natural smirk. A pair of handcuffs dangled from his forefinger, the cuffs swinging like twin nooses.

Cash got the point. Would've had to be blind not to. One noose for him; the other for his client. Shafer had all the subtlety of a sledgehammer.

* * *

The Wild West motif of Tapia's chambers harkened back to the days of Judge Roy Bean and frontier justice. Hang the sonovabitch first and then give the corpse a fair trial.

Oil paintings of cowboys, quarter horses, and cattle staked their claims to prime wall space. Above and behind the seated Tapia loomed a framed display of famous Texas brands, with her family mark dead center: a circle around an upside-down T. A well-worn saddle hugged a wooden bench. A coiled rope hung from the horn.

The trappings reminded visitors of Tapia's nickname: *The Hanging Judge.* Not that Cash needed reminding of that.

"Mister McCahill, explain why you thought it permissible to cross-examine Agent Shafer on his investigation of an unrelated case, after I had warned you twice not to go there." The judge's tone was perfect for lecturing a third grader.

Cash chalked up Tapia's smooth brow to a recent round of Botox that had left her face, like the chambers, frozen in time. He looked around the room. Just the judge, Jenna, and him in a space that could easily hold twenty.

No court reporter in sight. Could be a good sign. Can't sanction for contempt without an official record, not for the finding to hold up on appeal anyway.

Or possibly a bad sign. No extra witnesses to the carnage to come.

"Of course, your honor." He stalled, looking to Jenna for a lifeline. She dodged eye contact. No help there. Hail Mary time. Lean on the loopiest of loopholes. "I have reason to believe that Shafer has recently been disciplined by his agency for hiding exculpatory evidence from the prosecution and, by extension, from the defense."

"In this case?" the judge said.

"In an investigation being conducted at or near the same time as this one."

Tapia tensed for the kill. She placed both elbows on the rough-hewn desk, steepled her forefingers and rested her chin on the peak. "How does that not violate my order prohibiting you from questioning the witness about alleged *Brady* violations?"

Cash didn't blink, nor miss a beat. "I don't intend to ask Shafer if he has violated the Supreme Court's landmark ruling in *Brady versus Maryland*, which he has done repeatedly throughout his checkered career. Instead, my question is whether he failed to follow the procedures set out in the IRS manual and has been disciplined on that score. Totally different line of inquiry."

Tapia's eyebrows twitched. Probably the closest simulation of a frown she could manage. "That's cutting it mighty close, Mister McCahill."

"While all the time following the letter of your ruling."

"What about the spirit of my ruling? Did you abide by it?"

"I believe in letters, Your Honor, not spirits."

"Then I'll make my new ruling crystal clear and put it in writing this time. I'm barring any inquiry outside this particular investigation of this specific indictment. That means no questions to the agent about violating *Brady*, the agency manual, the Ten Commandments, or any other rules, regulations, or laws in connection with other investigations. Do I make myself clear?"

"Painfully clear, and may I have my objection to your *new* ruling placed on the record?" No reason to let temporary relief over dodging a bullet deter him from playing another round of Russian roulette.

"Of course. Now let's move on. I'd like to finish this trial before my grandkids have grandkids."

Back in the courtroom, Cash caught his client talking to the agent, still on the stand. He pulled Benanti away. "What did I tell you about talking to the government?"

Benanti's neck veins bulged. "We weren't discussing the case."

Cash pointed to a smiling Shafer. "When that cold-hearted bastard goes to bed at night, he dreams of ways to put you in prison. And when he wakes up the next day, the first thing on his mind is how to fuck you over. When he says hello, you say goodbye and run like hell. Better yet, don't bother saying goodbye. Just run like hell."

The defendant snorted. "Funny, but the way he's looking at you now, I could swear that he's thinking of ways to send you to the big house."

# CHAPTER THREE

*Two years, five months, and one day ago*

A black butterfly landed on Cash's shoulder.

"Don't move," Larry Benanti shouted.

Cash froze on the porch of the Highland Park mansion. *Screw this.* He flicked the butterfly away. It loop-de-looped before fluttering to freedom.

"You shouldn't have done that." Benanti sounded bat shit serious. "I just lost a rare species, but you lost a lot more."

"What are you talking about?"

"Legend has it that the black butterfly steals the souls of sinners and sends them straight to hell."

"I'll have lots of company." *Present client included.*

Benanti shuddered, a sign he bought into the legend. "If you'd gotten here five minutes earlier, you would've run into that bitch from probation."

"Sandy Robinson?" Cash said.

Benanti nodded.

"What was she doing here?"

"Said it was a court-ordered home visit."

That struck Cash as odd. Not the home visit part, which was routine. But after hours? What government worker does that?

"Now she's someone who really will steal your soul," Cash said, "along with your body."

He followed Benanti inside. The ostentation of the place never ceased to amuse him. Greco-Roman palace, meet Jersey Shore.

A nude statue of Mariposa, his current wife, greeted guests in the foyer. The statues of wives one and two collected dust in the attic, banished there by Mariposa. Busts of Roman emperors lined the long hallway. The last and largest bust, a flattering likeness of Benanti.

The passageway split into two forks, wrapping around a glass-enclosed hothouse and indoor pool. The hothouse teemed with a jungle of plants and flowers of every size, shape, and color. An ever-changing kaleidoscope of butterflies bathed the enclosure in a rainbow of hues. More species than Cash could count.

Benanti had stolen a page from the Bellagio Botanical Gardens. Not the only thing he had lifted from the Vegas landmark.

In a black string bikini, Mariposa cut clean strokes though the cobalt water. In a past life, she had been the lead dancer at the Bellagio in a midnight revue called *Leather and Lace*, the act heavy on the leather part. Her Vegas stage name had been Wicked Wanda, but her real name and arrest record remained buried in some bought-off bureaucrat's dead files.

Mesmerized by Mariposa's flip turn, Cash fell another step behind Benanti. She barely broke the surface. Just a flash of leg visible for a nanosecond. But enough of a sighting to cloud his judgment.

Cash caught up with his host in the split-level study. Benanti closed the double doors and sat behind a massive mahogany desk on an elevated platform. The higher ground allowed him to look down on Cash.

Even had they been on equal footing, the concave couch would've wiped out Cash's height advantage. His eyes swept across rows of hardback classics lining three walls. None read, few ever opened. The books, like the wife, there for show.

A large map of the Americas dominated the fourth wall. On the map a half-dozen red arrows flowed from points on the Northeastern seaboard of the United States, converged in Central Texas and petered out in the Sierra Madre Mountains of Mexico. Cash mistook it for a weather map until he made out the caption:

MIGRATION PATTERN OF THE
MONARCH BUTTERFLY.

"What's the deal with you and butterflies?" Cash said.

Benanti's eyes lit up. "What other creature on the planet begins life so ugly and blossoms so beautifully?"

"You tell me," Cash said.

"They're like the women I rescue from lives of poverty and despair. I take caterpillars and turn them into butterflies."

*Yeah, that's one way to describe a sex trafficking ring.*

"But don't butterflies have a short lifespan?" Cash said.

"Isn't a brief burst of beauty better than a long life of ugliness?"

"Not sure about that," Cash said, "but I'm willing to bet that a short life on the outside is better than a long one in prison. So let's focus on the trial and make sure you get to stick around to enjoy all the beauty you've created."

Benanti frowned. "The trial, it's not going well."

Cash sighed. Not this again. No resting on laurels with the underworld's biggest ingrate. Nor could he take comfort in the calmness of the client's tone, not given his hair-trigger temper. The wrong word, even an untimely pause could set him off.

"I understand that you don't enjoy being put on trial. That's rational. What's not is second-guessing the lawyer who has gotten you off twice before."

"Those two victories came in state court. This time we're up against the feds. This is the big leagues."

"Look, you pay me to win. State or federal court makes no difference. Same bottom line. Win and you go home. Lose and you spend the rest of your life in prison."

"Do I need to remind you how much I pay you to win?"

Cash shook his head. "You bring that up every day, and I've already had today's reminder."

"For the fortune I'm shelling out, I own you, body and soul."

"Except that according to the legend, my soul is gone." Cash smiled.

Benanti didn't. "You owe me your undivided attention, and I'm not getting it. Not sure what's occupying your mind these days, but your zipper problem is no secret. Got something you want to get off your chest, Romeo?"

Cash's heart stopped. Moment of untruth time. Because in the circumstances, the truth would not set him free. At best it might buy him a quick death, rather than a slow, agonizing one.

So he fell back on rule number one: never cop to anything until you know what the other side has on you.

"Like what?" Cash said.

"Like why you're playing footsy with the hot prosecutor. Maybe that stuck-up bitch has got you thinking with the wrong head...has you confused over which team you're on."

Cash breathed easier. He was still pissed that Benanti questioned his loyalty, but at the same time relieved to have him barking up the wrong bed.

"It wasn't that long ago you shared an office with her." Benanti's voice took on a harder edge. "Maybe you're angling to get your old job back, along with the snatch that went with it."

"That's ancient history," Cash said. "My old job wouldn't cover my car payments now, and Jenna and I, we split up years ago. Sure, the sex was great, but her holier-than-thou sermons got old."

Benanti rose from behind the desk. Bad move. The closer he came, the less imposing he seemed. "If I don't go home after the trial, no one does."

"Really not helpful to threaten your lawyer at this stage of the proceeding. I told you from the get-go that there are no guarantees in my business."

"There are in mine," Benanti said.

Cash sprang to his feet but stifled his instinct to tell Benanti where to shove the threat. No way to win a war of words with this client—to win a war of any kind with him.

Cash sat first. "What say we get down to the business at hand? The prosecutor called after court today. Her final offer stays on the table until nine a.m. tomorrow. If you cop to the conspiracy count, she'll drop the rest of the charges. That's five years max, but you'll do only four inside. Maybe three if I can squeeze you into a halfway house early."

"Tell your girlfriend I won't do three hours behind bars and give her my final offer. If it's a body she's after, my bean counter will do the time."

"You want your accountant to take the fall?"

"Yeah, and he'll go away for ten years if that's what it takes to get her off my back. That way she has her precious stat, and I keep my freedom. Win-win."

"That's not how it works," Cash said. "You can't trade down. You can only trade up."

"What the hell does that mean?" Jersey roots surfaced in his voice.

"Jenna's not in the market for a flunky. To hook her, you'd need to offer a target she wants more than you. That means someone higher on the food chain."

Benanti's eyes narrowed. "Not going to happen."

Cash knew it wouldn't. Much as Benanti liked to dress in black and play the godfather role, he answered to higher powers outside the country. But he'd never admit to playing second banana, and Cash couldn't call him on it.

"That leads to the next decision point. I expect the government to rest its case tomorrow."

"So you start putting on my defense then?"

"No. I plan to rest right after the government does and get the jury deliberating as soon as possible." A long silence felt like a lifetime.

"Are you telling me that I'm paying you two million dollars to put on no evidence for me?"

"You're paying me two million dollars to know when to take our case to the jury, and I'm worth every cent of it."

The door to the study banged open, and Mariposa stood at the threshold. She looked stunning, even swallowed by a terry cloth robe, wet hair, and no makeup. An olive complexion allowed her to pass as a native in a host of hot-climate countries. Her cheekbones could cut ice. Green eyes locked on her husband, as if Cash were invisible.

"I'm going to a late movie with Elena. Don't wait up for me." The hard-to-pin-down accent hinted at a globe-trotting youth. Tonight, a dash of Puerto Rican swagger mixed with Valley Girl vanity.

"Don't wake me when you come in," Benanti said. "Big day in court tomorrow. My mouthpiece is going to catch the feds flat-footed, so wear something nice."

"But conservative," Cash said. "A dark blue suit. Not too short, not too tight, and—"

She left before he could finish.

"Almost be worth taking the lousy deal," Benanti said, mostly to himself, "just to get away from...."

Cash did a double take. "There are less drastic ways to leave a spouse. I can recommend a good divorce lawyer."

"Yeah, that'd be one way to do it." Benanti's tone made it clear it wouldn't be his.

"What say we get you out of this jam before you jump into another?"

Benanti shrugged.

Cash took his silence as a green light to the game plan. "So you're on board with resting our case right after the government does?"

"What choice do I have?" Benanti sounded resigned to his fate. "But dammit, I had my heart set on testifying."

Pure, unadulterated bullshit, but Cash didn't call him on it. No way did this client, or any other for that matter, really want to take the stand. They just needed someone to play daddy and tell them no. If Benanti were to make the fatal mistake of testifying, Jenna would beat him like a piñata.

"I count at least five jurors leaning our way," Cash said, "and we need only one to stay strong. We rest our case tomorrow."

Benanti banished him with a whisk of the hand. Meeting over. Trial nearly so.

On the way out, Cash couldn't help but glance at the pool. Empty now. The last ripples of the swimmer's wake gently lapped the deck. A funnel cloud of butterflies swept across the hothouse.

Cash slipped into the driver's seat of his Carrera and reached for the gearshift. His hand touched something cold and damp. He pulled back.

A black string bikini draped the shift.

No question who had put it there. Or why.

The black butterfly landed on the windshield. Cash gunned the Carrera, and the butterfly took off.

# CHAPTER FOUR

*Two years, five months, and one day ago*

"Liar."

Not a trace of anger in Eva Martinez's voice. Just rock solid certainty that her B.S. detector had caught Cash in a lie. Tonight's whopper, that he'd been about to call her when she got him on the line.

On the cusp of downtown Dallas, Cash slowed the cherry-red Carrera to twenty miles an hour over the speed limit. "How could you possibly know I was lying?"

"Your lips were moving."

*Shit.* Busted by his bloodhound of an assistant and only blocks from the Ritz. Sure, he should've called her from Benanti's mansion, but if he had, she would've told him to come straight to the office.

Would've been game over for him. Do not pass go. Do not shell out three hundred dollars for a junior suite. And definitely do not carve another notch on the bedpost.

"I've been cooling my heels at the office for over two hours," Eva said, "and our jury instructions are due by nine a.m. tomorrow. You can't afford to piss off the judge, again." A trace of panic spiked her voice. "So why the hell aren't you already here?"

"Well, I had to—"

"And don't lie to me again."

Damn, she was good. Gave him no choice but to resort to a half-truth.

"I have one more appointment tonight. Very important. But I'll be there in under an hour."

"Who is she?"

He slipped back into the defense lawyer's default mode. Flat-out lying, forgivable in the circumstances because she wouldn't buy a word of it anyway. "No one you know. Besides, a gentleman never tells."

"I'll keep that in mind in the unlikely event I encounter a gentleman while working for you. We're on deadline, so I don't give a rat's ass if you're in hot pursuit of Penelope Cruz. You don't have time to chase tail tonight, and I don't have time to hunt you down."

"If only you were more flexible in your choice of bedtime companions, I wouldn't be forced to search the city for a soul-mate with benefits. Remind me why we've never hooked up."

"I've got a brain, and you're not my type."

"I just hope that when you get past this experimental phase you're going through and fall head over heels for me, it's not too late." He pulled into the circular drive at the Ritz and parked behind a Bentley. "Now hammer out a draft of our jury instructions. Use the Crawford case as a go-by. I'll be there in an hour or less to review it."

He dropped the call before she could bust his balls and tossed the keys to the valet. "Pull my wheels out of sight, Stevie. And for the record, you haven't seen me tonight."

"Sure, Mister McCahill, or whatever your name is this evening." Stevie flashed a you-dog-you smile.

Intoxicated by the scent of top-shelf perfume in the lobby, Cash regained his swagger. A quick survey of the talent on display, weak even for a Wednesday. At least three horny dudes hovered around every hottie at the bar. Plying their not so helpless prey with hard liquor. Laughing too hard at her lame jokes. Trying too hard, period.

*Hard* being the operative word here.

But Cash liked his odds anyway. With his target set, no need to cull the pros from the cons at the bar. Or wade through the horndogs with wads of bills stuffed in one pocket and packets of Trojans in the other.

The only glitch, no Mariposa in sight. Odd, she'd left the mansion minutes before he had. She should be on her second Vodka Collins by now. Liquored, lubed, and looking for love.

Or as close as she'd come to it in this lifetime.

He landed at a table far from the bar action and ordered a scotch and soda. Checked the messages on his iPhone to see if she'd been forced to scratch the date. Nothing.

After a second drink, he was about to leave when a woman emerged from the shadows and approached him. Not Mariposa, but not bad. And vaguely familiar. The freckled face more so than the tight body. And growing more recognizable by the step.

She reached the table and extended her hand. He took it before clicking on her identity. She was Juror Number Ten.

The looker in the lot and the best bet to buck the initial rush to convict.

Ten pulled her hand away. "This concludes the business portion of our meeting."

Cash recoiled. "I don't—"

Twin laser dots, red as blood, jitterbugged across his chest.

# CHAPTER FIVE

*Two years, five months, and one day ago*

"Hit the floor! Get down! Down!"

Agents shouted on the run, arms drawn. Their choppy words echoed across the Ritz lobby.

The din of iniquity froze. A pianist stopped mid-tune, bringing an abrupt end to "The Days of Wine and Roses."

Fearful of being caught in the crossfire, Cash backed away from Juror Number Ten. The first agent hit him high. The second went low, sweeping him off his feet. He landed face-first on the marble floor.

Dazed, Cash processed the takedown as an out-of-body experience. The swirl of action unfolded around him in slow motion. Shouts and screams topped each other.

Cash's head-butt to the floor dulled his senses, sparing him from a world of pain. Or so he thought until a knee dug into his spine, and his arms were roughly pulled behind his back.

*Click. Click.* The metal teeth of cuffs bit into his wrists. The harder he struggled, the deeper the bite. Tears blurred his vision of a forest of black boots. The forest parted to make way for a pair of scuffed wingtips.

The takedown team yanked him to his feet, wrenching his shoulders. He gritted his teeth to keep from screaming in pain. Kept them clenched while a third agent frisked him, seizing an iPhone, a Montblanc pen, and a wallet.

IRS Agent Marty Shafer, rocking back and forth on the wingtips, grabbed Cash's wallet. "Let's see how the crooked half lives." He thumbed through the bills. "Looks to be about seven hundred bucks. Plus, a half-dozen credit cards to stores I can't afford to set foot in. A bar card, which fortunately you won't have much longer. And hello, what do we have here?" He fished out two Hard Rider ribbed condoms. "Size, extra-large." He snickered. "Don't flatter yourself, McCahill."

Shafer opened his jacket to reveal a pistol on one hip and a pair of handcuffs on the other. His thin lips curled into the same shit-eating grin he'd flashed in the courtroom earlier that day.

"Dammit, the FBI was supposed to let me slap on the cuffs." Shafer's ire sounded real. "Guess I'll have to settle for the honor of booking you."

"Step back, Marty," Cash said, "or at least have the decency to suck on a breath mint."

Shafer's face turned red. "That's right, funny man, keep running your mouth. That'll go over big in prison."

"Whoa!" Cash kept his voice steady, but his heartbeat raced ahead of his tongue. "Since when did bumping into a juror by coincidence draw time?"

"You call it coincidence," Shafer said. "I call it jury tampering."

Cash resisted the urge to blurt out a denial. For every suspect who talked his way out of trouble, a thousand dug themselves a deeper hole.

Shafer tucked the condoms back in the wallet. "Don't bother trying to feed us some cock-and-bull story about coming here to get lucky. The only person you'll end up fucking tonight is yourself." He turned to the FBI agents. "Take him away."

The perp walk wound through the lobby. Cash took a last look around, searching for a friendly face. Finally settling on a pretty one.

Actually, two pretty ones.

Evidently Juror Number Ten had just been elected prom queen. Beaming, backslapping agents clustered around the blonde. The geezer in the takedown squad fetched her a drink from the bar, while a striking, six-foot female agent rifled through her purse.

Cash recognized the Amazon Agent. Maggie Burns, a.k.a. MagDoll, counted aloud the fat wad of cash she had pulled from Ten's purse. He caught Maggie's eye and gave her a knowing smile. She blushed and started the count over.

After placing the bills in a clear evidence packet and sealing it, Maggie removed from Ten's purse a metallic object not much larger than a credit card. No doubt a recorder, government-issue.

Only a half-dozen or so words had passed between Cash and Ten before the bust. Nothing incriminating. Or was there?

He replayed the exchange in his mind. First in slow motion. Then at double-speed.

Ten's reference to *the business portion of our meeting*, yeah, that could be twisted. But who knows if the recorder even picked it up?

Given the feds' penchant for paying top dollar for bottom-drawer goods, Cash gave the device only fifty-fifty odds of capturing the one-sided conversation. Might be his only break tonight.

For a nanosecond the scrum around Ten parted, and Cash made eye contact with her. Just long enough to silently ask: *what the fuck?*

She shrugged her nonverbal message: *shit happens.*

The pianist went back to business. His parting song for the heavy tipping Cash, a dirge-like rendition of "Jailhouse Rock."

In the parking lot, Cash and his captors weaved through a gauntlet of reporters and camera crews. Hands cuffed behind his back, he suffered the sting of questions fired from all sides.

The feds must've tipped off the media. More than likely, Shafer the snake. Either he or Moore the showboat. U.S. Attorney Tom Moore played the leak game perfectly, scoring free publicity by bribing reporters with tips and occasionally even exclusives.

Though Cash also fed the media beast regularly, tonight tested his core belief that there was no such thing as bad press for a defense lawyer. He aced the test. Instead of the standard duck-the-head-and-drop-the-eyes approach taught in Perp Walk 101, he slowed his pace, held his head high, and nodded to the reporters.

He knew all but two of the vultures who had dragged themselves from bars to pick his carcass clean. Had plied most of them with liquor and stories for years. The seasoned reporters, more interested in booze than news.

As the agents shoved him into a black SUV, the blonde babe from Channel 11, Ginger something, scored the last question. "You've just been arrested for obstruction of justice. What happens now?"

"I'm going to Disneyworld," he said.

Sound bite on tape, the reporters rushed across the lot, where Moore posed on the curb, basking in the glow of portable lights. He would stay on stage until the lights dimmed and the last reporter left.

Maggie shoved Cash into a middle seat and strapped him in. "The last time we were together," he whispered to her, "the cuffs were on you."

"I've got a gun," she said through clenched teeth, "and I'm not afraid to use it."

"You're breaking my heart, but what hurts even worse is being upstaged at my own arrest by a blowhard like Moore."

"Get used to it." Maggie slid next to Cash, their hips bumping. "The most dangerous spot in Dallas is between him and a TV camera."

* * *

The all-night vigil had taken a toll on Eva. Even filtered through the smudged glass partition at the visiting room of the Dallas County Jail, she looked rocky and ready to fall apart. Her mascara had a hit-or-miss texture, and eyeliner had slalomed down her cheeks. Either she'd been crying or planned to audition for a Kiss tribute band.

Still, of the dozen or so early morning visitors, she had a lock on the coveted title of First Choice for a Conjugal Visit.

Low bar.

"Do I look as bad as you do?" he said.

"Worse." She forced a smile. "Can't they find a jumpsuit that fits you?" The sleeves of the uniform fell inches short of his wrists.

"How quickly can you get me out of here?" He surprised himself by keeping his voice steady.

"Your initial appearance is scheduled for three this afternoon."

"In front of?"

"Tapia."

He groaned. If there was a way to keep him behind bars, Tapia would find it, aided and abetted by her co-conspirator, Sandy Robinson of Pretrial Services. "We drew the wrong judge, but tell me we caught a break on the prosecutor."

"Wish I could, but the Big Cheese is handling your case."

He did a double take. "Moore?"

Eva nodded.

*Holy shit on a stick.* The U.S. Attorney personally handled only one or two cases a year, hand-picked to be surefire winners with massive media coverage. The tough cases, close calls, and no-press nothings flowed down to his hundred plus assistants.

"Guess it could be worse," he said. "We could've drawn Jenna, who actually knows how to try a case."

"She called me this morning."

"To gloat?"

"To give you a message. Said for you to hire the best damn defense lawyer you can't afford and tell him to cut a deal."

# CHAPTER SIX

*Two years and five months ago*

The nightstick jabbed Cash's ribs. Harder than necessary to get his attention.

"Stand up, scumbag." Bailiff Dewey Delahunt, the pudgy arm of the law in Judge Tapia's courtroom, lived by a simple code: *Speak loudly and swing a big stick.*

Cash shared the front row of the jury box with five Mexican mules, ages eighteen through twenty-four, as disposable to the cartel as they'd be in the system.

All six prisoners wore orange jumpsuits that were either comically large or painfully small. Cash's outfit fell into the latter category. With every move, the collar cinched like a noose. When he sat, the pants crept halfway up his shins.

The defendants were chained together ankle-to-ankle, putting the con in conga line. The chains jangled as they rose for the judge's grand entrance and again as they sat on command.

The press routinely buried drug cases on the back pages of the metro section or the tail end of early morning newscasts, if they made the cut at all. Drug busts were dog-bites-man material in a border state like Texas. All the more so for a transportation hub like Dallas. So the five Mexicans about to get shit-canned for life were invisible to the reporters crowding the courtroom.

But Cash's fall from grace garnered top-of-the-newscast coverage and drew a full house of press and prosecutors. He divided the audience into three groups: those who took pleasure in his downfall, those who derived extreme pleasure from it, and Eva.

Based on Tapia's smug grin, she nestled comfortably in the second camp. Same for U.S. Attorney Tom Moore, who arrived for the arraignments fashionably late and sat at the government's table next to Jenna.

Like she really needed his help.

As always, Moore rolled into court camera-ready, his cotton-candyish hair teased to transparency and wearing more makeup than a drag queen. The contrast between his navy blue suit and maroon tie would pop on the tube tonight.

Moore leaned over and whispered to Jenna, lingering too close and too long. She bit her lower lip, a sign she was struggling not to say what was on her mind.

Hard to figure which camp Jenna fell into. Probably didn't know herself.

"Is the government ready to proceed?" Tapia sounded uncharacteristically chipper and managed to look stylish and chic in a black robe. Common knowledge among the defense bar that she charged *rent* on her courtroom. The rent paid for in years stacked onto the sentences of the foolhardy few who put up a fight.

Moore placed a hand on Jenna's shoulder and rose. Not clear whether the hand had been planted to help him up or hold her down. "Yes, your honor."

"I have a number of defendants to arraign this afternoon." The judge paused for effect. "So I'll start with Bennie Ayala."

A collective groan from the crowd greeted the announcement. Good thing too, as it drowned out the "shit" Cash uttered under his breath. It was going to be a long afternoon. Rather than do the humane thing and dispose of the solo defendant first, Tapia would do everything in her power to draw out his ordeal and deepen the humiliation.

Moore turned over to Jenna the disposal of the druggies. No opportunity to mug for the press there.

Tapia questioned each of the Mexicans individually and with an interpreter before delivering the inevitable ruling, denying bail across the board and sending them to jail pending trial in two months. Not that anyone on either side of the courtroom or the border expected a trial to take place.

The five would plead guilty. No testimony and no cooperation translated into no harm to their families back home.

Though the outcomes for the fucked-over five were preordained, Tapia managed to drag out the routine proceedings more than an hour before calling a fifteen-minute break, sparking more groans from the reporters, fearful the delay would cut into their happy hour.

During the break Eva made a beeline to the jury box. Dewey the Dumbass stood and said in a comically high-pitched voice, "Go back to your seat, little lady, and stay away from the prisoners."

Cash smiled. On neutral turf the *little lady* remark would've cost Dewey his right nut. Both nuts, if Eva was having a bad day.

She stopped ten feet from Cash but stood her ground. "I have a message from Mister McCahill's attorney, and I'd strongly advise you to get out of my way. If you don't, you're violating his Sixth Amendment right to counsel, and you personally will be the reason my boss walks out of this courtroom a free man. Try explaining that to *your* boss."

Cash's smile widened. He couldn't have bluffed better himself. Especially since Dewey wouldn't know the difference between the Sixth Amendment and *The Sixth Sense.*

Dewey blinked. "Okay, you've got two minutes."

Eva motioned for the bailiff to back away. After he moved out of earshot, she turned to Cash. "Looks like the judge is immune to your boyish charms."

"Are you kidding? She's taking me last so she can feast her eyes on me longer."

"Riiiiight."

"Enough small talk," Cash said. "Did you get hold of Racehorse? Can't wait to see Moore piss his pants when Race waltzes in."

"He can't take your case. He's double-booked with murder trials in the Valley."

"Then get Rusty."

She shook her head. "He didn't even offer an excuse. Just said no and that he'd see you in hell."

"Guess he's still pissed that I poached Duffey. Did you tell him that I did him a favor, since Duffey stiffed us on the fee?"

"Yes, and he doesn't care. Rusty's out."

"Okay, who's next on the list? Meadows? Finn?" A hint of panic crept into his voice.

As if on cue, Gary Goldberg entered the courtroom. A five-foot-five-inch bantam rooster, strutting as if he were six-six. The Stetson, the snakeskin boots, and most of all, the swagger created the illusion of a bigger man.

"Elvis has entered the building," Eva said, "and in time to make an official appearance on your behalf."

Cash's heart bungee-jumped between his bowels and his throat. "Are you kidding me? I wouldn't trust that has-been to handle a traffic ticket."

# CHAPTER SEVEN

*Two years and five months ago*

Goldberg flung open the office door. "Guess who kicked butt in court today."

As Cash and Eva followed him into the office, they exchanged a look. His, of annoyance. Hers, amusement.

The startled temp dropped the paperback and tried to look busy by shuffling papers on the desk. Thick glasses magnified her eyes. "I didn't expect you back so soon, Mister Goldberg." She sounded even greener than she looked.

"What happened to Hilda?" Cash said.

"Oh, she up and quit last month." Goldberg made it sound like no big deal. "Didn't have the decency to give a reason, but you remember how flighty she was."

No, Cash didn't remember that at all. Just the opposite, in fact. He considered Hilda the rock of the office. A saint who had put up with an incorrigible boss longer than anyone else on his payroll had.

And way longer than any of his wives lasted.

Goldberg loosened his bolo tie and undid the top button of his shirt. "Anyway, meet my trusty temp, Judy."

"Julie," the newbie said softly.

Goldberg muttered under his breath, "Looks more like a Judy."

Cash rolled his eyes. Classic Goldberg. *Never in doubt, often wrong.*

Goldberg herded Eva and Cash into his private office and closed the door behind them. He tossed the battered briefcase onto a swayback sofa. Not an inch of wall space had been spared from print and pictures heralding the lawyer's high-profile acquittals.

Here a crooked politician cut loose by a bamboozled jury. There a drug kingpin who beat the rap on the ticky-tackiest of technicalities. Throw in an accused wife-killer or two for good measure.

A young Cash lurked in the background of a few photos, jockeying for position while bearing the boss's briefcase. Not as battered in those days, either the briefcase or the boss.

But mostly Cash had been invisible back then. Cropped from the shots, if not by the papers, then by Goldberg.

Story of his life as a young attorney.

"Now that the new girl can't hear us, let me take a wild guess." Cash heaped on a heavy dose of sarcasm. "You screwed Hilda, literally and figuratively, so she walked out on you."

Cash stood by the door, primed for a quick exit. Eva sat on the sofa, legs crossed, the toe of her right shoe tapping the floor. Lightly at first, then more forcefully. Warning sign of her rising temper.

Cash turned to her. "While I was working for this walking hard-on, he managed to bed his married secretary, two paralegals, and a first-year associate." He wheeled back to Goldberg. "Did I leave anyone out?"

"The bookkeeper," Goldberg said matter-of-factly.

"Right," Cash said. "Forgot about Rose. Once again, impeccable timing. Drove off the best bean counter in the business during tax season."

"Not that you were any paragon of virtue," Goldberg said. "You weren't upset that I dipped my pen in the company inkwell, just that I beat you there."

"At least I learned at any early age not to shit where I eat." Cash upped the volume.

Eva's toe-tapping stopped. She planted both feet on the floor and pounced. "Shut the fuck up!" she shouted.

A stunned silence settled over the room. She looked from Cash to Goldberg and back again. "Peas in a pod. If you two boys want to whip 'em out for me to measure, do it now. If not, let's get down to business."

Goldberg retreated behind a boomerang-shaped desk. "I'm ready to focus on the case if he is."

Cash remained by the door. "I'll discuss my defense with the lawyer who will actually handle it, and that's not him. Come on, Eva, we're leaving."

"No," she said.

"What do you mean no?" More surprised than pissed.

"No means no, and don't act like you haven't heard *that* before." She settled back onto the sofa. "We're going to work out whatever beefs you two have with each other, so we can put all that shit behind us."

Cash turned to Goldberg. "I need to have a word with Eva."

"Sure," Goldberg said. "Permission to speak freely."

"Alone." Cash didn't try to hide his exasperation.

"It's my damn office. You want to talk in private, go out to the hall."

"Goldy, can we please have five minutes?" Eva's tone defused the turf war.

She had the old man at *Goldy*. Could've asked him to fly out the window, and he would've sprouted wings.

"I'm doing this for you, honey," Goldberg said, "not him." He limped toward the exit, stopping at the door. "Help yourselves to a drink. You know where everything is."

"We won't be here that long," Cash said.

Eva stood. "Thanks. Don't mind if I do." After Goldberg left, she went to the well-stocked bar. Bottles of booze outnumbered law books in the office three-to-one. "Sure you don't want me to mix you a drink? It's not every day you get charged with a felony."

"I'm the one who's been indicted, not you. And I'll be the one who picks my lawyer. Again, not you."

She prepared a Vodka Seven and took a sip. "I'll be damned if I'm going to let you torpedo your defense by passing on the best lawyer in Dallas."

"Second best," Cash said.

"No, he's still number one, and know why?" She didn't give him a chance to respond. "Because he had the smarts to learn under Charlie Tessmer, the top dog of his day. You blew your chance to work with the best when you walked out on Goldberg ten years ago."

"If you love the old fart so much, why the hell don't you go work for him? He'll be in the market for a new secretary any day now...soon as he hits on Judy or Julie or whatever her name is."

"Because right now you need me almost as much as you need him." The glass came down hard on the counter. "You haven't even thanked him for getting you released on bail today."

"Yeah, after surrendering my passport and posting a two hundred and fifty thousand dollar bond."

"You don't need a passport because you never take a vacation, and you work so hard you can't spend the money you make." She poured herself a second drink, heavier on the vodka this time.

"Since when did you start drinking in the afternoon?"

She checked her watch. "Since I started babysitting you. Besides, we'll be spending most of our waking hours in this office until we get you acquitted. Might as well make ourselves at home."

"Not me," he said. "I'm already gone." He headed toward the door.

"Unless you hear him out, I quit."

Cash's first instinct was to call her bluff. After all, she had threatened to quit more times than he could count. Mostly over his penchant for sleeping with clients, witnesses, agents, prosecutors, pretty much anyone off limits.

Anyone, that is, except prostitutes. They were actually off limits to him, for reasons more personal than professional.

But today's threat sounded different. Way too calmly delivered for his comfort. He cratered. "Okay, I'll sit through his B.S., but I'll never hire him to represent me."

Five minutes later, Cash signed Goldberg's engagement letter and handed him a retainer check for one hundred thousand dollars.

And it took Goldberg only two words to turn Cash around.

# CHAPTER EIGHT

*Two years, four months, and twenty-nine days ago*

"Reverse proffer."

The bait Goldberg had dangled to get Cash's signature on the engagement letter yesterday. The same bait that lured the two onto enemy turf today.

The walls of the windowless conference room at the U.S. Attorney's office were closing in on Cash. The odor of bad coffee and foul lies took him back to a past life as a prosecutor, when he'd broken many a defendant in this come-to-Jesus corner.

A reverse proffer, where a prosecutor lays out his case to the defense in detail, is a rare and precious gift. A peek at the cards in the government's hand. Bestowed only when the prosecutor trusts that the dog-and-pony show will push the accused to fold.

With a reverse proffer at hand, it would be beyond stupid to dump Goldberg before hearing out U.S. Attorney Moore. During the delay involved in changing counsel, the reverse proffer might fall off the table.

Moore kept them waiting in the conference room fifteen minutes. A tactic no doubt meant to build tension but serving only to tick off Cash.

Goldberg stopped whistling. "Remember, son, no matter what that blowhard says or does, keep your trap shut. He'll do everything in his power to provoke you, but we're here to listen, not talk."

"Got it the first six times you warned me."

"And no funny faces or weird body language. For the entire time we're here, you're deaf, dumb, and blind."

"I won't even breathe," Cash said.

Moore led his retinue into the room. In order came IRS Agent Marty Shafer, FBI Agent Maggie Burns, and Jenna Powell, who closed the door behind her.

Cash and Maggie had a history. One that went back years before she had cuffed him at his arrest. Not that he harbored hard feelings over her role in the bust. After all, turnabout's fair play, and he'd cuffed her in the past.

Jenna evaded eye contact, and it was all Cash could do to keep from slapping the shit-eating grin off Shafer's weasel-face.

No apology from Moore for being late. Not that Cash expected one. Being the big cheese meant never having to say he was sorry, not even for destroying an innocent man's life.

Rumor had it that the top fed kept a hair stylist and makeup artist on retainer. He must've visited both this morning. A fluffier comb over and fewer crow's feet than usual. The touchups certainly weren't for Cash's benefit. Probably for the TV trucks circling the courthouse like vultures.

"Once again, Goldy," Moore said, "I've got you outnumbered and outgunned."

"Wouldn't have it any other way, and only my friends call me Goldy. You can call me Mister Goldberg."

Moore signaled for the minions to sit while he remained standing. The floor belonged to him. "Before I get started, is there anything you or your client would like to say?"

Goldberg leaned back in his chair. "You offered to walk us through your case. We're waiting."

"Very well." Moore moved behind Jenna. His palms rested on the back of her chair, his thumbs bracketing her shoulders. She flinched at the touch.

"Then I'll lead with the punch line and work my way back to the overwhelming evidence that will send your client to prison for a decade. Jenna, show our guests the superseding indictment."

She slid two copies of the pleading across the table. Cash skimmed the three-page document. Same charges as the original complaint, obstruction of justice and jury tampering, but more meat on the bone. The new document included the name of the bought juror, Yvonne Strauss, and the amount of the bribe, twenty thousand dollars in cash.

Instead of spiking Cash's alarm, the pleading ratcheted down his fear. The more details in the document, the farther out on a limb Moore climbed. And the easier it'd be for Goldberg to saw off the limb.

"We plan to present this indictment to the grand jury for a vote tomorrow," Moore said, "and it'll be made public the next day."

Goldberg tossed the papers aside. "Indict your brains out, but no need to re-arraign Cash. We're sticking with our not guilty plea."

"Hold off making a decision," Moore said, "until you've heard our evidence. The lead-off witness will be the lovely and very credible Ms. Strauss. She'll testify to getting a call after day three of a trial that Cash was losing for a client who's not a good loser."

"Have you traced the number of the phone making the call to her?" Goldberg said.

"McCahill used a disposable phone and scrambled his voice. Your client got careless, but he isn't stupid."

Goldberg fake yawned. "You've got a call from someone you can't identify on a phone you can't trace. Color me underwhelmed."

The veins on Moore's temples pulsed, and his voice took on an edge. "Ms. Strauss did the right thing and contacted the trial judge, who brought in the FBI."

Maggie nodded on cue. Evidently she, like Cash, had been assigned a nonspeaking role.

"The Bureau coached Yvonne to play along with McCahill by demanding payment up front of ten thousand dollars. Half of what she'd been offered in return for voting not guilty and sticking to her guns. At worst the defense would get a hung jury. At best she'd sway the whole panel, or at least the males. Never underestimate the power of a beautiful woman."

As if to drive home his point, Moore patted Jenna's shoulders. "Here's where your client tripped up. Granted, he faced a tough choice. Does he make the payoff himself? That's risky. Or does he bring someone else into the conspiracy? Even riskier."

"Let me get this straight." Goldberg sounded incredulous. "Your theory is that my client, one of the most sophisticated criminal lawyers in the country, went to a public place and paid a bribe to a juror in front of dozens of witnesses." He slapped the table. "That's bad, even for government work."

Moore checked his watch. No doubt jonesing for his next media hit. "It's called hiding in plain sight."

"It's also called reasonable doubt when I convince a jury that Cash was at the Ritz, not to bribe a juror but to meet someone else."

Moore's smug air hinted at more aces in his hand. "I've never lost a jury trial, and I'm not about to break my streak now. Not that this case will ever reach a jury."

Goldberg snickered. "That line might work on a rookie, someone who's not aware of your track record of taking only cases where the defendant has confessed in writing and has the misfortune of being represented by a potted plant."

Cash leaned over and whispered to his counsel. "Mariposa Benanti left in my car a very personal invitation to meet her that night. An invitation that'll have her DNA all over it."

Goldberg nodded to Cash, then turned to Moore. "You were good enough to tell me your first witness, so I'll share mine. It'll be the mystery woman my client was waiting to meet at the Ritz, when your agents so rudely interrupted the date."

Moore's smile widened. "You won't have to call Missus Benanti to the stand because she'll be our second witness. She'll testify to having an affair with your client until she broke it off two weeks before his arrest."

Cash's face froze into a mask of indifference, but his brain warped into overdrive.

"Missus Benanti will also swear that on the night of the arrest, she was at the movies with a friend, just like she told her husband. She paid for the tickets with her credit card, and her companion for the evening will back her up. She had no intention of meeting McCahill, not that night or ever again."

The noose tightened around Cash's neck. A trapdoor had opened beneath him, and he was falling. Mariposa must've turned on him, and her cuckolded husband wouldn't be far behind.

Hell hath no fury like a client scorned.

"Both Mister and Missus Benanti are cooperating fully with our investigation," Moore said. "Mister Benanti, our third witness, will testify to McCahill's assurance of having one vote in the bag. Benanti didn't fully grasp the significance of that remark at the time, but certainly does now."

Moore picked up the pace of the proffer. "McCahill also told him about needing ten thousand dollars for a jury consultant. That sum got wired into your client's account and withdrawn the same day."

"Ten thousand is in the ballpark for a jury consultant." Goldberg sounded shakier. "I don't use those snake oil salesmen myself, but most jackleg lawyers swear by them."

"Except that the money winds up in the juror's purse." Moore's maximum smile bared his canines. "That's right, gents. I saved the best for last. Special Agent Burns will be our fourth witness." He moved behind her. "She searched Ms. Strauss head to toe, including her purse, before she entered the Ritz. The juror had exactly one hundred and fifty-seven dollars and thirty-five cents on her that night. After meeting your client, she had ten thousand, one hundred and fifty-seven dollars, and thirty-five cents."

Moore swatted an air backhand. "Game, set, match."

Cash kept a poker face. Quite a feat considering his insides were imploding.

*WTF*. One or both agents must've set him up. Shafer, he could believe. But Maggie?

"Is that all you've got?" Goldberg said.

The government side of the table erupted in laughter. All except Maggie.

Cash's chest swelled. His heart pumped like mad, stoked by anger.

And fear.

"As a matter of fact, it isn't," Moore said. "But I'll reveal the last piece of the puzzle to Cash and Cash alone, with everyone else out of the room."

Hard to tell which side of the table got caught more off-guard by the U.S. Attorney's closing gambit.

Shafer bolted to his feet. "Hey, it's my case."

Moore's glare shut him up and sat him down. Jenna bit her lip. Maggie stared at the table.

"There's no way I'd leave you alone with my client," Goldberg said.

"I have no intention of questioning him. In fact, I don't want him to say a word." Moore slid a single page to Goldberg. "But to put your mind at ease, here's a queen-for-a-day letter. This makes it clear we can't use anything your client might say today against him in court."

"Still not leaving him with you," Goldberg said.

Cash blindsided his lawyer. "Don't worry. I've got this."

"Bad idea," Goldberg whispered loud enough for everyone to hear.

"Give us five minutes alone," Moore said.

After Jenna and the agents left the room, Goldberg rose so angrily that his chair toppled backward. At the door he stopped. "Son, there are cleaner ways to commit suicide." He turned to Moore. "If my client isn't out in five minutes, I'm coming in."

Two minutes later Moore invited Goldberg back into the room. Cash didn't look his lawyer in the eye. Instead, he focused on the dozen or so typed pages spread out on the table.

"What's that?" Goldberg said to Moore.

"It's a plea bargain that lets your client cop to a five-year count of jury tampering. Cuts his prison time in half. With good behavior, he'll be out in four. This limited time offer expires in fifteen minutes. I'll leave the room so you two can chat."

"Don't bother," Goldberg said. "I can tell you right now where to stick that plea bargain."

Cash held out his right hand, palm up. "I'll need a pen."

# CHAPTER NINE

*The present*

"It's a matter of life or death." Cash's voice cracked, this time for real.

From behind a massive metal desk, Warden Marvin Stockman didn't react, not even a blink. The scowl carved into his leathery face straddled contempt and boredom.

The Spartan office mirrored the man. Not that there were any actual mirrors in the room. That'd be too frou frou for the hard-ass. Just a desk built to survive a bomb, a pair of folding chairs, and a lumpy sofa. No artwork, no photos, no diplomas. Everything was functional, impersonal, prison-made, and stamped with a six-digit number.

Cash and Big Black sank into the sofa. Big Black's weight caused him to sink a little lower.

"Quit whining, McCahill," the warden said. "No one has ever died from a stint in solitary. The peace and quiet might even do your client some good."

*I'm not talking about saving his life, you old fool, but mine.*

Big Black clenched his fists, veins snaking like cords along his massive forearms. Prison tatts of grizzlies covered both arms from elbow to shoulder.

Though hardly the first client to threaten Cash with a "win or else" ultimatum, this one set off major alarms. For starters, there was little to no chance of prevailing before Stockman, who divided prisoners into two camps: the few who were plainly guilty and the bulk who were guilty as hell. As a result, when a guard flagged an inmate for an infraction, the warden routinely rubber-stamped the finding.

For over a year, Big Black had protected his silver-tongued cellmate, and protection didn't come cheap in prison. In return, he expected, actually demanded that Cash clear him when charged.

Not if, but when. And the when was now.

Big Black must've sensed the futility of today's appeal. He began to seethe like a volcano about to blow. If he was acting, fork over an Oscar.

Cash inched away from the explosive client, painfully aware of his split personality. Big Black had a dark side and a darker side. Sometimes he was violent, like when he bitch-slapped the ancient prison barber for nicking his ear.

Other times he turned ultra-violent, like when he beat a punk to pulp for cutting in front of him in the chow line. Poor fool didn't die, but wished he had. He now took his meals through a straw.

Today threatened to turn into an ultra episode.

Stockman, in contrast, had only one personality. Barely one at that. The opposite of volcanic. More like Mount Rushmoric. Granite. Imposing. Unmovable.

"McCahill, I sure hope you're not planning to deny that your client assaulted one of my correctional officers, because C.O. Gomez has the bruises to prove it. Do I need to call him away from his rounds to repeat what he put in his report?" The warden spoke in a just-the-facts monotone.

Big Black leaned over and whispered, "I barely touched the screw."

"I can hear your client." Mount Rushmore almost cracked a smile.

"No sir, we're not contesting that he may have technically laid a hand on Gomez. Just pointing out that he did so not with any malice or forethought but in the grip of temporary insanity."

"Drop the word temporary," the warden said, "and I might buy your bullshit argument."

"Warden, as you're well aware, Big Black couldn't read a lick when I got transferred to Seagoville last year, and it became my duty and privilege to tutor him. Happy to report, sir, that he took to reading with a religious fervor. Like the Catholics always say, there's no convert like a late convert."

Cash paused for effect. Not seeing any, he went on. "That's when I made a miscalculation." He patted Big Black on the shoulder. Like hitting a brick wall. "I underestimated his passion for the written word and urged him to tackle *Great Expectations*. Well, sir, that was like giving liquor to a teenage boy. He drank deeply from Dickens' most moving novel. Became intoxicated by the prose. Captivated by the characters. The book came alive for him."

The warden's eyes glazed over. Better reel him back in.

"Have you read the work, sir?" Cash said.

"A hundred years ago, in high school."

"Then surely you remember the passage where the social climbing Pip, ashamed of his humble roots, turns his back on poor Uncle Joe. The same gentle Joe who had shown Pip such care and affection." Cash's voice broke again. This time, for show.

The warden nodded warily.

"When Big Black reached that chapter, he was overcome with compassion for Joe and disappointment in Pip. Distraught and practically out of his mind, he was not himself. Unfortunately, at precisely that moment, Gomez tried to take the book from Big Black, who ever so gently pushed him away. Not out of disrespect for authority but from a deep love of literature. Rather than punish such passion for the arts, shouldn't we instead reward it?"

A flicker of a smile flitted across the warden's lips. A first. "That's a helluva defense, McCahill. Easy to see how you helped so many scumbags beat the rap on the outside." He pounded the desk. "I'll take the matter of the proper punishment under advisement."

Cash jumped up and motioned for his client to follow. "Thank you, sir." He tried to hurry Big Black from the office before the warden could change his mind and rule on the spot. Came close but didn't quite make it.

"Deliberation over," the warden said, "decision made." The inmates froze at the door. "Thirty days in the hole starting tomorrow, followed by the loss of PX privileges for thirty days, capped off with the suspension of library privileges for a year."

Translation: a death sentence for Cash. Why else would Stockman wait until tomorrow to toss Big Black into solitary? Soon as Cash set foot inside the cell, his life expectancy would shrink to seconds.

A rising tide of bile burned Cash's chest and throat. He instinctively leaned toward the metal waste basket. False alarm. The danger of heaving passed, but that was the only danger which did.

He turned to Big Black. "Let me have a word alone with the warden."

"I'll be waiting outside for you," Big Black said.

After BB left the office, the warden said, "You're wasting your breath if you plan to ask me to reconsider."

"You have to transfer Martin Biddle to another prison immediately," Cash said.

"I don't have to do anything."

"Bad as it is for Biddle to share a cell with Big Black," Cash said, "it'll be worse for him when Big Black's not around to keep the wolves at bay."

The warden massaged his temples. "I can move Biddle into the hole with Big Black. Defeats the purpose of solitary, but I'll do it if Biddle formally requests it. Call it protective custody."

"That the best you can do?" Cash said.

The warden nodded.

* * *

Soon as Cash emerged from the warden's office, Big Black grabbed his collar and dragged him down the corridor. "Dead man walking." Big Black's warning echoed throughout the cellblock.

The death sentence drew no reaction from the one-eyed guard escorting the pair to the place of execution. Prisoners emerged from the shadows of their cells to line the route of Cash's last mile. Not as a show of support or even sympathy, but to take a last look at a lawyer who had lost his final appeal.

Cash slowed the pace while his brain went to warp speed. "It could've been worse." Not that he could think of a worse outcome.

Big Black flashed a get real look. "Don't hardly see how. Before the hearing, I had a choice of thirty days in the hole or thirty days without script. And I done come away with both."

Cash stopped fifteen feet short of the cell. "Let Stockman cool off for a day or two, then I'll get him to reconsider."

Big Black laughed. "You ain't got a day or two left."

One Eye prodded Cash with a nightstick. He didn't budge.

"Step into the cell and take what you got coming like a man." Big Black laced his fingers together and cracked all ten knuckles. "Or I'm gonna drag your sorry ass in here, and it'll be a damn sight worse."

Cash silently called bullshit on the threat. Again, no way it could get any worse.

# CHAPTER TEN

Big Black shoved Marti, a.k.a. Marty, a.k.a. Martin Biddle from the cell before shutting the door and trapping Cash inside. The eight-by-twelve-foot cell shrank with each heartbeat, and Cash's ticker pumped like there was no tomorrow.

"You girls have fun now." One Eye tapped his nightstick on a metal bar. "And Big Black, clean up your damn mess this time. After your last party, it took me an hour to swab down the blood and guts."

One Eye whistled a tune as he sauntered away. So off-key that it took Cash several bars to recognize the *Rocky* theme.

Big Black grabbed Cash by the throat with one hand, lifted him off the floor, and slammed him against the wall. Cash would've begged for his life if he could've gotten the words out.

Big Black drew back his left arm. His fist loomed as large as an anvil, eclipsing the lone light in the cell. The letters tattooed onto his fingers blurred before Cash's eyes.

B-E-A-R dissolved into T-E-A-R, then to F-E-A-R.

One Eye's mobile phone chirped. He took the call and turned toward the cell, frowning. "Shit. Looks like the mouthpiece gets a reprieve. He has a visitor. You girls will have to postpone your last dance."

The balled fist had a mind of its own. It shook from the strain of holding back. Finally exploded with a fast, furious blow. At the last instant, it spared Cash's face but drilled his gut.

Cash crumpled to the floor and curled into a ball, bracing for a flurry of kicks. When none came, he struggled onto his hands and knees. Fought to catch his breath as he crawled from the cell.

"Your visitor best be a priest," Big Black said, "here for your last rites."

It might've taken Cash two minutes or twenty to stagger to the visiting room. His insides scrambled, he lost all sense of time. Except for the knowledge of living on the borrowed kind.

One Eye left Cash alone in an eight-by-ten-feet sound-proof room reserved for attorney visits. But not before cuffing his hands behind his back and shackling his feet to an eye hook in the floor. The pain from the punch still radiated from his gut.

Since Cash didn't have a lawyer on retainer, he smelled an ambush. Someone must want a piece of him before Big Black finished the job.

The stench of sweat and fear gave way to the odor of cheap aftershave. Cash had smelled the buy-by-the-gallon brand before. It was popular among the federal courthouse crowd, bureaucrats who valued quantity over quality.

IRS Agent Marty Shafer entered the room and sat across the table, trademark smirk in place. Off-the-rack suit a size too small, check. Coffee stains on the throwback tie, check. Frayed collar and cuffs on the faded white shirt, double check.

"What're you doing here?" Cash said. "Come to pay your final respects?"

Shafer snorted. "You can thank me later for saving your life."

"I'll be sure to put you on my Christmas card list."

"You're not likely to make it to Christmas." A smile swallowed the smirk. "Hear you've got roommate trouble."

Cash wouldn't give the prick the satisfaction of hearing him beg. "Yeah, the big lug snores something terrible."

"I can take care of that problem for you."

Cash didn't lunge for the lifeline. Nothing came free in Shafer's world. "In exchange for what?"

"Benanti." Shafer leaned forward. "Give me his head on a platter, and I'll whisk you out of here right now. Grease a transfer to a minimum security facility, maybe even a camp. Put you on the fast track to an early release."

"If I turn on Benanti, how long do you think I'll live?"

"How long will you last if you don't?" Shafer sat back, ensured a win whichever way Cash went.

"Besides, I was his lawyer, so our conversations are privileged. He can waive that privilege, but I can't."

"Fuck the privilege," Shafer said. "Whatever you tell me will fall under the crime-fraud exception. Benanti can't fart without breaking three laws in the process."

Cash hesitated. Not about where he'd wind up but how he'd get there. Partly he prided himself on being a stand-up lawyer, one who didn't roll over on clients. But mostly he didn't trust Shafer. Wouldn't put it past the agent to be on Benanti's payroll. This could be a test.

"Can't help you," Cash said.

"Then help yourself. I thought you'd jump at my offer of an early out. Or maybe you prefer the company of men to women."

"Not all men." Cash kneed the call button under the table until One Eye returned. "Agent Shafer is leaving."

The agent rose. Started to speak but shook it off.

"See you on the other side," Cash said.

"Don't bet on it."

With Shafer out of sight, the guard unshackled Cash and led him down a dark corridor. One Eye whistled a new tune. The theme from *Jaws*.

"This isn't the way to my cell." Cash couldn't decide whether the detour was good news or bad.

One Eye took a circuitous route to the warden's office and knocked on the door. "Last stop on your farewell tour," he said, "before Big Black tucks you in for the night." He shoved Cash into the office and closed the door behind him.

Warden Stockman shot Cash a look of disgust. Cash moved slowly toward the couch, still suffering from the punch.

"Don't bother sitting, McCahill. You won't be here long." The warden signed a document and pushed it across the desk, as if it were toxic.

"By *here*, do you mean your office or Seagoville?" Cash said.

No answer.

"Are you transferring me to another prison?" Cash could barely hear the words over the pounding of his heart.

"Nope."

"'Cause I could sure use a transfer now, and I'm willing to go anywhere...even SuperMax."

"Wouldn't matter where we sent a low-life scum like you. Half the prisoners would hate you because you represented them. The other half, 'cause you didn't."

"What did you just sign?" Cash said.

"Much as I wish it was your death certificate, it's an early release form. Now get the hell out of my sight and out of my prison."

Air rushed from Cash's lungs, and his knees buckled. His faculties returned before his voice did. He knew his release date down to the hour, and he wouldn't be eligible for another six months and four days.

"Is this some kind of joke?"

"Am I smiling?" The warden couldn't have been farther from it.

"Am I being released for good behavior?"

"Don't make me laugh."

*Fat chance of that.*

"The fucked-up federal prison system has exceeded its maximum capacity population." The warden made it sound like no big deal. "So some bleeding-heart judge in Pennsylvania had a hissy fit and threatened to hold the BOP in contempt unless we start springing nonviolent offenders who are within a year of their release date. The early outs have to continue until we fall below ninety-five percent. Lucky punk that you are, you fit the profile."

"My release papers, were they on your desk while I was here earlier with Big Black?"

The warden nodded.

"And you couldn't have given me the good news before I died a thousand deaths on the way to my cell?"

"Decided to let you sweat awhile."

"Which makes me wonder why you didn't wait until Big Black had beaten me senseless before pulling me out."

The warden let out a loud sigh, making it clear he'd been tempted. "Like I said, we've got a bleeding-heart judge breathing down our necks."

"While the Bureau of Prisons is in a generous mood," Cash said, "how about cutting Biddle loose? He's the poster boy for nonviolence."

The warden shook his head. "He's not within a year of release, not even close."

"I have to talk to him on my way out."

"No time for that," the warden said.

"Five minutes...that's all I need."

The warden nodded.

* * *

Cash found Biddle in the first place he looked, the prison chapel. He was alone and on his knees, praying to a crucifix on the wall. His hands were clasped, the purple nail polish chipped and cracked. Purple was Big Black's favorite color.

Cash knelt beside him and whispered, "I'm getting out."

Biddle stopped praying. "I know. Bad news travels fast behind bars."

"I was hoping you'd see it as good news."

"Good for you, not for me." He turned to Cash. Tears had clumped his makeup. "I can't make it here without you."

"Hang on," Cash said. "Your brief is almost done, and we've got a real shot at the Fifth Circuit."

"Can you file it under your name and not *pro se?*"

"Not without a law license." The doomed look on Biddle's face prompted Cash to spell out plans B and C. "If I can't get my license back immediately, I'll find a hotshot lawyer to sign our brief. And if I can't persuade some Good Samaritan to sign it, we'll have to go *pro se.*"

Cash started to rise, but Biddle grabbed his sleeve. "The warden has given me a choice. Check into solitary with Big

Black or stay in gen pop and take my chances. What should I do?"

Cash stared at the crucifix. Neither Cash nor Christ had a good answer. It was like being asked to choose between a long, slow death by crucifixion or a longer, slower death by a thousand cuts.

Cash bought a little time for his brief to work its magic.

"Go with Big Black."

# CHAPTER ELEVEN

Eva gunned the Carrera on Highway 175. Thickets of fast food franchises clogged both sides of the road.

"So which whorehouse do you visit first?" she said.

Cash kept his eyes on the road. "You know I don't go there."

"Except to pick up clients," she said. "Besides, I thought prison might've changed you."

"Not on that score. Drop me off at the SMU Law Library."

She mouthed a *what-the-fuck*. "And I thought you said you didn't go for prostitutes. By the way, you're welcome."

"For what?" he said.

"For picking you up today."

"Part of your job."

"Except that I happen to work for Mister Goldberg now, and he doesn't know about today's field trip." Her voice had an edge. "He was good enough to take me in after you left me high and dry."

Better change the subject before one or both said something they'd regret. He leaned over to check the odometer. "I asked you to take care of my baby." He patted the dashboard. "Not take her around the world."

"Did you expect me to put your car in cold storage until you returned? Was the world supposed to stop spinning until you came back into circulation?"

He sighed. "Can we not do this today? Would you give me twenty-four hours to celebrate my freedom before you start busting my balls again?"

She downshifted on the outskirts of Dallas. "Sure, you've got a day pass from the doghouse. Any idea where you'll stay and what you'll do? Not that it's any of my concern." The tone betrayed her concern.

"Thought I might crash with you for a few days, until I get my own place."

"My girlfriend's going to love that." Spoken with sarcasm to spare.

"You never know. Maybe she's into an audience or, even better, a three-way."

"Afraid you're not her type, but knock yourself out trying. Nothing amuses me more than seeing you shot down."

"By the way," he said, "thank you."

"For what?"

"For visiting me. The first few months, I had a steady stream of visitors, but then they petered out. You were the only one who hung on to the end. Most of the guys back there had no one. I always had you."

"Not always. I skipped a stretch of five weeks during the first year. In case you were too dense to figure it out, that happened after you royally pissed me off."

"I remember," he said, "but I knew you'd come back."

"Cocky sonovabitch, aren't you?"

"Not as cocky as I was two years ago."

At SMU she slowed to the posted limit. Not because campus cops would target her ride. Carreras were nothing special at a college crawling with Porsches, Benzes, and Beamers.

She slowed to search for an empty parking space, which was rarer at the private school than a student without a trust fund.

Cash waved to the blonde catching rays on the stairs of the Underwood Law Library. Sandaled feet, crossed at the ankles. Long, lean legs, mocha tan. A decade or so older than the law students. A decade or so younger than the faculty.

Jenna Powell stole his breath every time he saw her, from his very first sighting here twenty-two years ago. She had the same effect today.

Eva must've seen her too, because she braked hard and turned to Cash. "You stupid sonovabitch. You never learn."

\* \* \*

"Was that Eva peeling out in your Porsche?" Seated on the steps of the law library, Jenna Powell sounded amused. "Whoever it was flipped me the finger."

Cash loomed over her. "Her parting shot was aimed at me. You got caught in the crossfire."

"You sure about that? The whole time we were together, she tried to break us up." Jenna's brow furrowed. "Maybe I should thank her for that."

"She wasn't the only one pulling us apart. On your father's list of potential spouses for his princess, I fell between Osama bin Laden and Charlie Sheen."

He took her hand and pulled her to her feet. Her palm fit snugly inside his. Made it hard to let go.

She was taller than he remembered. Or perhaps two years in prison had whittled him down a notch or two.

Pushing forty-five, she still had the whole blonde-haired-blue-eyed-head-cheerleader-for-life thing going. Hot enough to draw second looks from the drones trudging to and from the library.

"Tell me I wasn't your first call upon release, because that would be pathetic."

"Relax," he said, "you were my third."

"Still unbearably sad. But now that you've ruined my day off, what did you just have to say in person?"

He looked around. "Not here."

"Let's duck into the library." She smiled. "Be a whole new experience for you."

"I'd burst into flames if I set foot in there. How about the Starbucks across the street?"

It took ten minutes to claim an empty table and another ten for Cash to return with the order. "Skinny latte, light on the foam, two Splendas." He handed the cup to her. "As you like it."

"You still an espresso man?"

"After the swill served inside, the hard stuff would send me into orbit. Starting out with decaf."

"Still don't know what I'm doing here," she said.

"I need your help."

Her eyes narrowed. Jaw tensed. Defense mechanisms. "You should've thought of that before you bribed a juror."

"I never...." He completed the sentence silently. *Never had to, not to beat your office.*

"Then why did you plead guilty?" she said.

He fought the urge to come clean and confess his innocence. "I had my reasons."

"I'd like to hear them." Her voice turned brittle. Less like a hard-nosed prosecutor, more like a hurt lover. "Actually, I need to hear them."

"Some other time." He doubted there'd be another time. "I need your official help."

"Let me guess. You want to set aside your guilty plea, vacate the conviction, and start over at square one."

He shook his head. "What's done is done. I just want my law license back."

"That shouldn't be a problem, not after you finish your term of supervised release. Even murderers have gotten their meal tickets back, eventually."

"I need it back now, so I can file an appellate brief for an inmate named Biddle. He's hanging on by a thread."

Her eyes widened at the mention of Biddle's name. Cash had hit a nerve.

"You can still prepare the brief and have him file it *pro se*," she said.

"*Pro se* briefs go straight to the shredder. You know that. So does he."

She started to speak but shook it off.

"Your office can petition the court to end my supervision immediately."

She massaged both temples. Evidently even head cheerleaders got headaches. "At the same time, we can ask Judge Tapia to turn her chambers into a halfway house for the cons. None of which will ever happen."

"How do you know until you try?"

"For starters, Tom would have to sign off on that." She placed a hand over his, warm from cradling the cup. "You don't want to go there. He'd be more likely to ask Tapia to extend your period of supervision."

"Are you trying to protect him or me?"

"Both."

"In the past that hasn't worked out so well for me."

She pulled back her hand. "Whose fault was that?" She took a swig. Lowered the cup too fast, sloshing coffee onto the table. "Guess this is as good a time as any to break the news that Tom and I are engaged."

His turn to take a drink. The bitter aftertaste lingered. "I'm sure that makes your father happy."

"That's not why I'm marrying him."

"I'd love to hear the reasons."

She threw his words back at him. "Some other time."

Conversation dead. Relationship, on life support.

"Can I give you a lift?" she said.

"Thanks, but believe it or not, I'm actually going into the law library to finish Biddle's brief. The poor guy was set up to take a fall by some real crooks."

"Never heard that one before," she said on her way out.

# CHAPTER TWELVE

ash fixated on the noose swaying hypnotically in the windowless room. So much so that he lost eye contact with Probation Officer Sandy Robinson and missed most of her litany of dos and don'ts.

More don'ts than dos.

He cupped a hand behind his ear. "Sorry, lost my train of thought."

"Can't look away from it, can you?"

"From what?" The words no sooner left his lips than he regretted denying the obvious. The hangman's noose sucked all the attention in the office.

Not that there was much else to see. A diploma from El Centro Community College and a framed poster of the Grand Canyon on beige walls badly in need of a fresh coat. No photos of family or friends. Could mean she had no family, no friends. Or simply a safety precaution by a bureaucrat whose job involved making the hard lives of felons a little harder.

She swiveled her chair to face a coat-rack in a corner, the noose dangling from the top limb and dancing to the beat of an oscillating fan. "Judge Tapia sent it to me after the *Observer* dubbed her 'The Hanging Judge' in a trashy cover story. Became an inside joke here at the courthouse."

"I'm sure it has the defendants in stitches," he said.

The strange gift dredged up an old rumor about Tapia and Robinson. Courthouse gossip dating back to Cash's stint as an Assistant U.S. Attorney. He'd dismissed it then. Even if one or both of them batted for the other team, Tapia could do better, and Robinson should be so lucky.

But now he saw the P.O. in a new light. Noticed her recent efforts. Foundation slathered across her broad face, caulking the pits. Pink lipstick to accentuate the kisser. Rapid blinking from a recent conversion from glasses to contact lenses.

She was primping for someone, and it sure as hell wasn't him.

"Fail to find a job and a place to stay pronto," Robinson said, "and you can see for yourself if the judge deserves the title."

"I'm working on it."

"Work faster." She flipped through a stack of papers on the desk, too quickly to read them. Speed-signing pages flagged by post-its.

"On Monday I report to the court on whether you've satisfied the conditions of release. If you haven't, it's back to Seagoville."

He wasn't about to tell Robinson that a return trip to prison spelled certain death. Why give her more motivation to piss on his welcome home parade?

"In case you haven't noticed," he said, "the job market out there sucks."

She continued to process paperwork, her hand on auto-pilot. It took all his self-control to keep from sweeping the papers off the desk.

"Also, in case it has slipped your mind, I happen to have a law degree."

"But not a license," she said, "which means you can't go back to your old racket of helping bad guys beat the rap."

"Well, you don't expect me to work at McDonald's, do you?"

She stopped signing and stared at him. "Of course not. I expect you to start out driving for Domino's and work your way up to McDonald's."

\* \* \*

After three years away from the courtroom, Cash couldn't resist a detour to the fifteenth floor of the federal building. Maybe catch a snippet of a trial before returning to Goldberg's office. Get a second-hand high from watching a real, live trial lawyer in action.

Instead, he bumped into the opposite of a trial lawyer. Tony Dial, a.k.a. Terrible Negotiator Tony. TNT for short. A butterball bottom feeder with decades of malpractice behind him.

Rumor had it that upon rising to deliver the opening argument in his maiden case forty-five years ago, he fainted, banged his head on the defense table, and wound up at Baylor Hospital with a concussion.

The prosecutor offered the client a sweet deal out of sympathy, pity, or whatever, and TNT had been pleading out clients ever since. Avoiding trial at all costs. Cutting deals right and left. Some good, most bad.

TNT had only one special skill: conning suckers into swallowing his shitty deals. Today's sad sack client slumped on the bench outside Judge Tapia's courtroom. His dazed look meant Tony hadn't closed the sale.

"Hey Cash," TNT called out, "I hear you're still out of the game."

"On injured reserve. Be back by the playoffs."

TNT waddled over and grabbed Cash by the arm. "Help me persuade my main man Tommy to take the best deal of his young life."

Tommy and Cash shook hands. The baby-faced defendant held the grip like a drowning man clinging to driftwood. Hope had drained from his watery eyes.

"What are you charged with?" Cash said.

"False statement to a bank." Tommy stared at the floor. All but shouting he was good for it.

"That sucker carries a thirty-year max." TNT sounded perversely upbeat. "But I pulled strings, and the prosecutor will recommend probation if Tommy pleads to only one count. Helluva deal."

"Any priors?" Cash said.

Tommy shook his head. Good, still a category one defendant under the sentencing guidelines.

"How old are you?"

"Twenty-two."

"Married? Kids?"

"Married two years. Sixteen-month-old son and a daughter on the way."

Cash had one last question. "How much did the bank lose?"

"Nothing," Tommy said. "They turned down my loan before turning me in."

Cash handed TNT a ten-dollar bill. "Get us three coffees while I talk some sense into the kid."

After TNT left, Cash sat next to Tommy. "Scared?"

"Yes, sir."

"Bet you're almost as frightened as your counsel. When you're Tony's age and you haven't gone to trial in forever, the prospect of facing a jury is terrifying. That's why he's pushing the deal so hard."

"Is it a good deal?"

"For a repeat offender, yes. For you, no." Cash paused until Tommy looked him in the eye. "Here's what you're going to do. Tell Tony that you're taking this to trial unless he gets you pretrial diversion."

"What's that?"

"A slap on the wrist. Most important, it means no record."

"What if the prosecutor won't go along with it?" Tommy said.

"Trust me, Tony can and will deliver if a trial is his only other option." He clapped Tommy on the back. "No matter how much Tony pleads and begs, don't fold. It's pretrial diversion or trial."

"Wish you were representing me."

Cash stood. "You and me both."

# CHAPTER THIRTEEN

The parking lot behind the courthouse was nearly empty, which made Cash all the more suspicious of the black limo with tinted windows. With scores of spots open, why had it parked next to his Carrera?

He stopped short of the lot, turned around, and bumped into a solid wall of muscle. The bruiser towered six-foot-eight, give or take an inch. Weighed three hundred pounds, plus or minus ten. An ex-Dallas Cowboy nicknamed *The Manster*.

Manster's dimensions made it easy to overlook his sidekick, who was a foot shorter, one hundred and fifty pounds lighter. But the shiny pistol in the shoulder holster boosted his stature.

"Where you going, McCahill?" Shorty said. The Jersey accent pegged him as one of Benanti's tools.

Cash looked around. No one in sight. "Left my phone in the courthouse."

"You can get it tomorrow." Evidently Shorty did all the talking. The brains of the duo. Low bar.

Cash considered a fast break but recalled that Manster had led the league in sacks several seasons. And throwing a punch wasn't an option. It'd be like hitting the building.

"You boys don't want to create a scene," Cash said, "not here at the courthouse."

"No, we don't," Shorty said.

Manster locked Cash in a bear hug, and Shorty jabbed his neck with a hypodermic needle.

"Hey," Cash shouted, "what the fuck!" The protest died on his lips, and the world went dark.

\* \* \*

When Cash came to, it was still dark. The black bag over his head stank of drool and vomit. He hoped it wasn't his.

He jerked on his limbs, but his wrists and ankles were lashed to a wooden chair. No give there. His heartbeat spiked. Breaths escaped in hot bursts.

"Where am I?" No way to drain the fear from his voice.

"Tell you that," Benanti said, "and we spoil the surprise."

Didn't take Cash long to figure it out, the techno beat from the floor below being the first clue. Whistles and catcalls from a liquored-up crowd, the clincher.

"*Metamorphosis?*" he said.

No response. Cash had his answer.

The locale set, he knew the layout of the command center from past visits. Too many wasted days and wasted nights here.

Benanti would be bunkered behind a bulletproof desk, with dueling wet bars to the right and left. An entire wall of live action screens scoured every corner and crevice of the so-called gentlemen's club and its grounds.

The cameras captured enough blackmail material to keep the city, county, and state off Benanti's back. Probably the feds as well.

Based on the shuffling of footsteps, Cash pegged at six the number of henchmen milling around the room. Give or take a goon.

"Lift the bag off his head," Benanti said. "I want him to see it coming."

The bag stayed in place as heavy footsteps approached to his right. A mouth breather with B.O. loomed over him.

Cash leaned away, far as the ropes allowed. The music downstairs died, signaling a change of strippers on stage. The room turned quiet as a tomb.

A loud pop exploded in Cash's ear.

Soon as the bag came off, a spotlight struck Cash blind. Eyes watering, he couldn't tell whether his tears sprang from relief or despair. Either way, the future looked bleak.

Blurry shapes around him appeared more like apparitions than persons. Took forever for the room and its ghosts to settle into focus. Even longer to accept his fate.

He was a prisoner in the command center of *Metamorphosis*. Suspected of being a snitch by a sick, paranoid fuck. Tied to a wooden chair and surrounded by goons who knew how and where to bury bodies.

On the ground floor, the DJ launched a fresh assault on eardrums. Gangsta rap. Done down, dirty, and deafening.

The heavy beat from below raced against Cash's heart and lost. "I didn't talk." He kept the closing argument short.

"I know." Benanti handed down the verdict in an it's-just-business monotone. A thin veneer of civilization over the sociopath's deadpan delivery. "If you had, I'd have known."

Cash switched survival strategies. From taciturn to talking his fool head off. Desperate to keep the conversation going, he resorted to the obvious. "You have someone inside Seagoville, right?"

Benanti killed the spotlight. His hard edges took shape. The dark eyes were like sinkholes.

Cash took a stab at outing the mole. "Shafer?" Not exactly a wild-assed guess, given the agent's eleventh-hour prison visit. Could be on the take, sent there by Benanti to test Cash's loyalty.

"Nice try." Benanti turned to Shorty. "Okay, Mario, give it to him."

Mario had both hands behind his back. He showed his right hand first, the one holding a Dom Perignon bottle by the neck. His left hand brought forth a flute of champagne.

"Untie the mouthpiece," Benanti said, "so he can enjoy his drink."

His hands free, Cash took the glass.

"Drink up," Benanti said. "My girls are preparing a special dessert for you."

Cash lifted the flute for a toast. "To just desserts."

# CHAPTER FOURTEEN

After midnight Benanti's boys dropped Cash off at Eva's Uptown apartment. Given the odds against sleeping, he should've gone another round of drinks.

Eva's date turned out to be a moaner. And a marathon moaner to boot. Woke Cash around two a.m. and again two hours later. Who knew Eva had such stamina?

During lulls in the lovemaking, crowd noise from the sports bar across State Street kept Cash up. He stewed in the dark. It had been three days since Sandy Robinson's ultimatum to get a job and a place to stay by Monday, or else. Here it was early Saturday morning, and he had neither.

And not much in the way of prospects. A line on a part-time sales position with a national furniture chain (straight commission, no salary or benefits) and an offer to housesit for a month while a former client and his fourth wife toured Europe. It was the least the client could do, considering he had stiffed Cash on a 250k fee five years ago.

Not that Cash had expected the doors of Dallas to fly open for a convicted felon. Just not to be bolted shut and welded tight. Even without the racket from the bedroom and the sports bar, worry would've robbed him of sleep.

Come Monday, he faced a tongue-lashing from Judge Tapia at best. Worst case, a one-way trip back to Seagoville. Crazy thoughts of taking flight and living off the grid pinged his brain, like moths bouncing off a bulb. Not landing for a stay but not leaving either. Just circling and circling.

A sense of dread drove him to his feet. He paced a living room not much larger than the cell he'd shared with Big Black and Biddle. Five steps in any direction and he hit a dead end.

He passed by the desk three times before temptation got the better of him. He turned on a lamp and rifled through the drawers. A ledger and folder bulging with bank receipts contained a cache of records for two accounts: Eva's personal and Goldberg's business.

Good thing she handled the finances, because the old fool couldn't balance the books on a bet. He could score a six-figure fee one week and wind up broke the next.

*Broke* being the operative word here. Over the past couple of years, while Cash had been a guest of the feds, Eva's nest egg of sixty thousand dollars had vanished.

Goldberg started out paying her three thousand net every two weeks. Over time, the payments became fewer, smaller, and farther between. This year saw more installments missed than made.

Even worse, about six months ago she began plowing her personal funds into the practice to cover office expenses. Rent, transcripts, filing fees, travel vouchers, and the like. Advances that were turning into charitable contributions to the nonprofit institution known as Gary Goldberg, Esquire.

Eva never met a charity case she didn't fall for.

Last month she'd bounced a check. Must've been traumatic for a fussbudget like her. And she had fallen behind on just about everything, including installment payments on her beloved wheels.

Not like her at all.

The only constant in the ledger was the seven hundred dollars she wired to her mother in Tuxpan every pay period. Support for a widow with five mouths to feed.

Which was exactly like Eva.

Red ink riddled the most recent pages of the ledger, a sign that both she and the business were bleeding out. All the more reason Cash had to get his law license back, soon.

She had suffered in his absence, financially and otherwise, and a small sense of relief swept over him. Okay, maybe more than a small sense. Gave him an opening to ride to the rescue.

The patter of bare feet on a wooden floor aborted his audit. He dumped the records in a drawer, killed the light, and dived onto the couch.

Darkness sharpened his sense of hearing. The footsteps stopped in the kitchen, where a cabinet creaked open and ice cubes clinked into a glass. A faucet sputtered and cleared its throat.

"Eva," he said softly. Even odds of being right. Not sure whether he wanted to be right or wrong here. With Eva, he had lots of history and no shot. With her GF, no history and almost no chance.

"Go back to sleep," Eva said.

He sat up on the couch and turned on a lamp. Her place had been tricked out like a man cave, what with the poster of the bikinied blonde on a Harley above the flat-screen TV. Pennants for local sports teams bandaged the walls.

Cash recognized the hog on the poster, an Iron 883 with a candy-red custom shell. The model Eva had bought three years ago over his objection. Way too much bike for her, he had warned. A miracle she could hold it up.

Tonight, she seemed smaller than usual. An oversize T-shirt fell almost to her knees, and her dark hair corkscrewed wildly.

"Can't sleep with all the racket inside and out." He flashed her a knowing smile. "Read me a bedtime story."

"What are you, five?" She looked toward the bedroom. "Oh well, Paula's down and out for the night, so if this will shut you up."

She rubbed her chin. "How about the tale of the Big Bad Wolf and the Three Little Lawyers?"

"I thought they were three little pigs."

"Isn't that what I just said? Now don't interrupt me." She sat on the edge of the couch and held her arms at ninety degree angles, palms up, cradling an imaginary book in her hands.

"Once upon a time, there were three little lawyers. The first little lawyer built her practice on Daddy's connections. Let's call her Jenna. The second lawyer made a bundle on bluff and bullshit. We'll call him Cash. And the third lawyer relied on sweat and savvy. His name is Goldy."

"Not sure I like where this is heading," he said.

She shushed him and pretended to turn the page. "A Big Bad Wolf came upon the office of the first little lawyer and said, 'I'll huff and I'll puff and I'll blow your office down.' And he did."

"So Jenna sought shelter with the second little lawyer, but the Big Bad Wolf soon arrived at Cash's door and said, 'I'll huff and I'll puff and I'll blow your practice down.' And again, he did.

"So both Jenna and Cash took refuge at the office of the third lawyer. The Big Bad Wolf made the same threat to Goldy.

But this time when he huffed and puffed, he couldn't shake the rock-solid structure."

She air-closed the book. "Now go to sleep and dream about what you'll do when you get your license back." She pulled the sheet to his chin and kissed him on the forehead.

"What *we'll* do when I get my license back." He grabbed her arm as she started to rise. "You and Moana Lisa in there, how serious?"

"She's the one." No hesitation. No waffling.

"Have I met her?"

"No," she said, "because I'm trying to hold onto this one. So I'll thank you in advance for not making a play on Paula and embarrassing all three of us."

"Be bad form for me as a guest to steal her from under your nose."

"In your case, true to form."

"Well, you know what they say. Once you've been with a lawyer, all others lose their appeal. So where'd you pick her up? The nearest biker bar?"

"Worse. A legal conference."

He did a double take. "You swore you'd never date lawyers."

"Yeah well, I've learned never to say never. Now get some sleep." Her tone now maternal. "You've got a big day ahead. Starting at breakfast with your new boss."

Cash bolted upright. "What? When were you planning on telling me this?"

"In about four hours," she said.

"When and where am I meeting him? Who is he?"

"You're meeting him in five hours at the Original Pancake House on Lemmon, and that's when you'll find out who he is."

"How will I recognize him?"

"Oh, he'll recognize you." She smiled. "But he might hire you anyway."

# CHAPTER FIFTEEN

Cash smelled an ambush the instant he entered The Original Pancake House. That and smoke-cured bacon.

On the subject of pork, he hadn't seen so many cops under one roof since his booking on jury tampering charges three years ago. His arrest had brought together every cop he'd destroyed on the stand in a classless reunion.

This morning Cash couldn't throw a shoe in the restaurant without hitting one of the boys in blue. All of them packing heat and most bearing a grudge as well.

But the biggest grudge in the place belonged to a civilian with no weapon, other than his razor-sharp tongue and an annoying habit of whistling off-key. Gary Goldberg waved Cash over to his back booth.

As Cash weaved through a maze of tables, he couldn't help but turn his back to one enemy or another. Every clink of silverware sounded like the cocking of a pistol. Every cough, like a shot.

Nor did the booth offer safe refuge for the pair of pariahs. In a contest for the title of the lawyer most likely to be dumped in an alley, bloody and unconscious, Goldberg edged Cash by a whisker. Both had track records of ripping cops a new one on the stand, but Goldberg had been at the game longer. More notches on his alligator belt.

And unlike Cash, Goldberg had never taken a time-out for a trip to Club Fed. Karma still hadn't caught up with the old man.

Goldberg didn't rise to greet Cash or even offer to shake. He was too busy attacking a tall stack of blueberry pancakes floating on a syrup slick. "Because you're late," he mumbled with a full mouth, "I took the liberty of ordering for you."

Cash stared at the plate before him. "Pigs in a blanket?" He looked around the room. The number of cops seemed to have doubled. "Really?"

Goldberg belched.

"For the record," Cash said, "I'm not late. Eva told me to be here at eight, and it's eight on the dot. If she had been straight about who I was meeting, I wouldn't be here at all."

"Desperate for a job as you are, you should've been early."

"Not desperate enough to work for you, old man."

"Eva begs to differ."

"She has a sick sense of humor." Cash pushed away the plate. "And this must be her idea of a joke."

"Won't be a laughing matter if you don't have a job by Monday." Goldberg downed his coffee in three gulps, then raised the cup for a refill. The waitress shot him a dirty look, then resumed flirting with a bulked-up cop two tables over.

Goldberg turned back to Cash. "Tapia's itching to send you back to the slammer." He shook his head. "Don't know how you manage to piss off so many women."

"Learned from the master."

Goldberg lifted the cup higher. The waitress didn't budge, but Muscle Cop swaggered over. Up close it looked as if every breath threatened to split the seams of his uniform. The badge read: A. Conant.

*Damn.* Cash had heard of the ape. Nothing good. Called "Conant the Barbarian" by his buddies. Worse, by everyone else.

"Unless you're holding that cup for exercise," Conant said in a cut-the-shit cracker accent, "you're wasting your time. MaryAnn's big brother was my partner until you tripped him up on the stand and put him in I.A.'s crosshairs. Your scumbag client walked away to lie, cheat, and steal another day, while my boy Bobby got busted to the graveyard shift. Ain't justice grand?"

Goldberg lowered the cup to the table. Slow, cautious movements, as if he were putting down a loaded pistol. Kept both hands above the table.

Conant glared at Cash. "And you, cocksucker, a fucking miracle you made it out of the big house alive. Be an even bigger one if you make it out of the parking lot without a ticket."

"For what?" Cash said.

Conant grinned. "Broken tail light, for starters."

"But I don't have a...." Cash didn't finish the sentence. He'd be lucky to limit the damage to a tail light.

As a parting shot, Conant swept Cash's plate into his lap. He strutted away, pausing at the next table to high-five a fellow cop. Then turned back toward the booth. "Oh, and enjoy the secret sauce that went into your breakfasts."

Cash brushed the food off his lap and onto the floor. Goldberg went back to work on the pancakes.

"Tell me you're not going to eat those now," Cash said.

"Ah, he was just pricking with us." Goldberg poured more syrup onto the stack. "All in good fun."

"Well, I've had all the fun I can take this morning." Cash rose. "See you...uh...never."

"Don't you want to hear about the job offer?"

"Not if it involves working for you." Cash dropped a twenty-dollar bill on the table.

Goldberg looked up. "What if it involves working against Benanti?"

# CHAPTER SIXTEEN

"Okay, so like, what's it going to cost me?" Taylor Donovan sat across the desk from Goldberg, with Cash flanked to her right. Her flip-tone rubbed Cash the wrong way.

She crossed her tanned legs, hiking the skirt halfway up her thighs. A Jimmy Choo pump dangled from her elevated foot, holding on by a toe. Her perfume cut through the fog left behind by decades of cheap cigars.

At first blush, she could've been a pampered coed facing a minor violation. Like speeding. Smoking pot. Littering.

Then again, she wasn't blushing.

"In dollars," Goldberg said, "or years?"

Cash rolled his eyes. The old man must've borrowed his bedside manner from Attila the Hun.

Besides, Cash knew Goldberg's weakness. If the looker played her cards right, the case could end up costing the old fool more than it would her. Not only in dollars out-of-pocket, but also in years shaved off his ticker.

Cash pegged Taylor's hourly rate at eight-fifty, give or take a hundred. Five grand for an entire night of fun and games, but only if she could stomach staying over. Twenty-five thou for the best week of a man's life.

Or a woman's.

Double that for a kinky couple.

Which more or less matched Goldberg's fee structure. As well as Cash's, back in the day. Stripped of his law license, he now pocketed fifty dollars an hour, half of what clients shelled out for his services as the most overqualified paralegal on the planet.

It struck Cash as funny that the price tag for an ace defense lawyer and a top-drawer hooker tracked so closely. Must say something about the professions. Or the society.

"I was thinking of dollars," she said, "instead of years."

For someone who'd received a target letter from the IRS only yesterday, Taylor sounded as calm as if she were discussing what to wear to the Crystal Charity Ball. Coolness under fire made her special. What made her extra special, a *date* could take her to a formal event, and no one would suspect her of being on the meter.

Well, no one but Cash, but then he had a lifetime of experience with the Taylors of the world, starting with a mother who had taught him to stay still and quiet inside his locked room when her *dates* came around.

One fall afternoon, at the not so tender age of eight, he had waited in his room for hours. Darkness fell. His stomach growled. When he finally ventured out, she was gone.

From his first days as a defense lawyer, he'd kept a steady stable of prostitutes as clients. Had a soft heart for them. A soft dick too. They were the only clients who remained truly off-limits.

Taylor's shoe slipped off, nailing the floor and jolting Cash back to the present.

With her auburn hair pulled into a ponytail, she looked younger than her twenty-four years, but her husky voice registered older. So it all balanced out nicely.

"Just tell me what it'll take to get the feds off my back." Businesswoman brusque.

Goldberg held a calling card at arm's length, squinting. "This the agent who handed you the target letter?"

Taylor nodded.

"Shafer's bad news." Goldberg looked up at her. "In addition to being a royal S.O.B., he's career C.I.D. Meaning you're S.O.L."

She gave him a quizzical look. "C.I.D.?"

"Criminal Investigation Division. The tax goons who keep score in years, not dollars." He returned the card to her. "Did he try to interview you?"

She nodded again.

"You talk to him?"

She shook her head. "Said my lawyer would contact him."

Cash smiled. Perfect. Clearly not her first brush with Johnny Law.

"Good girl," Goldberg said, "because that snake will twist your words against you. He can turn a simple howdy-do into a full-fledged confession."

"Doesn't he have anything better to do than hassle me?" The first hint of emotion rippled through her voice.

"Not when you happen to work for Larry Benanti." Goldberg rocked back in his chair and swung his snakeskin boots onto the desk. "Shafer's been chasing Benanti for two decades. Almost had him three years ago, till a more enticing target popped up and distracted the prosecutors." He winked at Cash.

Cash bristled. So much for his vow to keep his mouth shut and let Goldberg do the talking. "For Shafer to chase Benanti twenty years without catching him means one of two things. Either Shafer's the sorriest agent on the planet, or you and he both work for the same man."

"Don't know about the agent," she said, "but in my case, it's *worked*. Past tense."

"Well, that could explain your problem with the IRS," Cash said. "I can't see Benanti letting you go, not in your prime anyway. When you're thirty-five going on sixty, then he might cut you free. That is, if he can't make a buck by auctioning off your body parts."

Goldberg cleared his throat. "There's a way to find out if Shafer's bent. If you were to crawl to Benanti on your hands and knees and beg him to take you back, would your tax problems magically disappear?"

"I'm never going back to him," Taylor said.

Cash caught himself wanting to believe her. Dangerous territory for a defense lawyer to buy anything a client said, especially at the first meeting. "Why'd you leave Benanti? Can't be the money. He pays top dollar."

"In the interest of full disclosure," Goldberg said, "Cash has first-hand knowledge of Benanti's deep pockets and fat payroll."

Cash leaned forward. "In the interest of fuller disclosure, I represented Benanti in the past. Not proud of that and don't work for him now, so there's no legal conflict to prevent me from working on your case. But if my past representation causes you any heartburn, I'll bow out."

"No problem for me," she said, "if it's not one for you."

Cash eased back in the chair. "Then we're square. Tell us why you bailed on Benanti."

"I got sick and tired of the constant sexual harassment."

Cash waited for the punch line. None came. Now he'd heard everything. Since when did call girls start complaining about sexual harassment by their pimps? Wasn't that part of the deal?

"Reality check," Cash said. "By and large, pimps aren't real good about drawing the line between business and pleasure."

"I wouldn't call Mister Benanti a pimp," she said.

"I would." Cash beat Goldberg to the obvious comeback.

"Besides, he was never less than a perfect gentleman to me," she said, "but his wife...she couldn't keep her hands off me."

Goldberg let out a loud guffaw and looked from her to Cash. "Well, I guess that gives you two something in common."

# CHAPTER SEVENTEEN

A man could set his watch by Mariposa Benanti's workout regimen. Six a.m. sharp, five days a week, she clocked into the Preston Hollow Equinox for two hours of extreme cross-training, followed by a deep tissue rubdown.

While Cash had been away, she had upped her security. Or perhaps it had been tightened since his release. Because of his release.

In an underground garage beneath the health club, she emerged from a black limo and whispered to the chauffeur. She held his hand a beat too long before letting go.

The vehicles parked in the lot were empty, except for Cash's conspicuous Carrera. He made a mental note to ditch the obnoxious license plate: LITIG8R.

The lights in the lot burned bluish and bright, giving Cash a clear view of Mariposa. His first sighting in nearly three years dashed any hopes that she had aged horribly in his absence. Or aged at all.

Damned unfair. No forty-four-year-old should look that good at this hour under any lighting. Certainly not after a steady diet of cocaine, caviar, and champagne. The silver warm-up suit showcased a body that'd be the envy of women half her age.

The chauffeur's presence made Cash consider taking off and waiting for a better opportunity to confront her. But he'd already waited three years.

He had to know if she had set him up on the obstruction charge. Also whether she had put Taylor Donovan in the IRS's crosshairs. Besides, who knew if he would ever catch her without a shadow, and the day he couldn't handle a simple driver....

Cash sprang from the Porsche and intercepted her before she made it to the elevator. If the ambush alarmed her, she didn't show it. Hardly acknowledged his presence. A nod and half-smile, that was all.

He spoke only after it became clear she wouldn't. "I see you're still hitting it hard every morning."

"Good habits are hard to break," she said.

He took a step toward her. "In my experience it's the bad ones that are hardest to break."

She stood her ground. "You always had trouble separating the good from the bad."

"Occupational hazard. Lawyers are trained to divide the world into legal and illegal. Doesn't always translate into good and bad."

The chauffeur sprinted to Mariposa's side. He moved more like a bodyguard than a driver. The flattened nose and facial dings marked him as a brawler not afraid to lead with his mug.

"He bothering you, Missus B?" The accent shouted Jersey Shore, the breeding ground of Benanti's brass knuckle goons. Most of the mobster's legal firepower hailed from the Garden State as well. Cash had been the exception.

"Wait for me at the elevator, Bobby." Her tone busted him back to gofer status. "I'll be done with Mister McCahill shortly."

"After I frisk him." Bobby's clenched fists dared Cash to resist. Cash didn't take the bait, mostly because he liked his face the way it was.

"That won't be necessary," she said. "The only way Mister McCahill could harm me is by talking me to death."

Bobby's shoulders slumped. He trudged to the elevator.

The bruiser out of earshot, Cash breathed easier. "So it's Mister McCahill now. There was a time when we were on less formal footing."

"It's not healthy to live in the past. You'd best get on with your life. Never know how much of it is left."

"Thanks, but if I want clichés from a life coach, I'll watch *Dr. Phil.*"

"If you're not in the market for friendly advice," she said, "why are you here?"

Good question. Cash had a real reason and a pretext. He went with the pretext. "Taylor Donovan. Name ring a bell?"

Mariposa's brow furrowed but just as quickly smoothed. Her reaction told Cash more than a hundred polygraphs.

"She's a very troubled girl." Her voice betrayed concern. "Has a hard time seeing what's good for her and what's not. A lot like you in that regard."

Cash glanced at Bobby, who was hammering the up button on the elevator with his fist. As if overkill would kick it into higher gear.

Cash turned back to Mariposa. "Seems Taylor has the IRS nipping at her heels. Know anything about that?"

Her brow furrowed deeper and longer this time. "Taylor has made her bed." Her tone turned cold, sounding less like an ex-boss than a jilted lover. "But are you really here to ask about her? Or are you still trying to figure out who turned you in?"

Busted. "I was winding my way to that question."

"A little obvious," she said, "even for you. As for Taylor, what makes you think I'd want to finger her?"

"*Finger her*...interesting choice of words. But right off the bat, I can think of one reason. Seems like every time you get your ass in a crack, someone else takes a fall. SOS. Same old strategy. Lose a pawn, save the queen."

The elevator pinged its arrival. "Elevator's here," Bobby shouted.

"Your boy has a keen sense of the obvious," Cash said.

"Hold the elevator," she shouted to Bobby. "I need another minute with Mister McCahill. Forgot that he's a slow learner."

"You're already late for the trainer," Bobby said.

"She'll wait." Mariposa turned back to Cash. "A parting lesson for both you and Taylor. Don't blame me for your legal jams. Sometimes bad things happen to bad people."

"I'm counting on it," Cash said, "and I've got a parting gift for you." He reached into his coat pocket.

Big mistake.

"Gun!" she shouted.

Bobby broke toward him. The clap of soles on cement echoed like gunfire in the garage. He launched himself, his forehead nailing Cash's sternum.

Cash went down hard, leaving him dazed and breathless. When his vision cleared, Bobby loomed over him, pointing a pistol at his chest.

"Take the gun out of your pocket," Bobby said, "slow and easy. Lay it on the ground and push it toward Missus B."

Cash slowly pulled his hand from his pocket and opened it to reveal a black string bikini. He turned his head toward Mariposa. "I believe this is yours."

She knelt and took the bikini. Checked the label, then dropped the swimsuit on Cash's chest.

"Wrong again," she said.

"You sure you don't want me to teach this prick a lesson, Missus B?" Close as Bobby could come to begging.

"Not today," she said, "but be patient. This won't be your last crack at Mister McCahill. Like I said, he's a slow learner."

# CHAPTER EIGHTEEN

A larger-than-life oil portrait of Taylor Donovan, posed like Goya's *Naked Maja*, greeted Cash and Goldberg in the foyer of her penthouse apartment.

*Naked* being the operative word.

A black cockapoo skittered toward them, its nails *clickety clacking* across the marble hallway. The dog braked too late and bounced off Cash's leg, then backed away, yapping like its tail was on fire.

"That's odd," Taylor said, "because Carmen usually takes to everyone. Must be a lawyer thing." She scooped up the pet. "I'll put her in the bedroom."

Goldberg held his tongue until Taylor was out of sight. "One thing for sure, if we do decide to meet with Shafer, it damn sure won't be here."

Cash nodded. "If that pit bull ever set foot inside this place, he'd have an orgasm. And not the good old-fashioned bust-a-nut kind but the twisted shit high he gets from slapping the cuffs on someone."

Goldberg lowered his voice. "This palace practically begs for a tax investigation. No twenty-four-year-old should live this well. Not without a trust fund or a sugar daddy, anyway."

"What's wrong with my apartment?" Taylor said from the hall.

Busted. Cash wondered how much of the conversation she'd overheard.

"Absolutely nothing," Goldberg said, "and therein lies the problem."

Cash pulled Goldberg away from the painting and into a split-level living room. "What's wrong," Cash said, "is that the income you claimed on your tax returns wouldn't cover the utilities here."

Cash and Goldberg staked out opposite ends of a white leather couch, while Taylor sat cross-legged on a yoga mat on the wooden floor. A midmorning workout had left sweat stains on her Lululemon top.

"So amend the returns," she said, "and I'll pay the difference."

"Honey," Goldberg said, "you lost that option when the IRS opened a criminal investigation. Amending your returns now would be confessing to tax fraud."

Her legs pretzeled into lotus pose. "Well, since my business is strictly cash basis, I don't see how the feds can prove my returns are false."

"It's called a net worth case," Cash said, "which happens to be Shafer's specialty." He picked up a vase on the coffee table. "Take this, for example. Looks like real crystal."

She nodded warily.

"What did it set you back?"

"I don't know. Five hundred maybe. Six tops."

Cash looked around the room. "Shitload of artwork here. You got receipts for all the paintings and knickknacks?"

"Sure...well, most of them anyway...scattered here and there." She sounded less certain by the word.

"The Beamer in the garage, you making monthly payments on it?"

"It's paid for." Came off less like a boast than an admission.

Cash whistled. "Throw in these digs, and you've got a net worth case Shafer could make in his sleep. He adds up all the money you blow on toys and shit. Tells jurors living hand-to-mouth that there's no way anyone could afford this lifestyle on the income you've sworn to."

"So what are my options?" The first hint of panic crept into her voice.

"There are no good ones," Cash said. "Our job is to pick the least bad plan."

Goldberg cleared his throat, a signal for Cash to shut up and let the lawyer with a license lay out the alternatives. Cash eased back on the couch.

"For starters," Goldberg said, "we can do nothing and pray for Passover."

"Does that ever work?" she said.

Goldberg nodded. "More often than you might think, but not when Shafer's on your tail."

Her legs still in a lotus knot, she leaned back until her shoulder blades touched the mat. Tucked her chin and tailbone and extended her arms at her sides, palms up. "Next option."

"We go to trial and force the government to prove its case."

"What are my odds at trial?"

"You have a five percent chance of an acquittal and a one hundred percent certainty of pissing off the prosecutor and judge for wasting their precious time."

Her chest rose and fell steadily. Six beats up. Six down. Eerily calm for a kid with one foot in prison and the other in Benanti's trap.

"So what's my best play?"

Goldberg placed his Stetson on the coffee table. "Cut a deal. The sooner, the better. The less work the agent has to do, the less time he'll want from you. Plead guilty and pay your back taxes, plus interest and penalties, even if you have to sell everything you own to do it. Bat those baby blues at the judge while I beg for mercy. Best case, you shave a year or two off your sentence and end up doing a year or two at Club Fed."

The pace of her breathing quickened. Three beats up. Three down. "I can't do prison."

Cash couldn't contain himself any longer. "There's a fourth option." He didn't look at Goldberg. Already knew the old fart's reaction.

"Toss Shafer a bigger fish," Cash said, "and he might let you slip through the net. Even if the Benantis didn't get you into this mess, and I still believe they did, they can get you out of it."

"Cash, a word with you...in private." Goldberg snatched his Stetson and stormed to the foyer. Cash took his time catching up.

"What the hell are you doing?" Goldberg said.

"Trying to help our client make an informed decision."

Goldberg fell about six inches short of going nose-to-nose with Cash but still managed to get in his face. "You can't be serious about having her roll over on Benanti."

"That's her only shot at avoiding prison, and she ought to be told that."

"Why don't you just tell her to buy a shotgun and blow her brains out? That'd also keep her out of the pen, and it'd be a lot quicker and cleaner than your way."

STING LIKE A BUTTERFLY

Cash cocked his head toward the living room. "You think her dance card is full on the outside. Wait till she hits Dykesville. Be like tossing a filet into a dog pound."

"You can't sacrifice that poor girl in your private war against Benanti. Don't let your desire for revenge get the better of you."

Goldberg had hit a nerve. Cash lashed back. "Don't let your fear of Benanti get the better of you."

Goldberg laughed. "Son, at my age there's only two things left to fear. Forgetting where I put my car keys and stumbling into a coven of my exes." He donned the Stetson. "I won't be a party to sending that girl to an early grave."

"That's not the issue," Cash said. "It's whether she has a better shot at surviving on the outside or inside. And she has to make that call."

# CHAPTER NINETEEN

The noose dangled from the top limb of a coat rack in Sandy Robinson's office. It swayed gently, as if waving Cash in.

It would be the warmest greeting he'd receive.

Cash didn't wait for an invitation to sit. "Do you keep all your clients waiting an hour?"

"Helps them learn patience," Sandy said. "Besides, you're a felon, not a client."

No apology from her. No small talk. Just an opening shot across the bow, followed by another. "One who needs to get a real job real fast."

"I have a job."

She snickered. "You call carrying Goldberg's briefcase a job? I had something more socially useful in mind for you. Busboy, dishwasher, maybe work your way up to janitor."

Cash shifted from defense to offense. "If you're so concerned about my employment status, don't force me to come down to the courthouse every week and cool my heels in the waiting room. Let me phone it in."

She shook her head. "There's that impatience again. You really need to work on it. Continue coming to my office at ten sharp every Monday morning and wait until I'm ready to see you."

Cash bit his tongue. Arguing with a probation officer was like debating a judge. No way to win. The only issues were how much to risk and how badly to lose.

A P.O. could make life easy for an ex-con or turn it into an endless nightmare. Robinson had consigned Cash to the lowest rung of hell, the depth reserved for baby rapers, con artists who prey on the elderly, and criminal defense lawyers.

"Speaking of work," Cash said, "I'd better get back to mine. Wouldn't want to slow down the wheels of justice."

Her complexion turned two-tone, the face flushing red, the acne pits purple. No amount of makeup could hide her disgust.

"Don't flatter yourself," she said. "Your life is about stopping the wheels of justice dead in their tracks. World would be a better place if I could bar you from being a paralegal."

"Ah, but you can't."

"What I can do is make sure you're not practicing law without a license. If I catch you playing lawyer, you'll go back to prison, with a lifetime ban from the bar."

He feared she had learned of his work on Biddle's brief, but she dismissed him without going there. Freed from her clutches, the fear faded. He gravitated to the fifteenth floor, where a cloud of cheap cologne and flop sweat made him nostalgic for his days as a trial lawyer.

Four of the six courtrooms on the floor had warnings posted outside the doors: "Judicial Proceedings in Progress." Judgespeak for "tread lightly, mute your cellphone, and shut up."

Cash peeked inside three courtrooms before finding Jenna Powell on her feet in the fourth, lodging an objection to a doper's presentence report. He slipped onto the back pew, swelling the ranks of spectators to one.

"Your honor," Jenna said, "the defendant's rap sheet understates his true criminal history. For that reason, we object to treating him as a category one offender and request that he be deemed category two under the guidelines." Her monotone telegraphed an objection being made for the record and not from any deeply held conviction.

"Your objection is duly noted, Miss Powell, and overruled." Judge Watkins' voice carried even less passion than hers. "We'll break for lunch and resume the sentencing at one-thirty."

Cash ambushed Jenna on her way out. Her initial flash of panic gave way to a long, slow burn. No shortage of passion now.

She brushed past him without a word, but he caught up to her in the hall. "I thought we might grab lunch," he said. "Been a while since we talked."

Jenna pulled free of his grip. "You shouldn't be here."

"Last time I checked, the courthouse was a public building. Or has Moore changed that to by invitation only?"

"I'll ask him at lunch." Her eyes swept the lobby before landing on his. "My father and I are meeting him at the Petroleum Club."

"Perfect. The president and vice president of my fan club dining together."

"If you're serious about getting your license back, this is not the way to do it. Tom can hurt your chances with the bar, and my father can kill them."

Copy that. "Last time we talked," Cash said, "I got the impression you wouldn't lift a finger to help me."

She scoured the lobby again. "I'm waiting for the right time to approach Tom. Closer to the wedding will be better."

"I'm betting you call the whole thing off."

Her eyes flashed. "Won't happen."

"You have a track record of bolting at the last minute," he said. "You and I were engaged once, remember?"

"Yeah, but then I sobered up."

Jenna's father emerged from the elevator, looking every tailored inch the name partner at a white-shoe law firm, the go-to counsel for Fortune 500 companies, and the fixer for big-shot politicians. Three-piece suit, the perfect shade of gray to match the salt-and-pepper hair. French cuffs and fancy monogram on a cream-colored silk shirt. Powder blue tie to bring out his eyes, the same hue as Jenna's.

"Please go," she whispered.

Cash stuck out his hand. "Good to see you, Mister Powell."

Powell walked past Cash and spoke to his daughter. "We're late for lunch."

Cash lowered his hand. "Would love to join you, but sadly I've got another engagement. Some other time. I'll have my associate call yours."

He beat the father-daughter duo to the elevator, rode down eight floors with them in an awkward silence before bailing on the seventh floor. Not that seven was his lucky number, but the criminal side of the IRS set up shop there.

Marty Shafer's office made Robinson's seem like a ballroom. Though both cookie-cutter rooms were roughly the same shape and size, stacks of cardboard boxes turned Shafer's into a maze leading to a metal desk. With only two chairs in the office, Shafer sat behind the desk, and Cash took the hot seat.

"Who's he?" Cash pointed to a framed black-and-white head shot on the wall behind the agent. Best guess, the bald, bespectacled subject was Shafer's father. Or grandfather.

"Why, that's Frank J. Wilson." Shafer's tone suggested that the name alone should do the trick.

"The singer?"

Shafer snorted. "The Treasury agent who took down Capone on tax charges. Ness got the glory, but our boy Frankie made the case."

"Kinda like today," Cash said. "You work up the cases, and the U.S. Attorney takes the credit."

"Exactly like today."

"You're probably wondering what I'm doing here," Cash said.

The agent shook his head. "Word travels fast in the courthouse. You want your license back, and you're willing to throw your mother under the bus to get it." He pulled out a pad and pen. "Okay, let's start the dance. Whose scalps can you deliver?"

"I'm here to ask questions," Cash said, "not answer them."

Shafer put down the pen. "That's not how this works. You of all people should know that."

"This won't take long," Cash said. "Fact is, I've got only one question. Do you really want to nail Benanti, or are you in his pocket?"

# CHAPTER TWENTY

Taylor Donovan stood in the doorway of her penthouse apartment. Hallway lights cast her in a honeyed glow. Made her look otherworldly. Angelic.

Cash knew better.

An oversize T-shirt bared her right shoulder and fell north of her knees. The message on the Vegas souvenir shirt said it all: *I Saw Nothing at the Mob Museum.*

The black cockapoo in her arms growled at Cash. Or as close to a growl as a cockapoo could come.

"Carmen really doesn't like you," Taylor said. "Wait here while I put her in the bedroom." Off they went.

"I'm an acquired taste," Cash said to the empty hallway.

Taylor returned to the foyer. "I wondered which of my lawyers would circle back here first."

"Well, technically I'm a paralegal, not a lawyer."

"I keep forgetting that distinction. Suspect that you do as well."

Cash couldn't dispute that. "Sounds like you've been talking to my pain-in-the-ass boss."

"Not yet," she said, "but I have no doubt he'll turn up shortly."

Change the subject. The less said about Goldberg tonight, the better. If the old man learned of Cash's after-hours visit, he'd blow a gasket.

"You always answer the door dressed like that?" He strained to sound paternal. "Or should I say undressed like that?"

"Never had a client complain before."

"I'm not complaining," he said, "and I'm also not the client here."

"Remains to be seen." She led him to the living room, where she sat on the leather couch. "I'm still not clear on who's paying whom for this call."

He took the chair farthest from the couch. "We'll call it a wash."

"Does your boss know you're here?" Her tone suggested she knew the answer.

*Damn.* She kept bringing up Goldberg. "I'll give him a report tomorrow. It's past his bedtime."

She checked her diamond-studded Rolex. "Past mine too, which leads to the question of what's so important that it couldn't have waited until morning."

Though he had rehearsed a longer answer, he rushed to the bottom line. "I can get you a walk."

Her eyes widened, then narrowed. "No prison time?"

"Not a day. You pay back taxes, plus penalty and interest, promise to be a good girl going forward, and put all this behind you."

"Who would I have to fuck to get that deal?"

"Benanti." He locked eyes with her. "You have to turn on him."

Her lips mouthed *no way*, but confusion clouded her eyes. Cash cut her some slack. The reality that her high-flying days were behind her would be hard to accept. Bitter pill for a twenty-four-year-old to swallow. Hell, at twice her age, he had choked on the same hard truth.

"The life you're living...it can't go on." Though meant to comfort her, his words fell far short.

Her misty eyes invited him to hold her, at least through the first stage of grief. In different circumstances he would've jumped at the chance, but her profession kept him at arm's length. Though he'd represented scores of prostitutes, he'd never slept with one. A line he didn't cross, for reasons more personal than professional.

Her eyes turned hard. The threat of tears passed. "When do you get to the part where I change my name and hair color, pack on forty pounds, move to Bumfuck, Utah, and wait tables at Denny's?"

"I'm not pushing the witness protection program," he said. "That's a shitty deal. You don't want to go there."

"Why not? Might be just what I need...a new start."

"Movies make it look romantic, like a big adventure, but it's more like a slow death march. Not one in a hundred can hack the red tape. You have to sever all ties with the past. No contact with family, friends, anyone you knew. One slip, and the feds can bounce you from the program. Can you really walk away from your parents and never see or speak to them again?"

"No parents left," she said. "Only a stepmother, and she's close to my age. Never seeing her again wouldn't break my heart. Or hers. But leaving my kid brother behind, yeah, that'd be tough."

"Hard as you think it'd be, the reality will prove a hundred times worse."

"What does Mister Goldberg think of the deal?"

"He won't like it."

"Why not?"

"Because it's not his idea," he said.

"That the only reason?" Again, asked as if she already knew the answer.

Cash hesitated too long to lie. "He'll think it's too dangerous."

"And you don't?"

Another telling pause. "Sure, it's plenty dangerous. But you have to decide which gives you the best shot at survival: testifying against Benanti and staying outside, or clamming up and doing time. In prison you'd be lucky to last a week. Benanti would know your only way out was rolling on him."

"What if I swear to him that I'll never snitch?"

Cash shook his head. "He's not big on trust."

"I could talk to Mariposa. She and I have a history."

"She and I have a longer history." He tried not to sound bitter. "It taught me she can't be trusted any more than her husband."

"You're not giving me many options."

"No good ones left. Our job is to find the least bad one."

"Let me sleep on it."

Cash tensed, determined to turn down her overture, no matter how tempting.

"Alone," she said.

He relaxed, relieved that the temptation had been removed. "Call me tomorrow."

"Before making a decision, I'll want to talk to you and Goldberg together. He tells me one thing. You, another. Hard for a girl to know what to do." She closed her eyes. "Set up a meeting. You, me, and your boss. But not too soon. I'm tied up most of the week."

"The agent gave me until five p.m. tomorrow to get back to him."

"Agent?" Her voice cracked. "You gave my name to an agent?" She paled. "Then I'm dead already."

"Chill," Cash said. "I kept your name out of it for now, but is there something about Shafer you need to tell me?"

The color returned to her face. "I don't know that it's Shafer, but Benanti has a mole in the courthouse."

Cash would've been surprised if Benanti didn't have more than one. "How do you know that?"

"Something Mariposa let slip one night."

"Who is it?"

She shook her head. "Don't know, but nothing happens in the courthouse that they don't know about in advance."

"That doesn't narrow it down much," Cash said. "Could be a judge, a prosecutor, an agent."

"Or all of the above," she said.

# CHAPTER TWENTY-ONE

Cash stared at Paula over the breakfast table. Eva had left on her morning jog, giving him a rare chance to clear the air. So much to say. So little time to do it. And no easy way to start.

"Do you own a Harley?" Cash said.

Paula took a sip of her latte, in no rush to respond. "No."

"Didn't think so. You don't look the type."

"Neither do you."

Hog or no hog, it wasn't hard to see why Eva had fallen for her. An M&A attorney and rising star at the prestigious firm of Powell, Ingram & Gardner, the statuesque brunette had six inches, twenty-five pounds, and fifteen years on Eva.

Broad-shouldered and no bullshit, Paula commanded attention. The crow's feet flaring from her gray eyes testified to a string of all-nighters, probably dating back to law school. Definitely not laugh lines.

"Do you know why I stuck around this morning to talk to you?" she said.

Judging from the steel in her voice, Cash bet it hadn't been to enjoy his company. "Probably to ask me to move out of Eva's apartment."

"You need to get out of her life."

Cash recoiled. "Hey, if you're worried about our relationship—"

She cut him off. "You're not a threat, not in that way." Another sip of the latte. "Eva should work for a real lawyer at a firm with a future."

Cash laughed. "If you think Eva would be happy sitting behind a desk and shuffling papers all day, you don't know her."

"Your world is too dangerous for her." Paula's voice stayed rock steady. "You're too dangerous for her."

She'd hit a nerve. Cash was slow on the comeback. "I hired Eva when she was a kid. Barely sixteen and scraping by on the streets. We've been a team for more than a decade. She's closer to me than a...."

"Than a what? What is she to you?" Paula pushed back from the table and stood. "The sister you never had? The daughter you'll never have? The mother you lost?"

"All of the above," Cash said.

* * *

When Cash entered the office, Goldberg checked his watch. "Ten-thirty. Nice of you to show up."

"Ran some errands." Cash didn't bother trying to sell the excuse. No way would Goldberg buy it anyway. Eva, even less likely.

Perched on the edge of Goldberg's desk, she tossed out the first question of the morning. "Do either of you know where your client is?"

Jump ball. Up for grabs between two white guys who couldn't leap for shit.

Cash and Goldberg glared at each other from across the desk. Neither blinked.

Cash cracked first. "She'll be here." His voice, more confident than his gut.

Goldberg rocked back in his leather-bound chair and plopped his boots onto the desk, the heels docking in well-worn grooves. The snakeskin Tony Lamas had aged better than the desk, and both had fared better than their owner.

"I still don't know what the hell this meeting's about." A toothpick twitched to the beat of Goldberg's twang.

Cash had run out of time. Every stall, evasion, and diversion deployed and spent. His plan had been to spring the news on Goldberg in Taylor's presence, with her head nodding and body language behind the deal all the way.

Roll the old man, two to one. Three to one, if Eva piled on.

But the client's no-show forced Cash to resort to the truth. Well, a half-truth anyway. "I ran into Shafer yesterday."

Goldberg surged forward, boots flying off the desk, heels hammering the hardwood floor. "Meaning you met with the agent behind my back."

"That's not exactly how it went down." Cash matched his mentor's decibel level. "I was in the courthouse for my weekly appointment with Robinson, and I—"

Goldberg cut him off. "And you just happened to bump into Shafer in a different agency and on a different floor."

"Something like that."

"Bullshit!" Goldberg rocketed to his feet. "That snake Shafer burrows so deep into his hole that it'd take dynamite to blast him out. And he doesn't budge from his office except to piss, shit, or nail someone. So you went out of your way to see him."

Busted. "Okay, I dropped by his office, and good thing I did. He'll offer Taylor a walk."

"In return for what?" Goldberg sounded skeptical.

A pause. "Giving up Benanti."

"Sheeeiiit!" The toothpick went flying in a stream of spit. "You just signed that girl's death warrant."

"The way I see it," Cash said, "I saved her life."

"Everyone knows Benanti has moles in every courthouse in the state," Goldberg said, "including the federal building."

Cash didn't waste breath disputing it. "Hell, that could be anybody, from the judge to the janitor."

"That could be *everybody* from the judge to the janitor." Goldberg chewed on a fresh toothpick.

"Not Shafer." Cash summoned all the confidence he could muster. "I'm not new at this game. I didn't give him Taylor's name. That's not why I went there. I had to look him in the eye. See how hungry he was to take down Benanti."

"You looked into his eyes!" Goldberg rolled his. "That's just beautiful. While you were gazing into his baby blues, he was blowing smoke up your ass."

Eva slapped the desk. The room fell silent. "I don't give a rat's ass what either of you thinks of Shafer or the deal. We need to find out what our client wants to do."

Goldberg sat as abruptly as he had stood. "She won't live long enough to decide. Unless she already knows what a damn fool thing Cash did, in which case she's probably in the wind. Leastwise, I hope she is."

He swiveled toward Cash. "You met with Shafer behind my back. Dollars to donuts, you lobbied my client on the sly too."

Busted again. "Yeah, I talked to her last night...briefly."

"Let me guess," Goldberg said, "you just happened to bump into her as well."

PAUL COGGINS

"I went to her place. Wanted to give her time to think about the deal before we hashed it out this morning."

Eva pushed away from the desk. "That the only reason you went to see her last night? Because there's this new invention called the iPhone that could've saved you the trip."

Taking fire from two sides backed Cash into a corner, literally and figuratively. "I didn't sleep with her, if that's what you're getting at. I don't sleep with prostitutes. Both of you know that."

*And both of you know why.*

"I'm sure that thought never crossed your mind." Eva proved Goldberg's match in the sarcasm department.

Cash held his tongue. Hard to answer that one with a simple yes or no.

"Cross his mind, hell," Goldberg said. "The thought of sticking his prick into every warm hole within a thousand-mile radius never leaves his mind. I'll bet the jackass made a damn fool of himself hitting on that poor gal. And her being young enough to be his daughter and all."

Cash came out of the corner counter-punching. "You're old enough to be her grandfather, and that wouldn't stop you."

Eva pounded the desk again. "Sorry I brought up Cash's zipper problem. But before we decide which of you two is the bigger perv, why don't we focus on finding Taylor?"

Goldberg pointed at Cash, his hand shaking. Could be anger. Or early Parkinson's. "Get out. Pack your things and get the hell out."

A buzzer sounded, and the temp's nasal voice crackled over the intercom. "Mister Goldberg, you have—"

"I told you not to interrupt me this morning." Goldberg killed the connection and turned back to Cash. "You've got

116

an hour to tell Robinson you were fired by the only fool crazy enough to hire you, or I damn sure will."

"It's a badge of honor to be fired by you," Cash said. "Means I did something right." Not that the judge or the probation officer would see it that way.

"It is so *not* the time for this," Eva said. "If we're going to keep a twenty-four-year-old alive and out of prison, you two have to work together."

"He's dead to me," Goldberg shouted.

Cash reached the reception area before Eva caught up to him. "Go to the apartment and cool down," she said. "I'll work on Goldy. It might take a day or two."

"I guess this is a bad time to ask the old man for a favor."

She gave him a you-can't-be-serious look. "What kind of favor?"

"I'm close to the deadline for filing an appellate brief for my cellmate at Seagoville, and it looks like I won't be getting my license back anytime soon. I planned to ask Goldy to sign the brief."

Goldberg limped toward them and shouted, "What's he still doing here?"

"Send me the brief," she said. "I'll see what I can do."

Before Cash left the office, the feds swarmed in.

# CHAPTER TWENTY-TWO

Four FBI agents herded everyone into Goldberg's office. Cash recognized the agent on point, the lone female.

Three years ago, Maggie Burns had been on the take-down team at his arrest. They had made eye contact that night. For just a beat her mask had slipped, giving way to a blush before she resumed her role as a badge-carrying ball-buster.

Today there was no blush, and the glint in her eyes dropped the temperature in the office ten degrees.

"I'm not leaving here without a scalp," Maggie said, "and I'm not too particular about which one I take."

She slapped an arrest warrant onto Goldberg's desk. Cash could recite the legal boilerplate but remained in the dark on the key detail: the arrestee's name.

No one picked up the warrant.

"Either I'm walking out with Taylor Donovan," Maggie said, "or one of you dirtbags will be taking her place."

At nearly six feet tall and with a moonlight-and-magnolia drawl from her Ole Miss roots, Maggie overcompensated for her beauty by talking down and dirty. That had never bothered Cash in the past and didn't now.

STING LIKE A BUTTERFLY

Backup agents fanned out to three corners of the room, either content to let Maggie take the lead or more likely, resigned to it.

Eva grabbed the document and flipped through it. "They plan to hold Taylor as a material witness to a felony."

Cash turned to Maggie. "What's the crime, and who's the target?"

"I'm here to ask questions," Maggie said, "not answer them. Question number one, where's Donovan?"

"We were just asking ourselves the same thing," Cash said.

The agent got in Cash's face. "You're thirty seconds away from facing charges, starting with obstruction of justice. Happy as it would make me to slap the cuffs on you again, Judge Tapia would be even more thrilled to see you back in her courtroom in chains."

Goldberg wedged between Maggie and Cash. "I sense that you two kids know each other, which never bodes well for McCahill. To know him is definitely not to love him. But, honey, that doesn't change the fact you've got no evidence on him or any of us."

Maggie towered over Goldberg. "No evidence, my ass. Your boy here talked to an IRS agent yesterday and found out we wanted to use anyone we could get our hands on to take down Benanti, including Donovan. Then he hustled over to her place last night, and now she's gone. Looks like McCahill has weaseled his way back into Benanti's good graces and onto his payroll."

Cash killed his first instinct, to ask how she knew he'd visited Taylor last night. Maggie wouldn't tell him, and the answer was obvious. He must've stumbled into a stakeout. What he didn't know was whether the Bureau had been watching Taylor, him, or both of them.

Cash went on offense. "I hear the same rumors about your colleagues...that one of them is on the take...maybe more than one."

If looks could kill, Cash would've fallen then and there. He weathered Maggie's glare. Saw her eyes harden from green to gray. Watched the blood drain from her lips.

"Any time you want to stack up your reputation against ours," Maggie said, "happy to oblige."

"Perhaps we should discuss this in private," Cash said.

Goldberg turned to Cash. "Given that you've got a target painted on your back, that's not a good idea."

"He's right, McCahill," she said, "you should hide behind your lawyer."

Cash snickered. "He's five-five. I couldn't hide behind him when I was ten." He walked to the door, then turned around. "*Special* Agent Burns, are you coming?"

"Stay here, fellas," Maggie said to her fellow agents. "I'll be back in five, with McCahill's balls in my briefcase."

She followed Cash to the oversize closet that served as his office and took a quick look around. Not much to see. "Quite a step down from your old digs."

Cash sat on a metal chair behind a metal desk not much larger than a TV tray. Maggie took the other folding chair in the room.

"Well, I'm a paralegal now, which means no window, no artwork, no room to breathe, and definitely no respect."

"Please stop before I dissolve into a puddle of tears." Her voice took on a lighter tone. Echoes of the prom queen from a past life. "Still, it beats a prison cell. Speaking of prison, why the hell aren't you still inside? Thought we had you off the streets for another year or two."

"Scored an early release, thanks to prison overcrowding."

She shook her head. "Hate it when that happens."

"Speaking of early releases, while I was in Seagoville, I thought a lot about our night together."

"Forget that night and focus on what I said at your arrest, especially the part where I promised to shoot you if you ever brought up my biggest mistake." She patted the piece in her shoulder holster. Her voice dropped back to brass knuckle business.

"I thought you meant not to tell a third party about it."

"Don't bring it up. Ever. Forget it happened. I sure as hell have."

"Riiiiiight."

Her blush told him all he needed to know. Better than a busted polygraph at exposing her lie.

"For what it's worth," he said, "I'm worried about Taylor too. We're on the same side here."

"Don't flatter yourself."

"You're the one who should be flattered," he said. "I'm about to share with you and you alone my best lead on her whereabouts."

She perked up. "Shoot."

"On one condition, we look for her together."

She stood. "That's not how the Bureau operates, and you know it. We take information. We don't give it out. Strictly a one-way street."

"Then cruise your road to nowhere without me." He let the threat sink in. "Besides, it's not like this would be the first time you broke Bureau protocol."

She patted the pistol, a reminder that a threat backed up by a gun carried more weight than words alone. "Give me your tip, and I'll call you in the unlikely event it pans out."

He stared until her eyes faded back to green. A signal for him to call her bluff. "No deal."

She made several false starts, her lips parting and closing, before folding. "If we were to do this together, no one and I mean absolutely no one can ever know."

"Agreed. Can't have my homies thinking I'm the Bureau's bitch."

As he stood, she slapped him, hard.

"What the hell was that for?" he said, more stunned than hurt.

"For leaving on the night that never happened without saying goodbye." She walked away but turned back at the door. "Besides, I've got a rep too. Want my homies to see my palm print on your face."

# CHAPTER TWENTY-THREE

**M**aggie and her magical, mystical search warrant strong-armed the super into opening Taylor Donovan's condo. All done legally and by the book, more or less. The warrant spared Cash from committing his first felony of the day: B&E.

"You sure her brother will show?" The agent sounded antsy. Good bet she hadn't followed Bureau protocol on a search and seizure. If she had, twenty of her closest colleagues would've crashed the party.

"You go through her things." Cash powered up Taylor's PC. "I'll take care of baby brother."

"What are we looking for?" Maggie said.

"A road map to Taylor."

It took Cash fifteen minutes to crack Taylor's password: *bluebutterfly*. Less than five to scroll through the folders before hitting pay dirt. A trove of messages to and from rdonovan@gmail.com.

The only Donovan that came up. Had to be baby bro.

The last string between the siblings ended yesterday. Cash responded for the missing sister: "Need to meet ASAP, my place."

Within an hour a poster boy for the preppy look let himself into the locked condo. Maggie and Cash ambushed him in the foyer. The nude portrait of Taylor hovered overhead. *The Naked Maja* knockoff.

"Ricky Donovan?" Cash said.

The kid froze at the door but finally nodded. Not that Cash needed to confirm the I.D. He could've picked Ricky out of a lineup. Or a yearbook. Same oval-shaped face as the sister. Same light blue eyes and disarming dimples. Same fresh-scrubbed look that could make even the most bald-faced lie ring true.

"Who the fuck are you?" Echoes of Taylor's East Texas twang surfaced in Ricky's voice. The accent, no doubt thicker when laced with fear. Like now.

Ricky reached for the door knob. "And what are you doing in my sister's apartment?"

"Settle down," Cash said. "We're here to help Taylor. Need you to tell us where she is."

"I don't have to tell you shit." The fear in Ricky's voice gave way to anger.

"You do if you care about Taylor," Maggie said.

"Is she in some kind of trouble?"

Good question. Either the kid didn't know about the tax investigation, or he could match his sister in the acting department.

Cash decided that two could play the lying game. "Not if we find her first."

"You still haven't told me who you are," Ricky said.

Maggie flipped open her badge. "Agent Burns, FBI."

Cash cringed. Yeah, that'll put the kid at ease. Sure enough, Ricky turned pale, and his hand drifted back to the door knob.

On the verge of losing their best lead, Cash took a stab at lightening the mood. "But her close friends call her *Special Agent Burns*."

Mission not accomplished. If anything, Ricky looked more spooked.

"Give me a minute with my partner," Cash said to Ricky.

He pulled Maggie into the bedroom and closed the door behind them. "The kid's a rabbit, and he's about to bolt. Let me talk to him alone."

"Bullshit. This is my investigation, and you're just tagging along. Now you want to run the show."

"The badge. The gun." *Not to mention the attitude.* "They're not helping. Give me five minutes with him, then he's all yours."

Maggie seethed, her eyes afire. "Five minutes, then I take over."

Relieved to find Ricky still in the foyer, Cash reached out his hand. Time to start fresh. Maybe even resort to the truth. "Cash McCahill here, and I'm helping your sister with a legal issue." But not the whole truth since he couldn't practice law without risking a trip back to Seagoville.

Ricky leaned away from the door to take Cash's hand. "What kind of legal issue?"

"It's a tax thing," Cash said.

Ricky broke the grip. "Then why's the FBI involved and not the IRS?"

Kid's smarter than he looks. Again, like his sister. "Long story," Cash said. "Let's make ourselves comfortable."

Cash led Ricky into the living room and onto the couch. Took the chair closest to him. "It's a complicated tax thing." He played a hunch. "Hey, are you in law school?"

"Pre-law at SMU." Ricky's voice gained confidence. "I've applied to law schools and plan to enroll next year."

Ricky's major explained a lot, like how he kept slipping off the witness stand and putting Cash on the hot seat. That was the downside for Cash. The upside, he had two points of connection with the kid: SMU and law school. Good start at winning him over.

"Small world," Cash said. "I was pre-law at SMU. Had a nice scholarship but still left school with a ton of debt."

"Tell me about it," Ricky said.

"You on scholarship too?"

Ricky shook his head. "Not exactly."

"Then you must've won the baby lottery by landing parents with deep pockets."

Ricky shook his head. "My father's dead, and my stepmother wouldn't spring for tuition at DeVry. Taylor's covering the tab, but I'm going to pay her back when I get my law license."

"Suh-weet." Good plan. Because his sister definitely needed a lawyer in the family. "When was the last time you saw Taylor?"

"About a week ago. When she's in town, which isn't often, we meet for dinner every Wednesday at Torchy's Tacos."

"And the last time you talked to her?"

"Two...three days ago. She called to see how I'd done on my European history exam."

"What else did you two talk about?"

Ricky eased back on the couch. "Said she was going out of town for a few days."

"Did she mention where she was going?"

Ricky shook his head.

"Sounds like she travels a lot," Cash said.

"It's part of her job. She's been everywhere. Knows everyone."

"What exactly is her job?"

"Best freaking gig in the world." Ricky's voice brimmed with a mix of pride and envy. "She's the executive assistant to one of the biggest hedge fund managers in the country."

It took all of Cash's self-control to keep a straight face. "Who's the hedge fund honcho?"

Ricky shrugged. "That's strictly need to know. She calls him Mister B. But whoever the dude is, he pays *primo dinero* and flies her all over the world in a private jet. Puts her up in five-star hotels. Even sprung for this place."

Cash reached a fork in the conversation. Play bad cop and bust the kid's bubble about his sister's occupation. Or stay on the high road. He took the latter route. After all, a real bad cop lurked in the bedroom, counting the seconds to her crack at the kid.

"Say Taylor had a few days off and needed some serious R and R," Cash said, "where would she hole up?"

Ricky looked down, deep in thought. "She travels so much for business that she's always saying how great it'd be just to crash here for a weekend."

"What about the two of you," Cash said, "ever travel together?"

Ricky's eyes lit up. "Yeah, we went to Santa Fe for my spring break. Stayed at La Posada, and it was awesome. She's planning to buy a second home there."

"Think she might've already sprung for that second home?" Cash said.

"I doubt she's had time to look. Plus, she would've told me if she had." Ricky's eyes clouded. "How much trouble is she in?"

"Nothing I can't handle, if I can get hold of her."

"Sorry I can't help with that," Ricky said.

Maggie burst from the bedroom. A belle on wheels. Cash intercepted her before she could get to Ricky.

"Tell me you got something from him." She spoke as if Ricky were not there.

Cash nodded. "Yep. The next stop in our magical, mystery tour."

# CHAPTER TWENTY-FOUR

The piñon scent in the lobby of La Posada stoked Cash's libido. Then again, what didn't?

With nature's aphrodisiac in the air and Maggie Burns at his side, he anticipated a weekend in Santa Fe of pleasure mixed with business.

Business first. The receptionist glanced at the photo of Taylor Donovan, then looked up at Cash and shook her head. "Don't recognize her."

He pushed the photo across the desk, closer to Alicia, the name on her badge. "Take another look, please."

He understood her reluctance to dime out a guest. In a past life, he'd counted on the discretion of hotel staff as his last line of defense against irate husbands and pissed-off boyfriends.

Alicia's nails drummed the desk. Her eyes, dark as the mahogany finish, betrayed nothing. She didn't blink. Forehead didn't furrow. Story didn't change.

"I told you this trip would be a waste of time," Maggie said, "and money."

Cash held his tongue, not wanting to fight in front of Alicia. Not wanting a fight, period. Maggie's reaction didn't surprise him. Typical Bureau bullshit. An agency quick to claim credit for the hits and dodge blame for the strikeouts.

Ought to change the handle from FBI to CYA. Truth in advertising.

He pulled Maggie outside Alicia's earshot and said, "I don't believe her. She's trained to see, hear, and speak no evil of guests. That means Taylor might be in Santa Fe, could even be staying here."

"I'll sweat the truth from her." Maggie whipped out her credentials. "No big deal to stonewall a defrocked lawyer, but it's a major no-no to lie to an agent. Let's see if little miss tight-ass sticks to the company line when facing a felony."

"Put the badge away," Cash said, "and don't even think about flashing your weapon. We can't afford to scare Alicia and risk spooking Taylor, so we play the scene my way. You and me, we're just a swinging couple on the prowl for a switch-hitting pro."

Maggie rolled her eyes. "Why am I not surprised that you'd come up with a plan involving a threesome?"

"Hey, this is strictly business." He kept a straight face, more or less.

He returned to the reception desk and played his best card. Actually Goldberg's credit card. Platinum AmEx.

"We'll take a room for the night," he said, "your most private suite. We tend to get a little loud." He patted Maggie's butt.

She slapped his hand away, harder than necessary. "Make that two rooms, and his will be loud only because he snores like a drunken sailor."

Not the image of a no-holes-barred couple Cash hoped to create. He scrambled to save the set-up. "Connecting rooms, of course."

Maggie and Cash walked in silence to their adjoining suites. While unpacking, they finally agreed on something. A first for the day.

If Taylor was in Santa Fe, she'd be drawn to gallery row. Based on the art collection in her apartment, her tastes were eclectic and expensive. Two words that captured the Santa Fe market.

With hours of daylight to burn, they started at the top of Canyon Road and worked their way down. Adobe galleries lined both sides of the narrow street, the shops crammed together like beads on a necklace.

Cash lost count of the galleries in their wake. Thirty, forty, maybe fifty. And still they were only halfway down the hill.

They could've moved faster if Maggie hadn't turned out to be an art major at Ole Miss. Figured. Art major, sorority sister, cheerleader, homecoming queen. The only mystery was how she had missed the next step in her natural evolution. Trophy wife.

At every stop she roped an owner or, better yet, an artist into bullshit conversations about light, color, texture, composition, blah-blah. Leaving the business questions to Cash.

The artsy crowd recognized Taylor from the photo. Though none copped to seeing her recently, all eagerly awaited her return. It seemed she was valued as a good customer with a keen eye, a quick wit, and a generous allowance.

At the Riggs-Freeman Gallery, nestled at the foot of the hill, Cash saw Taylor. Not the girl in the flesh but a nude portrait of her. Another *Naked Maja* knockoff. Even larger than the billboard greeting visitors at Taylor's place.

"She sure does like to flaunt her body," Maggie said.

Cash had no problem with that. He checked the price tag. Fifty thousand dollars, with "SOLD" written in bold across the sum. He dropped the tag.

An anorexic in a black dress walked stiffly toward them. Black-frame glasses swallowed her ferrety face. "I'm Gena Freeman." She extended a hand. "May I help you?"

"I was admiring this portrait." Cash took her hand. Detected the faintest pulse. "I've seen the artist's work before."

"You've got good taste." Gena's compliment sounded canned.

Maggie snickered. "Yeah, he's never seen a nude he didn't like."

The women exchanged conspiratorial smiles, flirting without saying a word. Maggie whispered to Cash, "Back off, boy. I've got this."

Not a chance. He couldn't resist crashing the party. "Did you mean good taste in women or art?"

Maggie rolled her eyes.

"They're not mutually exclusive," Gena said. "Marco is my best young painter, and this is by far his most popular work." Her gaze drifted from the painting to Maggie. "But I'm sure he could work wonders with your wife as a model."

Maggie shuddered. "He and I are business partners. *Strictly* business partners. He has money but no taste, and I have an eye for talent but no money. We do, however, share a common interest."

"In my artist?" Gena said.

"In his model." Cash wished he could swallow his words. Too blunt. Too soon. Maybe he should let Maggie do the talking.

"What my *silent* partner means," Maggie said, "is that we have an interest in purchasing a painting by your artist of this model."

Gena frowned. "Unfortunately, this painting was sold yesterday."

"To whom?" Cash said.

"We can't disclose the names of clients."

Maggie stepped in front of Cash. "Any other paintings of this model for sale?"

"I'm afraid Marco painted only two. This one." The owner pointed to the sold work. "And the model took the other."

"But he could paint another, right?" Maggie said.

Gena removed her glasses and teethed the frame. As close as she'd come to an afternoon snack. "Marco lives in Abiquiu, so I can get in touch with him today, but the model may be harder to reach. We can try to contact her and see if she's interested in posing again."

She popped the glasses back on. "Why don't you check back with me tomorrow, around noon?"

\* \* \*

"My feet are killing me." The noise level in the restaurant forced Maggie to shout. She kicked off her shoes and swept them under the table. The death march down Canyon Road, followed by a forty-five-minute wait for a table, had taken a toll.

"When we get back to the hotel," Cash said, "I'll treat you to my world-famous foot massage."

"The door between our rooms will be locked and bolted for the night. And remember that I have a gun, so don't even think about a booty call."

Too late.

Roughly an equal split of tourists and townies claimed every table at The Shed, while a pack of fifty or so paced the patio. Every year the restaurant seemed to shrink, and the crowd to swell. The ceiling sagged deeper, the walls crept closer together, and the doors forced Cash to duck lower.

But the fare made it all worthwhile. Prepared with fresh Hatch chili. Worth its weight in cocaine.

He recommended the green chili enchiladas with blue corn tortillas and a margarita. Maggie went with cheese tacos and iced tea.

Dinner conversation went downhill from there. Emboldened by his second margarita, he got personal. "Why did you join the Bureau?"

"Which is your not-so-subtle way of asking why a nice girl like me would waste her time playing with guns and handcuffs."

"The cuffs I get," he said, "but the guns throw me."

She shook her head. "I'll never understand how someone so good at reading jurors can be so bad at reading people."

"Enlighten me," he said. "What made you sign away your soul?"

She put down her fork. "During my senior year at Ole Miss, my parents got taken by a con man. A deacon in their church was running a Ponzi and hit up half the congregation. Wiped out the life savings of scores of retirees, including my folks."

"Sorry," he said.

"But not so sorry that you'd pass on defending the scum if he could come up with your retainer." Her voice had an edge.

He didn't bother denying it.

"I vowed then and there to protect others from being fleeced." She pushed her plate away. "Or if I couldn't bust the crook beforehand, I'd see to it that he spent the rest of his sorry life behind bars. Bonus points if I could block him from funneling the ill-gotten gains to his scumbag lawyer."

"Got anyone in mind to play the role of the attorney?"

"Present company included," she said.

Cash rarely talked about his childhood, but something about Maggie's story made him want to open up. Introduce her to the lonely child whose father had abandoned him at birth and whose mother had vanished years later without a trace.

"There are worse things than having your parents—" He stopped cold.

"What's wrong?" Maggie said. "You look like you've seen a ghost."

# CHAPTER TWENTY-FIVE

"Give me a ghost any day of the week," Cash said to Maggie, "over the psycho bitch headed our way."

Mariposa Benanti, with Bobby the Bodyguard in tow, wound through The Shed. Patrons and staff yielded to the pair. Conversations died in their wake.

Three-inch heels jacked Mariposa well over six feet. She held her head high, eyes forward. Like nothing to the right or left merited her attention.

Bobby wore...hell, who gave a shit what he had on? His dark eyes swept the room nonstop, like a Secret Service agent on speed. Searching for trouble or if none was found, stirring up some.

They took the table next to Cash's, the only empty one in sight. Mariposa faced Cash. With four chairs at the table, better than even odds she had chosen the view. Though if she saw him, she didn't let on.

Bobby parked his ass across from Mariposa, blocking Cash's line of sight to her. Again, he chalked this up to design.

Maggie looked over her shoulder to see what had captured Cash's attention. "She a friend of yours?"

"I once made the mistake of thinking so." Cash leaned left until Mariposa came into sight. Good thing as she rose and headed his way. Gave him a few seconds to brace for the showdown.

Bobby started to follow, but she signaled for him to heel. He slowly lowered himself back into the chair, seething.

"Are you tailing me?" Mariposa sounded more amused than alarmed.

"Funny," Cash said, "but I was about to ask you the same thing."

Maggie stood eye-to-eye with Mariposa and doled out the bare minimum by way of introduction. First and last names only. No mention of the FBI. No small talk. Sure as hell, no invitation to join them at the table.

Mariposa reciprocated in kind. First and last names.

"Benanti" sparked a reaction from Maggie. An arched eyebrow.

"I see you're finally dating someone more age appropriate," Mariposa said to Cash.

Cash nodded to Bobby. "And you still aren't."

"Oh, Bobby tags along to keep the creeps away. Looks like he's fallen down on the job."

Cash took a swig of margarita. "Which still doesn't explain what you're doing here."

"We have a second home five miles outside Santa Fe. I spend three months a year here, and everyone comes to The Shed for the posole." She took a sip of his margarita. "Try top shelf next time. Makes all the difference."

A waiter approached. "Would the four of you like to dine together? We'd be happy to seat you at the same table."

"No thanks," Cash said. "We're about to leave. *La cuenta por favor.*"

The waiter left.

Mariposa handed the drink back to Cash. "Don't run off on my account."

"Don't flatter yourself," Cash said. "It's getting late, and we have a big day tomorrow." He glanced at his watch. "Ten o'clock. Does your husband know where you are?"

"The better question," Mariposa said, "is whether your probation officer knows where you are."

\* \* \*

"You stupid sonovabitch." Maggie made it outside the restaurant before unloading on Cash.

He struggled to keep pace. "Hey, I can explain."

Not that she gave him a chance to. Her rant spanned the five-minute cab ride to La Posada. In the hotel lobby, her heels clicked to a furious beat, and her words flew faster. Cash trailed in pursuit, saving his defense for a pause that never came.

She locked and bolted the door between their rooms, only to throw it open a minute later. "How can you be so fucking dumb?"

The rant that refused to die.

*Slam.*

"Sweet dreams to you too," he said to the closed door.

It flew open again. Cash couldn't help smiling. The serial slamming of the door gave the scene a bedroom-farce feel.

"You think traveling outside the district without the judge's permission is funny?" Her tone made clear she didn't.

"Wasn't meant to be." Cash's foot propped open the door. "I'm trying to save someone's life here."

"Assuming she's not already dead."

"I have to act on that assumption," he said.

"Are you willing to go back to prison if you're wrong... maybe even if you're right?"

She walked to the fireplace, her back to him. The fire cast the only light in the room and gave her an otherworldly aura.

He followed her inside. "You know what they say. Better to ask forgiveness after the fact than seek permission in advance."

"I don't think Judge Tapia subscribes to that theory. She strikes me as more old school."

"More like Old Testament," he said.

She jabbed the logs with a poker. Sparks flew. "Like the Old Testament says, the judge giveth, and the judge taketh away. And this judge is about to take away your freedom."

She poked the logs harder. Embers fanned out. "Did it cross your mind that you've dropped me in the grease too? Not only do I have to explain to my boss what I'm doing here with you, but I'll also be forced to testify against you at the hearing to revoke your probation."

"If there's a hearing, I'm counting on you being a witness *for* me." Her back still to him, his hands bookended her shoulders. Gently. No pressure.

She tensed, then relaxed. The poker slipped through her fingers, clanging on the tile floor.

He kneaded her shoulders. "I'm the good shepherd, helping the angelic agent search for a lost lamb. That's our story, and we stick to it."

She laughed. "*You* helping the Bureau. That'll be the day."

She had a point. Any scenario where he volunteered to assist the FBI seemed far-fetched. Almost as unlikely as the idea that the agency would accept his offer to help.

He floated a backup plan. "Or we could chalk it up to a simple misunderstanding. You assumed I had asked the court for permission, while I thought you had. Sorry, your honor. Won't happen again." His grip on her shoulders tightened.

"The we-fucked-up defense plays a little better," she said, "but it still has a fatal flaw. Even if I could sell my boss on your new and improved story, the U.S. Attorney will never buy it, not given how he feels about you."

"I figure that Moore will sign off on whatever the FBI agrees to."

"You figure wrong." Her shoulders knotted. "He and my boss rarely see eye-to-eye. Fact is, Reyes hates Moore almost as much as Moore hates you."

"There are a million good reasons to despise the U.S. Attorney. I have my top ten thousand. What are your boss's?"

"For starters, the SAC lives to see his name in print and his mug on the tube, but Moore, being the political whore he is, hogs the spotlight. What's worse, every decision in his office boils down to who you know or who you blow."

Good intel. Any daylight between the Bureau and the U.S. Attorney could be exploited. If not now, maybe later.

His hands slid to her biceps. Remarkably strong for someone so slender.

She turned to face him, slipping from his hold. Crackling logs laughed at the couple. Flames fought the dark chill to a draw. From a daytime high near sixty, the outside temperature had dipped to the twenties. Sleet pinged the windows.

Not a night to sleep alone.

When he took a step toward her, she didn't flinch. The fire played shadow games on her face, turning her lips into a moving target. He leaned in. She stiff-armed him. Their lips didn't meet.

140

She pushed him away. "You've got to be kidding. You can't possibly think this will happen tonight."

"Hey, this could be my last night of freedom." Not too proud to stoop to a pity lay.

Her laughter gave him renewed hope, only to be dashed by the buzzing of his phone. It was Eva. That damn *bruja* had a sixth sense, an uncanny knack of snatching forbidden fruit from him.

He took the call. "This had better be good." Sounding as cross as he could.

"It's an emergency," Eva said. "Get to Baylor Hospital ASAP."

# CHAPTER TWENTY-SIX

"**Y**ou look like death warmed over." In a bed at Baylor Hospital, only a day after going under the knife, Goldberg still managed to fire off the first shot of the morning.

Cash stood on one side of the bed. Eva, on the other. No question who the target of Goldy's broadside had been.

Cash breathed a little easier. The old coot still had some fight in him.

"While you," Cash said, "have never looked lovelier. Course, given how butt-ugly you were from the get-go, the bar's set lower than a toad's ass."

Nothing better at breaking the ice than falling into their familiar pattern of putdowns. Beats running the risk of blurting out the truth that Cash had seen corpses that looked healthier.

Goldberg had aged twenty years in the last forty-eight hours. His complexion, chalky and gray. Breathing, weak and wheezy.

Cash gripped the safety handles of the bed. Man, how he hated hospitals. The stinging odor of disinfectant, disease, and death transported him back to the worst time in his life. His grandmother's last hours.

She'd been the rock who raised him from the age of eight on, after his mother's disappearance, and she had breathed her last in the same hospital, different floor.

Cash and Goldberg locked eyes, each silently daring the other to turn away. As if a battle of wills could keep both going.

Eva moved behind Cash and placed a hand on his shoulder, breaking the stalemate. She played the role of referee well. The peacemaker part, even better.

Cash took in the private room. A wilted floral arrangement and two get well cards kept a lonely vigil on the window sill. Occupational hazard of a criminal defense career, which had left in its wake a string of ungrateful clients and four pissed-off exes.

Clients who had been convicted of a small subset of their crimes invariably blamed Goldberg. Those who had beaten the rap by dint of his legal skill deluded themselves into thinking they never should have been charged in the first place, that any jackleg lawyer could've sprung them faster and cheaper.

In terms of the degree of delusion, however, clients couldn't hold a candle to ex-wives. Each of Goldberg's exes believed, against the great weight of history and common sense, that she would be the last *other woman* to topple the head that wore the crown.

Eva placed her palm on Goldberg's forehead. Held it there a good thirty seconds while her frown deepened. She grabbed a sippy cup and guided the straw into his mouth.

Goldberg spat out the straw. "Get me something stronger."

"You need to drink more water," she said. "Doctor's orders."

"Bullshit. Doc said I'm fit as a fiddle. Besides, nothing cures what ails you better than a shot of Crown Royal."

Eva turned to Cash. "Not even close to what Doctor Rosenberg said. Let's go to the coffee shop, and I'll fill you in."

As they were leaving, Goldberg lifted a hand. It fell back to the bed before Cash could decide whether he was waving bye or beckoning them to return.

"Did you find the girl?" Goldberg said.

Cash froze at the door. He considered lying to give the old guy a boost. Worried that his ticker couldn't take more bad news. But Cash doubted he could sell a happy ending, so he resorted to the truth. "Not yet."

Goldberg turned his face away from them and spoke to the window. "She's gone. Body will never be found."

"I'm not giving up hope," Cash said, "and neither should you."

Eva went to Goldberg and kissed his cheek. "Get some rest. We'll be back in a few minutes."

Goldberg grabbed her arm. A look clouded his eyes, bordering on panic. "Have you filed motions to continue our cases on Monday's docket?"

"Done," Eva said. "Now quit worrying and close your eyes."

\* \* \*

In the coffee shop on the ground floor, sleep-deprived friends and relatives played a game of musical chairs. Drawn by the aroma of fresh brew, like zombies to live flesh.

Cash and Eva pounced on an open booth and ordered a large pot of coffee. "Fair warning," she said, "that the coffee here sucks."

"If I can stomach your coffee, I can handle anything." He took a sip. "I stand corrected."

"Are you ever going to get around to asking about him?" Her tone made clear he'd already waited too long.

"No need to ask. You're going to lay out in graphic detail how poorly he's doing, and then you'll break down, and I'll comfort you. Two minutes later we'll go through the whole cycle again. Rinse and repeat."

"It's not good." Her eyes misted. "Yesterday was touch and go. Had no idea where you were, but several times I thought we'd lost him." She blinked back tears. "He's been on meds for years, but half the time he forgets to take them." Tears broke through.

Cash dabbed her eyes with a napkin. "He's too stubborn to die. He'll bury us both."

"If that's what you need to tell yourself to keep from facing the truth." Her voice took a hard turn. "The worst part, he's you in a few years."

"Thanks for the vote of confidence."

A grimace followed her first taste of coffee. "This stuff is lethal."

He managed a crooked smile. "When I told you he'd outlive us both, I didn't realize the coffee shop would do us in today."

"While you were in prison," she said, "he was like a father to me."

"More like a grandfather. I'm like a father to you."

She gave him a get real look. "You're more like my little brother. While you were gone, he looked out for me."

"Okay, we owe him for that," Cash said.

"And he took you in when no one in town would touch you. He's been like a father to you too. Only this one didn't desert you. You deserted him."

Cash winced. She'd hit a nerve. "I'll make it up to him."

"Better start soon because he's running out of time." Her phone buzzed. She checked the text message. "Shit. See what I mean. That's Meadows instructing me to transfer the Colby files to him." She put down the phone. "We're bleeding clients."

"When did that start?"

"About six hours after the heart attack," she said. "Bad news travels fast."

"How many clients have we lost?"

"We're well on our way to losing all of them."

"Hustle back to the office," he said. "I'll hold down the fort here."

"I can stall for a day or two before sending over files, but not much longer." She reached across the table and grabbed his hands. "You have to get your license back."

"I'm working on it."

"Work faster."

Cash recognized an FBI agent at the entrance to the coffee shop. Could be a coincidence. Perhaps he had a friend or relative in the hospital.

A second fed followed close behind. Not likely a coincidence now.

A third agent came in. No way.

# CHAPTER TWENTY-SEVEN

ash's hand had a mind of its own. It levitated off the table, itching to slap the smirk off Marty Shafer's face.

He held back for two reasons.

First, too many witnesses in the hospital coffee shop. A handful of staff and dozens of customers, eyes wide and mouths agape, followed the movements of the four federal agents as they fanned out to the corners of the room before converging on Cash's booth.

One punch, even a tap by Cash, and a prosecutor would need only a couple of witnesses to cinch a conviction.

The second holdup, the high stakes of a low blow. Shafer carried a badge minted by the Treasury Department. That'd be the *United States* Treasury Department. The gold-trimmed credentials meant that even the most well-deserved slug carried a prison sentence.

Too heavy a price for the fleeting thrill of putting Shafer flat on his back.

And the price climbed in Cash's case because his time would be stacked onto three years of supervised release. Wouldn't matter whether he scored a light slap of a year, caught a break with a deuce, or drew the full nickel.

The final tally would be academic because he'd never survive a night at F.C.I. Seagoville, not with Big Black lurking there. So Cash stayed his trigger-happy hand, and a little part of his soul died.

"If you're here to pay final respects to Goldberg," Cash said, "save your breath. He's going to pull through, and before you can say *not guilty on all counts*, he'll be back in court busting your balls."

Shafer invited himself to sit, hip bumping Eva deeper into the booth. The other three agents remained standing, stone-faced and statue still. Hard to tell whether Shafer had picked his backups for their broad shoulders or locked lips.

"Actually, I'm here to see you," Shafer said.

"In that case it'll be a few months before I can get back to kicking your ass in court."

"It'll be longer than that." Shafer slapped a document on the table, face up. Eva flipped through the pages.

"What is it?" Cash said.

Eva blanched. "The U.S. Attorney has filed a motion to revoke your probation and send you back to Seagoville."

"Hearing's set for tomorrow at ten a.m.," Shafer said. "We'll see who kicks whose ass then."

Twenty years in the trenches had taught Cash to keep a straight face, especially during the worst shit-storms. The greater the damage to his case, the more deadpan his expression. Litigators call the look *DILLIGAS: Do I Look Like I Give A Shit?*

"On what grounds?" Cash fought to keep his voice steady.

Eva pointed to a paragraph on page two. "Practicing law without a license."

Cash breathed easier. He could beat that rap. The line between lawyer and paralegal was razor-thin.

Her forefinger slid down the page, stopping near the bottom. "And leaving the Northern District of Texas without the court's permission."

Cash's lungs deflated, and he struggled to catch his breath. That charge, he couldn't beat. Not without a miracle.

"You've been served." Shafer smiled. "Fail to show tomorrow, and the marshals will pick you up and haul you into court in cuffs."

As Shafer rose, he placed a hand on Cash's shoulder. "Better bring a toothbrush with you tomorrow. By noon you'll be halfway to Seagoville, and your old prison pals have planned a blanket party to welcome you back."

* * *

Maggie fired six shots in the chest, all within a three-inch radius of the bulls-eye. Clustered so tightly that they obliterated the sternum.

Reloaded, and the next round blew away the target's crotch.

"Was that exhibition of marksmanship for my benefit or theirs?" Cash waved to the other agents at the firing range. None waved back.

Six pseudo-sharpshooters blasted away at full-body targets without coming close to Maggie's accuracy. The scene reminded Cash less of a war zone than a video arcade.

She removed earplugs and pressed a button. The paper target fluttered forward like a ghost.

"Remember what I swore to do if you ever breathed a word about the night I lost my mind?" she said.

He cleared his throat. "Technically, that would be two nights."

The crack didn't help her disposition. Or his cause.

"Well, the same goes if you ever show up at my place of work again." She took down the target, rolled it up, and handed it to him. "Keep this as a reminder that your balls are hanging by a thread."

"You call this a place of work? Looks more like a playground, but damn fine shooting anyway." He tossed aside the target.

Not that her aim surprised him, given her three-year reign as the champion marksman of the Dallas FBI office. Make that marksperson. Six hundred field agents and support personnel, and she could outshoot them all.

With this year's competition only a week away, the firing range had been the first place Cash looked for her. Not exactly the venue he would've chosen to make the hard ask, but with his revocation hearing tomorrow, he couldn't risk waiting for a better opening.

*Better* would've been any time and place that Maggie was unarmed and not surrounded by colleagues. But since the shooters wore ear protectors and were laser-focused on their paper foes, he and Maggie could've shouted without being overheard.

She didn't holster the Glock. "What the hell are you doing here?"

"I left you six messages. Couldn't wait any longer. We have to talk."

She looked around. "I can't afford to be seen with you. Get out of here."

"This will take only a minute," he said.

"You've got thirty seconds."

"I need you in Tapia's court tomorrow at ten to testify that I went to Santa Fe to help the FBI."

She turned pale. "You're insane."

"I can subpoena you." He broke eye contact. "Don't want to do that, but if you force me to...."

"You're asking me to commit career suicide."

"I don't see it that way," he said.

"Then you're not looking at it the FBI way."

"You didn't break any rules." He slipped into full defense lawyer mode. "There's no regulation against two single people spending time together."

"I broke the biggest unwritten rule in the book. The agency calls it DEB: *Don't Embarrass the Bureau*."

"Please don't make me subpoena you." He turned to walk away. A tap on the shoulder stopped him.

"Don't forget your goodbye gift." She handed him the rolled-up target. "This is the last time we'll talk and the last time you'll see me."

# CHAPTER TWENTY-EIGHT

"Welcome to the Thunderdome," Cash said, "where any-one can die at any time."

Not the first time he'd used that line in Tapia's courtroom. Could well be the last.

"Remind me to buy you a movie made in this century," Eva said. "Lord knows you need some new lines."

At the government table sat U.S. Attorney Tom Moore, flanked by his first assistant Jenna Powell and IRS Agent Marty Shafer. Moore and Shafer beamed, as if there was nowhere on earth they'd rather be. Jenna looked like this was the last place on the planet she'd choose to land.

Scores of prosecutors and agents, butt-whipped and bat-tle-scarred from past encounters with Cash, packed the pews behind the government table. The rows on the defense side of the aisle were empty.

For a nanosecond Cash considered doing a quick one-eighty and bolting for the exit. He turned to Eva. "When was the last time the Big Cheese handled a probation revocation hearing?"

She held tight to his arm, as if she'd read his mind about fleeing. "That would be, uh, never."

As Cash and Eva settled at the defense table, Moore pointed to the empty rows behind them. "I see that all your friends showed up to support you."

Moore's minions laughed as if their jobs depended on it.

"Pardon me for stating the obvious," Moore said, "but you seem to be an attorney short."

The minions laughed louder.

"Not to worry." Cash sounded more confident than he felt. "You've brought more than enough legal firepower to handle both sides."

Moore leaned closer and whispered, "Unfortunately for you, this time Jenna is on my side."

"Just because she's *by* your side," Cash said, "doesn't mean she's *on* your side."

Jenna did her best impersonation of Switzerland, remaining still and silent through the sniping.

The bailiff banged a gavel, and Tapia took the bench. Everyone in the courtroom rose, with Cash being the last to his feet and the first to sit.

Cash made a living by reading jurors but stayed alive by reading judges. Tapia had always been a tough call. Never more so than today. He'd expected to find her pumped at the prospect of sending him back to prison. Instead, she looked troubled.

"The first order of business on the docket," the judge said, "is the government's motion to revoke the supervised release of Mister McCahill." Brusque. Businesslike. Ready to bust the balls of anyone in her way. "Is the government prepared to proceed?"

Moore stood. "Yes, your honor."

"Is the defendant ready?"

Cash rose slowly. "No." Making a point of not adding the obsequious *your honor*.

"And why not?" Her voice rolled down from on high.

Lesser men than Cash would've quaked, as would greater men. But he stood firm. "Gary Goldberg, my lawyer, suffered a heart attack three days ago, and he's still in the hospital. The doctors expect a full recovery, but that'll take time."

"I'm sorry that Mister Goldberg has a serious health issue, but we can't postpone the hearing for a recovery that might take weeks or even months." Tapia didn't sound sorry at all. "What steps have you taken to retain substitute counsel?"

"I got notice of the hearing only yesterday."

Her jaw tensed. "You didn't answer my question, so I'll rephrase it. What efforts did you make since yesterday to hire new counsel?"

"None." An extra dose of defiance amped his voice. Eva slipped him a note that read *tone it down*. He crumpled the note. "Mister Goldberg is my counsel of choice, and I'm entitled to at least three days to see if he rallies."

"Based on what?" the judge said.

"Barring an emergency, the local rules require at least three days between service of a motion on a party and the hearing on it."

The judge looked to Moore for rebuttal. No help there. She turned back to Cash. "The three-day rule applies to discovery motions in civil cases."

Cash shook his head. "Read literally, the rule applies across the board. And it makes no sense to grant a grace period for a discovery dispute in a slip-and-fall case, while denying the same consideration to one whose freedom is at stake."

Tapia's glare finally forced Moore to his feet. He stood speechless for a full minute before dropping back into his chair.

The judge let out an exasperated sigh. "Mister Moore, you've never been more eloquent."

The spectators largely stifled their laughter, but a few titters broke through. Moore's face turned red. Tapia banged the gavel, and the courtroom fell silent.

"Although I do not subscribe to the defendant's expansive and novel reading of the local rule, I'll continue this hearing until Monday at ten a.m. At that time, Mister McCahill, you will appear with Mister Goldberg or another attorney. Alternatively, you're free to represent yourself. One way or another, this matter will be disposed of on Monday."

*Bang.*

\* \* \*

The continuance gave Cash three days to tie up loose ends, on the outside and inside.

He had to find some way to make peace with Big Black. Pay reparations. Promise the moon. Whatever it took to survive in Big Black's world.

Come Monday, it'd be Cash's hell too.

Monday loomed large, not only as Cash's judgment day before an angry goddess but also as the filing deadline for Martin Biddle's brief. If Cash couldn't persuade Goldy to sign the brief, he'd be forced to file it *pro se*, which was the kiss of death in the Fifth Circuit.

That meant two last-ditch visits to his least favorite venues: a hospital and a prison. In that order.

\* \* \*

Thursday morning Eva and Cash, both bearing gifts, caught Goldy on a rare good day. Eva brought a boxed set of Elmore Leonard's early westerns. Cash, a copy of Biddle's brief, ready for Goldy's signature.

Propped up in his hospital bed with his untouched breakfast on a tray, Goldy looked rested and restless. The color had returned to his face. His eyes were alive, active. His tongue, sharp as ever.

"Well, if it isn't beauty and the butthole." Goldy pushed aside the tray. "Eva, run downstairs and get me a breakfast burrito with chorizo and lots of salsa."

"Eat your oatmeal," she said, "or I'll be forced to feed you like a baby."

"How are you feeling?" Cash said.

Goldy stuck his chin out. "Like I could whip your ass."

With bigger fish to fry, Cash didn't take the bait. "Are you strong enough to read a twenty-page brief?"

"What brief?" Goldy sounded suspicious.

Cash went into detail on Biddle's background. The travesty of his trial, the horrors of his life inside, the family left behind, the points on appeal, and Monday's deadline. He placed the brief on Goldy's tray.

Goldy turned to Eva. "Have you read it?"

She nodded.

"Is it worth a shit?"

"I give Cash a B-plus," she said, "and Biddle a fifty-fifty shot at freedom or at least a new trial."

Goldy sat up straighter. "Fifty-fifty, those are good odds with the Fifth Circus, and B-plus is a damn sight higher than any grade Cash ever got in law school."

He held out his hand. "Give me a pen."

* * *

Saturday was visiting day at Seagoville. Cash stood out among the grandmothers, mothers, wives, girlfriends, and daughters herded through the metal detector into a windowless room, stinking of sweat and cheap perfume.

The large room was bare except for two dozen plastic chairs that looked like hand-me-downs from an inner-city high school. With more visitors than chairs, the lucky ones who'd scored seats didn't budge.

Well, not until Big Black swaggered in. Then the prisoners scattered as if their chairs had been hot-wired, and the noise level dropped from a dull roar to dead silence.

Big Black took center stage and tapped the empty seat next to his. Cash approached warily and sat.

"I knew you'd be back." Big Black licked his lips. "Not as no visitor neither but coming back for good. You musta missed me something awful."

"More than you can imagine," Cash said. "Missed our long conversations on life, law, and literature."

Big Black belly laughed. "And I've missed your special brand of bullshit. Even put together a little party to welcome you back next week."

"Don't go to any trouble on my account." Cash looked around to see if anyone was eavesdropping. Not that it mattered. No one would see or hear anything. Not unless Big Black told them to.

"You and me," Cash said, "are we square?"

Big Black rubbed his stubbly chin. "Me and my new bitch, we was watching this Jap film last night about the yazuka."

*New bitch?*

Cash assumed Big Black had tired of Biddle and moved on to fresh prey. "I believe it's called the *Yakuza*." He immediately regretted opening his big, fat mouth.

Big Black glared but went on. "Like I was saying, in the movie the big boss man of the Yazu...the Yaku...of the gang... he gets royally pissed off. His flunky done screwed up real bad. So to make amends for his fuck-up, flunky cuts off his little finger and gives it to the boss as a peace offering."

Cash swallowed hard. "You want me to slice off my pinkie?"

"Hell no. That pussy move didn't even work in the movie. Boss man threw away the bloody finger and chopped off the fool's whole hand."

Cash's heart bungee jumped to his bowels and back. "Are you seriously asking me to cut off my hand?"

Big Black smiled. "It's a start."

Cash left the visiting room without a clue that the trip to Seagoville would go downhill from there.

# CHAPTER TWENTY-NINE

unkered behind his desk, Warden Stockman looked grimmer than usual, if that was possible. He held Biddle's brief in the palm of one hand, as if weighing its worth.

Cash sat on the edge of the couch. "I don't see the problem. We filed the brief for Biddle on Friday, so it's available to the public. I brought him a file-stamped copy, but your people won't let me see him."

The lines on the warden's face deepened. "He's dead."

"W-w-what?"

"He hung himself in the chapel."

"When?"

"Last night."

It took a minute or so for Cash to trust his legs to hold. A thousand questions flooded his mind. None surfaced. He staggered toward the door.

"Take these with you." The warden pushed the brief across the table. Atop it lay the photo of Biddle's wife and twin daughters, the one he'd kept under his pillow.

\* \* \*

Cash hadn't touched the bone-in ribeye at Bob's Steak and Chop House. With only fifteen hours to his revocation hearing and sixteen to a one-way ticket to Seagoville, his appetite had deserted him.

As had his attorney.

Reality pummeled Cash with a flurry of blows. His last client, dead. His lawyer, knocking on death's door. His future, bleak and short.

Scratch Goldberg from appearing before Tapia tomorrow. This morning a raging case of vertigo had felled the old man. Halfway to the shitter in the hospital, his legs had turned rubbery, and the bladder had let go.

Cash had managed to catch him before he hit the floor. Not the first time Cash had cleaned him up and tucked him in.

Possibly the last.

"I should've filed the brief earlier and done it *pro se*." Cash had fasted for the day, sworn off everything but booze. At the restaurant he was on his third glass of the Shiraz.

"You can't blame yourself," Eva said. "Filing it *pro se* would've been like putting it in the shredder."

"I stalled too long in the hope of getting my license back, because I wanted my name on a winning brief." He killed drink number three and refilled the glass. "My pride got Biddle killed."

"It's okay to grieve his death," she said, "only not now." She pushed away her plate, the steak also untouched. "We should be at the office, preparing your defense."

"What defense? I'm down to one option: throwing myself on the mercy of a court that's never shown any."

"It's not like you to give up," Eva said.

"What do you want me to do? Ask the judge for another continuance?"

"That's a non-starter."

"Then I'm back to begging for mercy."

She poured herself a glass of wine. "Or you could choose what's behind door number three."

"Which is?"

"Subpoena the bitch who took you to Santa Fe. Much as Tapia would love to stick it to you, she'd hate to piss off the Bureau. That might jeopardize her shot at landing on the Fifth Circuit."

Cash shook his head. "Can't do that. Maggie would lose her job."

"Between her losing a job and you losing your life, not a close call."

"Drop it."

"Fine." Her tone made clear she wasn't about to. "If you won't subpoena her, I will."

"Over my dead body."

"Don't tempt me," she said.

* * *

Cash froze at the threshold of Tapia's courtroom. Good thing he and Eva had reserved seats at the defense table because those were the only ones left. An overflow crowd spilled into the jury box.

Cash's arrival amped the buzz in the room. A rush of last-minute wagers set the over-and-under on his sentence at two years. The over-and-under on his life expectancy, two days.

Preening in a pinstripe suit, U.S. Attorney Tom Moore worked the reporters on the front row. Pressing flesh. Cracking jokes. Soaking up the free pub.

At his side, an ashen-faced Jenna Powell pretended to read a brief. Her ploy would've been more convincing if she had bothered to turn a page every now and then.

The three-carat rock on her wedding finger caught Cash's eye. In a weird way, the ring comforted him. Proof he wasn't the only person in the courtroom to have made a bad decision.

The bailiff called the court to order, silencing the crowd and freezing the bets. The judge glided onto the bench, black robe flying behind.

"The only matter before me today is Mister McCahill's revocation hearing, which was continued from last week. Is the government ready to proceed?" Her cut-to-the-chase tone signaled a short hearing, quick sentence, and summary execution.

Moore announced ready.

"And the defense, are you ready?"

Every fiber of Cash's being screamed "no," but he said "yes." He crossed out the first word on his notepad. *Continuance*. Only one word left. *Mercy*.

"Before Mister Moore calls his first witness," Tapia said, "let the record reflect that Mister McCahill has elected to represent himself. So be it."

After being sworn in, Marty Shafer droned on about his background. Degrees, licenses, IRS postings, titles, commendations, awards, etc.

Shafer's shameless self-promotion finally forced Cash to his feet. "I'm sure Agent Shafer also earned a perfect attendance pin in the third grade." He paused for the laughter to die down. "But unless he has personal knowledge of my whereabouts on the dates in question, I object to this whole line of testimony as hearsay, irrelevant, and highly prejudicial."

Tapia didn't wait for Moore to weigh in. "Overruled. As you surely recall from your days as a federal prosecutor, Mister McCahill, hearsay evidence is admissible at a revocation hearing."

"Only at the court's discretion," Cash said.

"And this court exercises its broad discretion to allow Agent Shafer to testify fully as to his investigation."

It struck Cash as odd that Moore led off with an IRS agent without personal knowledge of the facts, rather than the FBI agent who had been at Cash's side in Santa Fe. Prosecutors generally call their best witnesses first or last.

And inside and outside the courtroom, Moore was nothing if not predictable. Meaning Maggie might be the last witness against him. Or even worse, she might not be called at all, in which case she had probably already been exiled to North Dakota for a permanent detail counting paper clips in a basement closet.

"Agent Shafer," Moore said, "where did you spend last weekend?"

"In Santa Fe, New Mexico."

"By the way, does Santa Fe fall outside the Northern District of Texas?" Moore's feeble stab at humor drew no laughs.

Shafer played straight man. "Why yes, I believe it does."

The judge did not look amused. "I'll take judicial notice that Santa Fe lies outside my jurisdiction."

Moore resumed. "Agent Shafer, what were you doing in Santa Fe?"

"Interviewing dozens of witnesses who saw Cash McCahill there a week earlier."

"Did you prepare memoranda of those witness interviews, which are commonly called MOIs?"

"Yes, sir."

"And did you bring those MOIs with you to court today?"

"Absolutely." Shafer pulled a stack of documents from his briefcase and handed them to Moore.

"Your honor," Moore said, "I've marked Agent Shafer's memoranda as government exhibits one through twenty-two, and I'll offer them into evidence at this time."

Tapia turned to Cash. "Any objection, Mister McCahill?"

Cash stalled. "May I see the exhibits first?"

Moore made a show of doling them out one by one. Slapping them on the table like a bank teller counting crisp bills.

Cash thumbed through the statements from waiters, gallery owners, artists, hotel staff, even Mariposa Benanti and her bodyguard. But zip from Maggie, stoking his fear that she had been sent to the Bureau's stand-in for Siberia.

A single witness statement could sink Cash. Twenty-two were overkill.

Cash rose. Might as well go down swinging. "Same objections. Hearsay. Lacks proper foundation. Violates the confrontation clause of the Sixth Amendment. Not best evidence. More prejudicial than probative."

"Overruled." Tapia swiveled toward the U.S. Attorney. "Any further testimony or exhibits, Mister Moore?" Her voice bristled with impatience. She had heard enough.

"Just one more exhibit." Moore handed a photo to Shafer. "Can you identify what I've marked as exhibit twenty-three?"

"Yes, that's a shot Mariposa Benanti took on her iPhone of Mister McCahill last Saturday night at The Shed."

"What's The Shed?" Moore said.

"A popular restaurant in Santa Fe established in 1953." Shafer came off like a brown-nosing student. "I highly recommend the blue corn enchiladas."

"I'll offer exhibits one through twenty-three into evidence," Moore said.

Cash took the picture from Moore. Maggie had been cropped out, confirming her new status as a nonperson.

"Same objections," Cash said.

"Overruled. Exhibits one through twenty-three are all admitted. Now, Mister Moore, are you ready to rest your case?"

The door to the courtroom banged open. Cash wheeled around to see living proof of the truth that anyone can die at any time.

# CHAPTER THIRTY

aggie Burns never broke stride on her march down the aisle. Didn't look to her right at the defense table, nor left at the government. Instead, she steamed straight to the stand.

The courtroom artist on the front row ditched the unfinished study of Cash to sketch the surprise witness. Maggie had that effect on people. Even in her bureaucratic blue blazer, matching skirt, and white shirt, she came off as too glam for a G-woman.

Her entrance caught the room off guard, but not for long. Cash scrambled to his feet, but Moore lodged the first objection. Cash glared at Eva, who gave a don't-look-at-me shrug.

Tapia quickly regained control of the courtroom. "What's the basis of your objection, Mister Moore?"

"Agent Burns isn't listed as a witness by either side, and the government has no intention of calling her."

Tapia turned to Cash, who said, "Same here."

"Agent Burns, while I applaud your willingness, even eagerness to come forward," the judge said, "you seem to be a witness in search of a sponsor. I'll have to ask you to step down."

Maggie didn't budge. "I have exculpatory evidence, your honor, and it would be reversible error under *Brady v. Maryland* for the court not to hear it."

A pained look crossed Tapia's face. She could safely ignore the bleating of defense counsel about *Brady*. Not so easy to blow off a warning by the Bureau.

"Very well, if no one else will do it, I'll call you to the stand." The judge laughed. "What am I saying? You're already there. Well, let me swear you in." She administered the oath.

Maggie nudged aside the exhibits and leaned forward until her lips hovered inches from the mic. The way the FBI taught agents to testify.

Or as Cash called it, *Testilying 101*.

"Agent Burns, what is this so-called exculpatory evidence that the court must hear?" Tapia sounded skeptical.

Maggie's cool façade crumbled. Cash jumped to his feet. He had caught her hesitation but doubted anyone else had. "Your honor," he said, "may we approach the bench?"

Tapia sighed. "If you must."

Cash and Moore rushed forward. Jenna and Eva held back, close enough to hear the sidebar without being sucked into the madness afoot.

Cash swallowed hard. "I'll stipulate for the record that I was in Santa Fe last week."

Moore smelled blood and leaned in. "Will you also stipulate that you didn't seek permission from the court to leave the Northern District of Texas?"

Eva tugged on Cash's coat. He ignored her and nodded.

"You'll have to answer verbally, Mister McCahill." Tapia would make sure the court reporter captured his confession.

"Yes, I'll stipulate to all that."

"In writing?" Moore said.

Another nod prompted the judge to remind Cash to speak up. "I'll sign whatever the government wants."

Tapia winked at Moore. A signal Cash caught, but the court reporter wouldn't. "Then there's no need to hear this witness or any other before I make my ruling. Do you agree, Mister Moore?"

The U.S. Attorney hesitated. He had a history of seeing traps where none were. Finally he agreed.

The judge shooed the lawyers back to their seats and addressed the restless crowd. "Ladies and gentlemen, the defendant will stipulate to leaving the district without permission, which brings this hearing to an abrupt end."

She swiveled to face the witness. "Agent Burns, in light of the stipulation, your testimony won't be needed. Please step down."

"I can't do that." Maggie's voice cracked. "The stipulation makes my testimony all the more important." She bit her lower lip, a telltale sign a lie was about to slip out. "Mister McCahill didn't seek permission to leave the district because he thought I had."

Cash slumped in his seat, his shot at saving Maggie from herself gone. His sole consolation was that Moore looked shell-shocked. The only thing more painful to the media whore than losing was losing in front of the press.

Moore climbed to his feet. "May I have a moment to confer in private with my witness?"

"A minute ago," Tapia said, "she wasn't your witness. You can't have it both ways, Mister Moore. Sit down. I'll hear her out."

She turned to Maggie. "Why would the defendant expect *you* to ask the court for permission for *him* to travel to New Mexico?"

Good question. Cash hoped Maggie had a damn good answer, because she had gone too far to turn back.

The door to the courtroom swung open, and Maggie blanched. Cash turned to see what had spooked her. Julio Reyes, Special Agent in Charge of the Dallas FBI office, glared at the witness.

Maggie did the lip thing again. Paving the way for another lie.

"Mister McCahill has been assisting the Bureau in locating a missing witness. This required his presence in Santa Fe, and he agreed to go there at my request. He thought I had cleared the trip with the court, while I thought he had. Chalk it up to a communication failure, more my fault than his."

Hell hath no fury like a judge scorned, and Tapia aimed hers at the U.S. Attorney. "Mister Moore, what made you think I wouldn't want to know that the defendant was working with the Bureau?"

Moore rose slowly, unsteadily. No doubt stalling to come up with an answer on the fly. Not his forte.

"This is the first I've heard of it, your honor. Neither Mister McCahill nor Agent Burns bothered to fill me in before the hearing."

"Did you bother to ask?" Tapia didn't wait for a response. "Of course you didn't. I strongly suggest, Mister Moore, that in the future you investigate matters more thoroughly before bringing them to my court."

Moore's face turned chalky. He nodded meekly and sat without a word. Following the maxim that faced with a pissed-off judge, the less said, the better.

Cash went with the same strategy, hoping to grab Eva and slip away to fight another day. He made it to his feet before the hammer dropped.

Make that, the gavel.

"Not so fast, Mister McCahill." Tapia's tone dashed any hopes that she had spent her anger on the prosecutor. It had to be tearing her up inside to rule in Cash's favor. "I don't know how many lives you've got, but you just burned your last one on my watch. *Capiche*?"

Cash nodded. Not defiantly but not as meekly as Moore had.

In the hallway, raised voices lured Cash past the elevators and around a corner. A string of *s*-words split the air. Shit. Slimeball. Sonovabitch.

Cash considered the most likely scenario. Two bullies were ganging up on Maggie. Playing bad boss/worse boss. Pummeling her with escalating threats. Reducing her to silent surrender.

He traced the source of the shouting to the no-man's-land outside Tapia's chambers and rushed to her rescue. He looked around. No Maggie. Only Moore and Reyes squaring off, as if about to trade blows.

# CHAPTER THIRTY-ONE

Cash's rollercoaster-ride of a day started on a high, thanks to the front page headline in *The Dallas Morning News*:

*"U.S. Attorney Stumbles in Rare Court Appearance."*

Cash laughed aloud at Judge Tapia's quote that "Moore should investigate his cases more thoroughly before coming to her court." The coverage was so cutting that Cash almost felt sorry for the publicity hound.

*Almost.*

Then again, always more pol than prosecutor, Moore knew the rule: live by the press, die by the press.

Cash's ride hit a rough patch when he set out to find Maggie Burns, the angel who'd saved him from a return to prison and certain death. Repeated calls to her work and cell phones went straight to voicemail, all unanswered.

At noon he gave up on a callback. With the marksmanship contest around the corner, he knew where to find her. Same place she'd been the last time he went looking. The FBI's outdoor firing range in the boondocks.

The month before the competition, Maggie practically lived at the range. Even aside from the contest, her favorite way of blowing off steam involved the trusty Glock, a full-body target, and enough ammo to reduce it to confetti.

Repeated bursts of gunfire almost spooked Cash into high-tailing it back to civilization. Not an ideal time to approach an armed and angry Maggie. If she didn't plug him, plenty of her colleagues would be more than happy to.

What sounded like a small army at the range turned out to be the work of only two heavily-armed agents and an endless echo. While one blasted away at a dancing target, the other shouted insults at the shooter. The smack talk drew more blood than the bullets.

Cash recognized the old hand at the range. Steve Baker, a.k.a. the Undertaker. The nickname had stuck throughout his career not because he'd ever sent anyone to Boot Hill, but for his pale skin and penchant for black suits. He just looked creepy and funereal.

Only months from retirement, Baker had downshifted from catching bad guys to not catching flak. Throughout his risk-averse career, he'd specialized in pinching low-hanging fruit. A course-of-least-resistance collector of quick, easy stats, he subscribed to the Bureau's unofficial mantra: big cases mean big problems; little cases, little problems.

Baker was certainly a better draw for Cash than his young sidekick, Marty Mendoza. Because Baker trolled for low-profile cases while Cash chased headlines, the two had never tangled in court. The hothead Mendoza, in contrast, still carried scars from Cash's stinging cross-examination.

Cash waved to Baker, who didn't wave back. Uh-oh.

"Hey, Marty," Baker shouted for Cash's benefit, "isn't it hunting season on scumbag lawyers?"

"Scumbag lawyer is redundant," Mendoza said, "and it's always open season on raging assholes."

Cash slowed his approach but rushed his pitch. "Look, fellas, I know you don't want me hanging around and spoiling your afternoon of fun with firearms." He stopped sixty feet from the pair. From this distance he doubted either could hit him but didn't want to test their aim. Or his luck. "Just tell me where Maggie is, and I'll leave."

Baker walked toward Cash. "She's where you sent her. Up shit creek. Suspended till hell freezes over. Far as the brass is concerned, she's dead to the Bureau."

"Don't tell that prick *nada*," Mendoza said before returning to the range.

"Suspended for what?" Cash said.

Baker gave him a cut-the-shit look. "Either she took you to Santa Fe on official business without clearance, which violated every rule in the book, or she didn't but lied on the stand to save your sorry ass. Either way, she's fucked six ways to Sunday."

Gunfire from Mendoza sent a shudder through Cash. An image of Maggie, Glock in hand, barrel in mouth, sent another.

"I've got to talk to her." Close as Cash could come to begging.

"In the highly unlikely event she wants to talk to you, she'll call."

Cash made a final appeal. "Look, I'm worried about her. Afraid she might...." He couldn't bring himself to say it. "Don't do it for me, but for her."

Baker shook his head slowly. Not in a get-the-hell-out-of-here way. More of an I-can't-believe-I'm-about-to-do-this resignation. He looked over his shoulder to make sure his partner was out of earshot. "No one can ever know I gave you her address. Least of all, MagDoll."

"I'll take it to my grave," Cash said.

"The sooner you do that, the better."

* * *

Maggie's third-floor apartment was two blocks north and several rungs below Taylor Donovan's penthouse suite uptown. The sprawling complex, a hive of entry-level millennials, banked on a pretentious name (*The Worthington Arms*) compensating for cut-rate amenities. Plastic sconces with fake flames lined mildewy halls.

One thing for sure, Maggie was painfully honest. No agent on the take would crash here.

Cash knocked on Apartment 317. No answer. Next stop, the fitness center on the ground floor, overlooking the pool.

The pool was deserted. The gym would've been too, but for Maggie.

Forty-three minutes on a treadmill and counting, she had slipped into a runner's trance. Dead eyes. Flaring nostrils. Locked lips. A drumbeat cadence that measured out life in miles, minutes, pulse rates, and calories burned.

His arrival broke the trance. The look that crossed her face straddled shock and anger. Heavier on the anger. Good thing they hadn't hooked up at the shooting range.

"The asshole who gave you my address is a dead man walking." Maggie breathed deeply but not hard. "So who dimed me out?"

"Let's just say a mutual friend gave me your address."

She slowed the pace to a brisk walk. "Given that I hang out with law enforcement types, we don't have any mutual friends."

"But we have a mutual enemy," he said, "which is a stronger bond."

She hit stop, and the treadmill ground to a halt. He offered his hand to help her down. She didn't take it.

"Why are you here?" she said.

"To make sure you're okay."

She laughed. "Any more help from you, and I'll wind up behind bars."

"Hey, I didn't subpoena you to the hearing. You came of your own free will."

"I had no choice."

"Bullshit." It came out harsher than intended. "You always have a choice. Just like I've got one now. First thing on my to-do list, get you out of the doghouse."

"You want to do me a favor? Then stay the hell away from me."

"I can't do that." he said.

"What part of *stay the hell away from me* do you not understand?" The deep voice came from behind Cash. The accent, straight from shit-kicker country.

Cash turned to face a bodybuilder in a muscle shirt and obscene shorts. Thick, blue veins coiled around massive biceps and triceps. A physique that owed more to steroids than to heavy weights. At least, Cash hoped it did.

Three inches taller than Bicep Boy, Cash had a longer reach, but that'd be his only edge in a fight that wouldn't last a round.

"Don't bother with him, Boone," Maggie said. "He's leaving."

Boone snickered. "I'll hurry him out."

Maggie tapped the bodybuilder's arm. "Not necessary, but if he's dumb enough to come back, he's all yours."

At the door Cash stopped. "What about Taylor Donovan? Are you giving up on finding her?"

"You don't get it, do you?" Her voice crackled with anger. "This is the agency's version of purgatory. I go nowhere and do nothing without clearing it first with Mother Bureau. I shouldn't even be talking to you."

Before Cash could respond, two messages jolted his iPhone. The first brought the dead back to life. The second sent the living straight to hell.

# CHAPTER THIRTY-TWO

E va f-bombed Goldberg into silence. She appeared poised to hurdle over the desk. The old man looked as if he were about to dive under it.

Cash's entry into the office brokered a cease fire. Temporary, at best.

"Fair warning, Goldy," Cash said, "that in fifteen years working with this *bruja*, I've never won an argument."

"And never came close," she said.

Goldberg harrumphed. "She doesn't frighten me." His tone said otherwise.

Eva had texted Cash to rush to the office. The ASAP in her message proved to be merited. No shit, Goldberg really did look like the walking dead.

Or in his case, the sitting dead. After losing ten, maybe fifteen pounds on hospital grub, he all but disappeared into the surroundings. The leather chair threatened to swallow him whole. The trademark Stetson rode low on his forehead.

"What the hell are you doing here?" Cash said to Goldberg. "You should be home resting."

Goldberg planted his elbows on the desk and propped himself up, best he could. He slid back into a slouch, then surged forward. The pattern repeated. Sliding. Surging.

"I'm fighting to save our practice," Goldberg said, "before you and that…that she-devil drive it into the ground."

Give the old man credit. Even in his weakened state, he had a set of pipes any mouthpiece would kill for. A low, rumbling baritone that seemed to belong to a warrior half his age.

"Doctor Rodriguez told the fool not to think about returning to work for another thirty days," she said, "and then only after passing a full checkup."

"He's a quack," Goldberg said. "Besides, with you two at the helm, we don't have thirty days."

Neither Eva nor Cash had a quick comeback. It was beyond dispute that the office was underwater. With three months' rent overdue, the landlord's serial letters had escalated from gentle reminders to eviction threats. Goldberg owed support payments to three of four exes, two of whom had already filed contempt motions.

To keep the lights on, Eva had burned through her savings and sold her Harley. A rich girlfriend was all that kept her off the streets.

Rattled by rumors of Goldy's imminent death, clients were stampeding from the fold and demanding refunds of retainers long since spent. Revenue dried up, while grievances and lawsuits piled up.

Cash took stock of their plight. Hard to believe that a practice forty years in the making could crater so quickly.

"What we have here is a temporary cash flow problem." Like his mentor, Cash had mastered the art of the understatement. "What we can't afford is for you to relapse and be out six months or worse. I can carry us for another month or so while you recuperate."

Eva shot Cash a quizzical look and mouthed *how?*

He tossed her a set of car keys. "Sell the Porsche and pay the landlord the bare minimum to get him off our backs."

"Are you sure?" she said.

He nodded. "And buy the cheapest bottle of champagne you can find for a celebration."

"What have we got to celebrate?" Goldberg said.

"Taylor Donovan texted me. She's in Dubai for two weeks."

"What's she doing there?" Eva said.

Cash gave her a get-real look. "The same thing she does here, only I assume for more dough."

"You don't sound all that overjoyed about the news," Goldberg said. "Are you disappointed that the Benantis didn't turn out to be the badasses you painted them to be?"

"The Benantis eat badasses for breakfast," Cash said. "Just wish I could be sure that Taylor had sent the message. Could be someone trying to convince us she's all right."

"If Taylor contacted you," Eva said, "odds are she got in touch with her brother too."

Cash nodded. "Good point. I'll see what the kid brother has to say." He pulled Goldberg to his feet. "Come on, old man. I'll drop you at the house on my way to SMU."

"I drove myself here, and I can damn well drive myself back." The grumpier Goldberg got, the more he reverted to his old self. "By the way, if she's really in Dubai, tell her to stay there. Sure as hell safer for her than Dallas."

* * *

Before Cash tracked down Taylor's brother, he had a stop at the cemetery. After all, it wasn't every day that he had a chance to send off a cellmate-client-suicide to the great unknown.

179

Cash had tricky terrain to navigate at Restland Park. He wanted to pay final respects to Martin Biddle while avoiding contact with the widow, fearful that anything he said to her would make matters worse. He knew too much about Biddle's time on the inside and too little about his life outside.

So he opted for the graveside interment over the memorial service. The outdoor setting decreased the risk of being trapped by Mrs. Biddle in a closed space. Despite the overcast day, he wore sunglasses. Less chance of being recognized.

Biddle had looked young for a thirty-four-year-old, which had proven a handicap in prison. His widow looked even younger. The twin daughters couldn't stop crying and clinging to their mother.

Though Biddle had been Catholic, an Episcopalian priest presided over the burial. Cash figured the Catholic Church had blackballed him over the suicide thing. The stand-in handled the cause of death well. Far better than Cash would've. He talked about not knowing what goes on inside another's head, not being judgmental, remembering the best of the departed.

During the service, the widow locked eyes with Cash. At least that's how he saw it. Despite hiding behind sunglasses and floating on the farthest orbit of mourners, he couldn't escape her judgment.

So he fled.

\* \* \*

Ricky Donovan proved almost as elusive as his sister. After striking out at the dorm, gym, library, student union, and Starbucks, Cash took a stab at the law school.

A long shot, sure, but Ricky had his heart set on burning three years there. And he would hardly be the first undergrad to turn into a law school groupie.

*Bingo.* Ricky had ambushed poor Professor Dodd on the steps of the Underwood Law Library. Even back in Cash's day, students had dubbed the ancient teacher "Professor Doddering." Behind his back, of course.

While Ricky angled for a recommendation to next year's class, Dodd probably had no clue he was wasting time on an undergrad.

Cash grabbed Ricky by the arm. "Hate to break up your brown-nosing session, but we have to talk." Pulled him aside. "Have you heard from your sister recently?"

"Yeah."

"When?"

"Yesterday." Ricky yanked free his arm and waved goodbye to Dodd. Hand leapfrogging hand on the rail, the law professor struggled up the stairs as if he were scaling Everest. He didn't wave back. No free hand.

"She texted me," Ricky said, "that she'd be in Dubai for a couple of weeks and not to worry."

"But since we last talked," Cash said, "have you actually spoken to her?"

Ricky shook his head. "That's no big deal. We text. That's how we keep up with each other when she's on the road and I'm swamped at school."

"The next time you talk to her, tell her to call me. I want to hear her voice." Cash handed him a business card. "And some free advice. If you go to law school here, give Dodd's class a miss. Boring as hell, and the twit gave me a C. I deserved a B for staying awake."

# CHAPTER THIRTY-THREE

Joey Lobello, a.k.a. Joey the Junkie, twitched like a puppet in the hands of a speed freak.

Eva had timed his entry into Goldberg's office to catch the old man doing his daily workout. Or more accurately, his sole, shaky pushup.

On cue Cash called out "thirty." His count had begun and ended on that mythical number.

Rheumy-eyed and runny-nosed, Joey whistled. "Not bad for a geezer. And here I heard you was knocking on death's door."

Goldberg crossed the floor on his hands and knees and climbed into the chair behind his desk. "Rumors of my death have been greatly exaggerated."

Joey stared blankly, the literary allusion surely lost on him. Then again, pretty much anything literary would whiz past the junior high dropout.

"What can I do for you, Joey?" Goldberg said.

The druggie's gaze darted back and forth between Goldberg and Cash, before finally lowering to the desk. Coffee swirls stained the wood. A poor man's Rorschach test.

"You been real good to me over the years, Mister G, so this here...what I got to do...well this ain't easy for me." He glanced guiltily at Goldberg. "But I come to get my files and my retainer."

"W-w-what?" Goldberg feigned shock. Acting as if the demand had been a bolt from the blue. Not letting on that a steady stream of clients had pulled the plug, emptying the firm's file cabinets.

And its coffers.

Cash erupted in outrage, only partly feigned. "You little worm. You fucking ingrate. Who got you off two years ago with a slap on the wrist?"

Joey's chest caved deeper. "Hey, I did time for that one."

"Ninety days when you should've pulled a nickel." Cash raised his hand, as if to bitch-slap the junkie.

Joey flinched. "Word on the street is that Mister G's hanging it up."

"Are you kidding me?" Cash said. "This man is a cockroach. He'll outlive you and me, plus all his detractors."

Joey looked even more lost than usual. "The tractors?"

"Dee-tractors." *Stupid shit.* "He'll damn sure outlive you unless you drop the dumbass request and get the hell out of here."

Eva opened the door and stuck her head into the office. "Mister Goldberg, Judge Robinson wants to know if you can play racquetball with him at six." Nailing her line.

"Tell the old fart that I'll be more than happy to whip his ass today," Goldberg said, "just like I did yesterday, and like I'll do tomorrow."

"Good enough for me," Joey said before leaving to commit his first felony of the day.

Cash would've high-fived Goldberg but for fear that the slightest touch, even a strong draft might knock him off the chair. The lone pushup had taken a toll.

So Cash slapped palms with Eva instead. The band, back together again.

"The good thing about holding onto our boy Joey," Cash said, "is that he's repeat business. Loser couldn't walk a straight line in a cattle chute."

"Maybe Joey can spread the word," Goldberg said, "that I'm back in the saddle and stronger than ever."

Cash let the puffery pass, allowing the old man to indulge in a moment of self-deception.

"While we're on the subject of rounding up strays," Cash said, "I have to go to Dubai."

Goldberg rocked back in his chair and heaved his boots onto the desk. "Last time I checked, Dubai fell a few thousand miles outside the Northern District of Texas."

"Not to mention that we don't have the dough to send you to Denton, much less Dubai." Eva the fussbudget, always the voice of reason.

"I'll fly coach."

"We can't afford to ship you cargo," she said, "and in case it has slipped your mind, Judge Tapia made it crystal clear at the last hearing. The next time you set foot outside *her* jurisdiction without *her* permission, it's back to Seagoville."

"So I'll get the judge's blessing." Cash sounded more confident than he felt. "Don't have a choice anyway, since her clerk has my passport."

Goldberg took a cigar from a wooden box. Before he could light up, Eva snatched it from him, snapped it in two, and tossed the halves in the trash. Her next stop, the office bar, where she poured bottles of booze down the drain.

"Stop, you crazy bitch," Goldberg shouted. "Doc Ramirez said I could have two cigars and two drinks a day. Aids the digestion."

Eva scoffed. "Before you drop another truckload of bullshit on us, get the name right. It's Doctor Rodriguez, and he said no such thing. It's cold turkey for you. And by the way, you're not even supposed to be back at work for another two weeks, so I'm letting you off easy."

Goldberg looked to Cash for help. Cash's shrug told him to surrender on Eva's terms.

"She needs to remember who's the boss around here." Goldberg sounded whipped and whiny. "You both do."

Cash paced the room. "I can't stay here and do nothing. It's been two weeks since anyone has heard from Taylor. Longer if the texts to her brother and me were sent by someone else. Two weeks of Taylor's time would bankrupt the entire Middle East. Plus, I can't see her staying interested in anyone or anything that long."

"What troubles me," Goldberg said, "is that I can't tell whether you're more interested in finding the girl or blaming the Benantis for her disappearance."

Cash stopped pacing. "They're one and the same."

Goldberg shook his head. "You don't know that. You assume a Benanti is behind everything that goes wrong in your car wreck of a life." He pressed both palms on the desk to steady himself as he rose to his feet. "Have I taught you nothing?"

"You taught me not to give up on a client," Cash said.

"That's not the only lesson you should've learned. With all the tools at their disposal, how do the feds ever manage to lose a case?"

Cash sighed, having heard the lecture a hundred times. "They lock onto a theory too early and refuse to let go, ignoring any evidence to the contrary."

"Which is exactly what you're doing now," Goldberg said. "Considering no alternative explanations and tossing out any evidence that doesn't feed into your obsession with bringing down the Benantis."

"What other alternatives are there?" Cash sounded defensive.

"For one, the girl could've felt pressured on all sides and simply taken off. She may be hiding from everyone, including you. Who could blame her?"

"She'd let her brother know."

"Maybe," Goldberg said, "maybe not. Once again, you're assuming."

Cash's iPhone vibrated. He checked the message. "Looks like my days of assuming are over."

# CHAPTER THIRTY-FOUR

Unlocked. That's how Cash found the door to Taylor's penthouse digs. Bad sign.

It triggered an internal alarm first set off by Ricky's message. Everything about the brother's text smelled wrong. From the place for the urgent meeting, Taylor's apartment, to the instruction to come alone.

Even in the relative safety of Goldberg's office, the *alone* part had seemed like a terrible idea. Possibly a fatal one.

Solo and unarmed hit the daily double of dumbass decisions. Cash had been tempted to bring the .357 Goldberg kept in the desk drawer in the event a pissed-off client went postal. As a felon, however, Cash had forfeited the right to carry. Toting a gun guaranteed a second felony and a return trip to prison.

With a push the door yawned open. Cash couldn't resist focusing on the larger-than-life painting of Eva in the foyer.

A whoosh from behind broke the spell of *The Naked Maja*. Cash glimpsed a glint of steel in the corner of his eye. A familiar scent set off alarms. Before he could wheel around to ward off the attack, metal struck skull, and he went down.

* * *

Hushed voices seeped into Cash's flickering consciousness. Hard to tell whether the words sprang from inside his head or out.

Scattered memories of the knockout blow pinged his mind. The twin shocks of total blindness and partial paralysis spiked his heart rate. Only the lockdown of his vocal cords kept him from screaming.

He awoke to the nightmare of being blindfolded and strapped to a chair. His wrists and ankles lashed to wooden arms and legs. Save for the blindfold, naked as *The Maja*.

As he struggled against the ropes, the chair clopped on the hardwood floor. Twice he nearly toppled over. The harder he twisted and turned, the deeper the bonds sliced into skin.

The captors' laughter hurt more than the rope. Mariposa Benanti's laugh cut deepest. Full-throated. Cruel. A promise that things would go from bad to worse.

Even if her laugh hadn't been as distinctive as a fingerprint, the perfume would've given her away. Clive Christian's No. 1. Three years ago the brand had set Cash back over two grand for a two-ounce bottle. Bought to celebrate a month of hotel hopping with the pet python of the most dangerous predator in Dallas.

An anniversary present for a woman he couldn't afford to be with. Certainly not get caught with anyway.

"Just like old times, Mariposa." Cash's parched lips popped on the *P* in her name. "Except that in the past, you were the one tied down."

The slap didn't catch him off guard. He'd braced for it. Still stung like crazy.

"I assume the love tap was for your husband's benefit." Cash's cheek burned. "Which means he must be here to enjoy it."

The gut punch did take Cash by surprise. If not for the rope, he would've doubled over and crumpled to the floor. His head bobbed. Strings of drool dangled from his mouth.

At least he hoped it was drool.

"The slap was for my wife's benefit." Violence brought out the Jersey Shore in Benanti's accent. "The punch, that was for me. Not that it settles the score between us. The penalty for fucking my wife is kissing your pecker goodbye. Tonight it will join my collection of scalps."

Cash stifled the comeback on his lips. Not the time, place, or predicament to mouth off.

Strain as he might, rope kept his legs pried open. His thighs spread in a *V. V* as in vulnerable. The family jewels there for the taking.

"Ricky texted me to meet him here," Cash said. "So where is he?"

A muffled scream to Cash's right. His head jerked toward the sound. The source close. Probably in the next room. Filtered through a gag and a wall.

The scream had been impeccably timed. No sooner had Cash asked about Ricky than the boy's torture began. Or more likely, resumed.

Probably Bobby the Bodyguard at work. He wouldn't be good for much, but a master at inflicting pain. Torture would be his thing.

A second round of muffled screams confirmed Cash's worst fears. Longer and louder than the first. Interrupted by spasmodic sobbing and unintelligible blubbering. Cash didn't have to make out the words to recognize someone begging for his life.

Or a quick death.

"If you're torturing Ricky to find out where Taylor is, you're wasting your time." Cash failed to drain the desperation from his voice.

"You and I know that," Benanti said, "but Bobby's a slow learner. Or perhaps by now even he has gotten the message, so he's butchering the poor boy for the fun of it. Either way, you'll tell us where she is. The over-and-under on how long you can hold out with Bobby is twenty minutes. I took the over."

"And I, the under." Mariposa sounded more confident in her bet. "Don't let me down. Let Taylor down instead."

Being tied to the chair had one advantage. The couple couldn't see the fear coursing through his body. At most they'd catch the tremor of his lips. Or the quiver in his voice.

"What makes you think Ricky or I know where she is, or would tell you if we did?"

The Benantis laughed in unison. She stopped before he did. Always did have more self-control.

"Both of you will spill everything you know," she said, "but only one will walk out of here tomorrow. Be the smart one for a change."

Cash bit his tongue. Didn't shake his head but didn't nod either.

Mariposa sighed. "I didn't think so."

She walked away. Ten clicks of her heels on hardwood, then five more on tile. The opening and slamming of a drawer. Fifteen clicks back.

She straddled him on the chair, sitting face to face, her bare thighs on his. Stroked his shaft, a forefinger strumming a pulsing vein. Coaxing an erection against his will.

"After your vacation at Club Fed," she said, "I wasn't sure you could still get it up."

"Prison didn't kill my desire for women." Knew he should stop there but couldn't. "Just for one particular bitch."

She squeezed his sac. "Last chance before your balls relocate from your crotch to your mouth."

Cold steel on foreskin killed the erection, along with his resistance. "Okay, I'll tell you what I know." His voice jumped an octave, as if anticipating a post-castration high. "I tried to talk Taylor into taking care of her tax problem by turning on you, but she bolted instead."

Cash paused, not sure how many words he had left. He made peace with his fate but steeled himself to save the client.

"Taylor's in the wind, and she's not coming back. She can't hurt you now, so be a sport and let her go."

"I can't do that," Benanti said.

"Sure you can. How many women do you own? A hundred? Five hundred? Five thousand? Throw this one back."

"You never did understand. I'm not the bad guy here. I'm more like the good shepherd." Benanti sounded deranged, as if he bought into his own bullshit. "When a lamb is lost, I leave the flock to bring it back into the fold."

Cash didn't buy a word of it. A butterfly freak with a net, that was the real Benanti.

With Taylor a lost cause, he focused on saving Goldberg, another loose end. Torn over whether to bring up his mentor or let it be, he finally decided that silence would likely leave more blood on his hands.

The Benantis subscribed to a strict policy of guilt by association. Better to kill nine know-nothings than risk letting a single witness live.

"By the way, Goldberg told her not to snitch on you."

"Why?" she said.

"You know why." The touch of cold steel on flesh prodded him to spill more. "He knew she'd never live to testify against you."

"Your boss is smarter than you are," she said.

"That seems to be the consensus."

"Is that all you know?" She sounded disappointed.

He nodded, not sure whether she was disappointed in him or for him.

She swiveled in his lap, her hip brushing his penis and reviving the erection. "What do you think?" she said.

Cash simultaneously had nothing to say and a thousand thoughts struggling to surface. Took him a few seconds to realize that the question was meant, not for him, but for her husband.

"I think he told all he knows," Benanti said, "but he didn't tell us anything we didn't already know."

"Right." She slid off him. "What say we show the condemned man a little mercy?"

"Your call," Benanti said.

"Cash," she said, "this is your lucky day."

He slumped in relief, the bonds again saving him from landing on the floor. "You're letting me go?" His faint words barely rippled the air. As if he'd thought rather than spoken them.

"Of course we're letting you go," Benanti said, "but your pecker stays behind. I'm keeping your balls in a glass jar to make sure you don't fuck my wife again. Or anyone else's wife, for that matter. World would've been a better place if you'd been fixed as a pup."

Cash froze, a plea trapped in his throat.

"But we're not monsters," Mariposa said. "We'll put you out before slicing it off. Better deal than you deserve."

Cash whipped his head from side to side but couldn't escape the chloroform-soaked rag pressed over his face. He held his breath until...until....

# CHAPTER THIRTY-FIVE

**C**ash came to, gagging on his own vomit. His head throbbed from a chloroform hangover. A snort cleared the caked blood from both nostrils. His eyes were caulked shut.

Curled in a fetal ball, he was naked and shivering. Cotton-mouthed. Sore all over. Wrists and ankles raw from rope-burns. His sense of smell returned first, followed in order by taste, touch, and sight.

A shaft of sunlight pierced the gap between parted curtains and burned the sleep from his eyes. He stared at the purplish blood pooled around him before taking in the room. The surroundings struck him as familiar but not overly so. He was neither a stranger nor a fixture here.

A rolled-up yoga mat in the corner grounded him in the present. Triggering an image of Taylor in the down dog position. Reminding him why he had walked into a trap and how he had suffered for it.

When he tried to push up to his hands and knees, he skidded on the slick and crashed face-first to the floor. His mug left an imprint in the viscous pool.

Heartbeat racing, he rolled onto his back and patted himself down. Checking the vitals. Starting with the all-important package. Everything intact and accounted for. No open wounds, not counting the busted nose and lip.

Relief swept over him. He rallied and rose to his feet. Paused a beat to steady his balance. Staggered to the guest bedroom, expecting to find Ricky Donovan in his own private pool of blood.

No body. No blood. The room, undisturbed. The bed, made.

Cash sat on the edge of the bed, lost in a sea of doubt. Paralyzed by a premonition that his next move would set him on a course of damnation or salvation. Even odds of landing in hell or heaven.

He forced himself to make a call.

* * *

Crimson swaths on the north wall of Taylor's bedroom ran from the headboard of the bed to the corners of the ceiling. The texture of the strokes was coarse, clotted. Some sick fuck had turned the white wall into a canvas.

"Is that blood?" Eva said.

A towel wrapped around his waist, Cash stared at the macabre design. He'd cleaned himself up, best he could, but his clothes had been shredded.

"Paint," he said, "mixed to look like blood."

"What's it supposed to be?"

"Butterfly wings," he replied, surprised by the certainty of his tone.

"What does it mean?" she said.

He shook his head, the fleeting sense of certainty gone. Hard-pressed to say whether he didn't know the meaning or couldn't face it. Silence forced his suspicion to the surface.

"Probably a message from the Benantis that Taylor has flown away, with the butterflies."

Eva dropped a pile of neatly folded clothes on the bed. "Make yourself decent, and by the way, you're welcome."

He pulled on the khaki slacks. "I was getting around to thanking you."

"Don't bother. Not like this is the first time I've had to bring you clothes in the wee hours of the morning."

"First time since my release from prison."

"You expect a medal for that?"

"Just a little understanding," he said.

"Oh, I understand all too well. But since Taylor's not married, who's the aggrieved party this time? Jealous boyfriend?"

"More like a pissed-off pimp."

"Benanti?"

"Bingo," he said.

"Then you're lucky to be alive."

"Luck had nothing to do with it."

"What the hell happened here?" she said.

"Still trying to figure that one out myself." Clothed, he threw open double doors to a closet the size of his bedroom. "But I'm no longer certain that the Benantis are behind Taylor's disappearance."

"Goldberg warned you against jumping to that conclusion." She followed him into the closet. "Must be tough for you to admit he's been right all along."

"I'm not conceding anything, not to him anyway. Just having doubts about my original theory."

"Big step for someone whose mantra is *never in doubt, often wrong*." She left the closet and returned with a damp washcloth. "Sit on the bed while I tend to the cut above your eye."

"This your way of trying to lure me into the sack? At least have the decency to get me drunk first."

"There's not enough booze on the planet to make me stupid enough to hop in bed with you," she said.

She shoved him onto the bed and doctored the most visible wound. He winced at her touch. "Not so hard."

"Don't be such a baby." She dabbed around the cut. "What made you change your mind about the Benantis?"

"My opinion of them hasn't changed. They'd snuff Taylor without losing a second of sleep. *If* they could get their hands on her. I just don't think they've found her yet. If they had, why bother torturing her brother and me to discover her whereabouts?"

"I can think of one good reason," she said. "What if they killed her but want to throw you and Ricky off their trail? A good acting job could send the two of you chasing a phantom."

"If they were acting, they deserve his-and-hers Oscars."

She bandaged the cut. "There, that should do it. Any more wounds to tend?"

"Just my pride."

"Lost cause," she said. "Speaking of Ricky, where is he?"

"Good question. He was gone when I came to. That is, if he was ever here." He ran his forefinger across the bandage. She slapped his hand away. "I never actually saw him last night, but someone got tortured in the bedroom. Could've been him. Could've been anyone."

"Might've been a recording," she said.

"One way to find out." Cash headed toward the door. "Let's hope Ricky is easier to find than his sister."

On the way out, he passed by the refrigerator and removed a black magnet in the shape of a poodle. Fine print advertised

The Canine Country Club, five-star boarding for a woman's best friend, with an address and phone number.

Evidently Taylor wasn't the only bitch missing.

"What are you doing?" she said.

"Going to see a man about a dog."

# CHAPTER THIRTY-SIX

**A**s things turned out, Cash saw a woman about a dog.

The familiar cockapoo growled at him. Would've been more threatening if she'd been larger than a mop head.

"Carmen doesn't seem to like you." Sami Ravens' tone made clear she trusted the dog's judgment.

"Seems to be the consensus," Cash said. "Good thing she's caged."

Holed up in hutch number seventeen of The Canine Country Club, Taylor Donovan's pet shared a wing with a yapping Chihuahua on her right and a cross-eyed cocker spaniel to the left.

As soon as Sami unlocked the cage, Carmen leapt into her elaborately-inked arms. Her left forearm featured a rainbow-colored cockatoo; the right, a smiling porpoise.

Eva stepped forward and made eye contact with the vet. "Cash seems to have that effect on the female of the species."

"Which species?" Sami said with a wink.

Eva winked back. "All of them."

Outnumbered two to one, three to one counting Carmen, Cash knew better than to cock-block his secretary. Besides, lesbians were proving to be his kryptonite.

He served up a line guaranteed to cement the bond between the new BFFs. "What can I say? Dah bitches, they just don't get me."

Eva touched the vet's forearm, gently stroking the cockatoo's golden beak. A fleeting touch so charged that Cash suffered sympathy goose bumps.

"You see," Eva said, "what I have to put up with?"

"You have my deepest sympathy," Sami said, "but this means you're either a saint or a masochist."

"They're not mutually exclusive." Eva held out her arms.

Cash wasn't sure where she was going with this.

"May I hold her?" Eva said. Sami handed the pet to her. "Does she miss her owner?"

"A ton," Sami said, "but Carmen spends a lot of time with us. We're her home away from home."

"Taylor Donovan is why we're here," Eva said. "We need to get in touch with her, or at least find out where she is and when she's returning to Dallas."

Sami frowned. "Afraid I can't help you there. Her job takes her all over the world, so we sometimes keep Carmen for weeks at a time."

Cash couldn't hold back any longer. "What would happen if Taylor took off and never returned?"

The vet's frown deepened. "We'd call the backup contact she gave us. Her brother. Why do you ask? Has something happened to her?"

Cash ignored the question. "Do you know Ricky?"

"Yes." Sami picked up the cocker spaniel. "Carmen's neighbor belongs to him." She nuzzled the pooch's neck. "His name's José."

Eva stroked the spaniel's chin. "Any idea when Ricky will come for José?"

Sami shook her head. "He dropped off this sweetie two days ago and said he needed to concentrate on finals. Guess he'll come back when they're over."

"You said Taylor often leaves Carmen with you," Cash said.

The vet nodded.

"How about Ricky? Does he board José here regularly as well?"

"No." Sami reached for a leash hanging on the wall. "This is José's first stay with us."

On the way out, Cash gave Sami a business card and asked her to call if she heard from Taylor or Ricky. He left the kennel with zero chance the vet would call him but good odds she'd ring Eva, whether or not the Donovans surfaced.

* * *

The rent-a-wreck Impala idled at the curb in front of the kennel, with Cash in the driver's seat and Eva riding shotgun. He squeezed the steering wheel until his knuckles popped.

"Big step down from the Porsche," she said.

"I'm adjusting to life in the slow lane." He eased onto the street.

"Where are we going?" she said.

"I'm taking you to the office. We can't leave Goldberg there unsupervised. Then I'm going to see someone about getting my license back."

"What about Taylor and Ricky? Are we giving up on finding them?"

"Not giving up, just not sure where to look now. We're back at square one." He pulled to the curb and parked. "We have a brother and sister disappearing act on our hands. Don't know whether they were kidnapped, killed, fled, or took off on a lark. No idea whether they're together or apart, whether they're working for the Benantis or against them, whether they're friend or foe."

"Why did you stop in front of a condom shop?" Her voice dripped disapproval. "Not that I really want to know the answer."

"To see if the black Lincoln, which was parked a block behind us at the kennel, pulls over." He angled the rearview mirror. The tinted windows of the Lincoln made it impossible to determine who or how many were inside.

"And it just did," he said.

# CHAPTER THIRTY-SEVEN

Cash couldn't shake the Lincoln, so he played cat-and-mouse with it.

After dropping off Eva at the office, he took a circuitous route to his destination, Inwood Village. He sped up. Slowed down. Sped. Slowed. Made illegal U-turns. Slipped down alleys. Even jumped a median.

The Lincoln stuck closer than a teen to a cellphone. Surveillance so open and obvious sent a can't-miss message. Someone wanted Cash to know that his every move was being watched.

He ducked into the Inwood Theatre and took his familiar seat in the large auditorium downstairs. Center seat, ten rows from the screen. His presence doubled the take for an afternoon showing on a weekday.

Ten minutes later Jenna Powell arrived and stood at the back of the theatre. Overdressed for a movie date with an ex-lawyer and ex-lover. Not that she'd call it a *date*.

Cash kept one eye on her, the other on the screen. He couldn't tell whether she had stalled to let her eyes adjust to the dark, or to give herself a last chance to back out.

He stood, and she moved toward him. The sequins of her black cocktail dress reflected the light from a chain of explosions on screen.

He sat. "You didn't have to dress up on my account."

"I didn't." She sat next to him. "Whatever you have to say, make it quick. I don't have time for a movie today."

"Not even *Taken 5*?" He tilted a popcorn bag toward her. A chaser of Coke Zero with two straws rested in the cup holder between them, and a box of Twizzlers bulged his shirt pocket.

"I see you're hitting all the major food groups." She waved off the popcorn. "I'm saving my appetite for a black tie event tonight. Reception at seven, dinner at eight. The Dallas Bar Association is honoring Tom as its Lawyer of the Year, so I can't stay for the film."

"A shame," he said.

"That I'll miss the movie or that the bar is honoring Tom?"

The word *both* popped into his mind. He managed to keep it there. Wasn't easy.

"A shame that you won't find out if Liam Neeson, going all kickass in his sixties, rescues his sexy granddaughter from white slavers."

"Are these the same bad guys who kidnapped his sexy daughter, sexy wife, sexy sister, and sexy girlfriend in *Taken 1, 2, 3,* and *4*?"

"More or less," he said. "I hear the family dog gets snatched in *Taken 6*."

"What's so all-fired important that I had to cancel appointments to meet you here?" Banter over. Business time.

"The here part is easy. This is where we played hooky from law school, back when we were the power couple on campus." He paused to gauge her reaction to the trip down memory lane.

*Nada.*

He jumped to the lone agenda item. "Have you made any progress on ending my supervised release? I need my law license back now."

She sighed loudly. "Be patient."

"Not my strong suit."

"You should've worked on that in prison."

Eerie how much she sounded like Sandy Robinson of the Probation Office. "I was preoccupied with staying alive." A recurring image of Martin Biddle hanging in the prison chapel returned to haunt him. "Not everyone managed to do that," he said more to himself than her.

"Then you really ought to tread carefully, because you're one misstep from a second dose of Seagoville."

His spine stiffened. "What do you mean?"

"We know you're looking for Taylor Donovan. So are we."

"We should look together," he said.

"That worked out so well for Maggie Burns, didn't it?" She grabbed a handful of popcorn. "If you get in our way, here's how it will go down. We arrest you for obstruction and put you on the next transport to Seagoville. Then you can kiss your license goodbye forever."

"That'd be a bullshit charge."

"Any doubt in your mind that it'd stick in Tapia's court?" Her tone made clear there was none in hers.

The plot on screen took a twist. The Russian cop who had been helping the hero suddenly turned on him. Flashes of gunfire illuminated an army of shadowy shapes, firing and falling in the night. Tough to tell the good guys from the bad until Neeson emerged from the smoke and slaughter.

"So instead of bearing good news," he said, "you came to deliver a threat."

"I'm here to tell you to back off," she said.

"Even if I do, Moore will never lift a finger to help me. Sure, I'm scared shitless of prison, but the thought of permanent exile from the courtroom scares me more."

She placed a hand on his arm. "Tom won't be U.S. Attorney forever."

"What are you saying?"

She looked around. Except for a sleeper on the back row, they had the room to themselves. "He's resigning to run for governor."

Cash did a double take. Good news for him. Bad news for the state. "And you're telling me this because...."

"You want your license back," she said, "and Tom won't be a roadblock much longer."

"When is he stepping down?"

"In a couple of weeks, a month at most. The timing's not nailed down. Big indictment in the works, and he wants to wring more headlines before bowing out." She patted his arm. "Can you keep your head low and mouth shut for a month?"

Good question. Not one he could honestly answer, so he asked his own. "Who's taking over?"

His question hung in the air. Her silence provided the answer.

"You're shitting me." He bit his tongue to keep from blurting out something he'd regret. Stewed in a fresh round of second-guessing his decision to bail from the U.S. Attorney's office and leave the business of justice to the likes of Moore. And Jenna.

He should've seen this coming. The way things had shaken out, she was the logical successor. Being the First Assistant to the Big Cheese gave her the inside track. Plus, her father had the juice to strong-arm both senators. The clincher, her upcoming marriage to Tom would keep the plum job in the family.

"Is it really so hard for you to picture me in the corner office?" Her voice, equal parts anger and hurt.

"The good news is that you're guaranteed to outshine your predecessor. Nice to have the bar set so low for you."

"Jealousy doesn't become you. Way past time to bury your beef with Tom."

"Show me a good loser," he said, "and I'll show you a loser."

She scooped a second helping of popcorn. "You'll get your chance to defend scumbags again. I have it on good authority that the next U.S. Attorney will prove more receptive to cutting you a break."

A monster explosion on screen interrupted them. A yacht burst into a fireball, seconds after the hero and his granddaughter had jumped overboard. Good guys in the drink. Bad guys baked to a crisp.

While Neeson made his escape, so did Jenna.

When Cash left the theatre, the Lincoln was gone. Game over. He had never felt more alone.

* * *

Maggie Burns refused to buzz Cash into her apartment building. On his first ring, she told him to fuck off. On his second attempt, she threatened to break his fingers, one by one, if he didn't leave immediately. The third time, she didn't answer the intercom.

Fortunately, the complex catered to a security-challenged clientele, most of whom defaulted to 1-2-3-4 as their code of choice, allowing Cash to crack it on his first try.

One hurdle down, one to go. He pounded on the door to Apartment 317.

"Go away," Maggie shouted through the door.

He hammered harder.

"Fair warning," she shouted. "I've drawn my gun, and I start firing in ten seconds."

Ninety-nine percent sure she was bluffing, Cash still sidled away from the door. "Give me five minutes, then I'm gone for good."

"Promise? Oh hell, what am I saying? Like the word of a defense lawyer means anything."

The door creaked open, and Cash rushed inside before she could change her mind. The odor from the kitchen almost drove him back to the hall.

"Garlic works for driving away vampires," he said, "not lawyers."

"As if there were a difference." A silk robe fell north of her knees. "You shouldn't have come."

"Had to check up on my new best friend." Better than admitting he had nowhere else to go.

"I'm not your friend, and you *really* shouldn't be here." More sadness than anger in her voice.

"We ought to console each other tonight. You've been benched by the Bureau on a bullshit charge, and I just got threatened with one." He took a step toward her. "It's that whole enemy-of-my-enemy thing."

"Are you armed?" she said.

He did a double take. "Where'd that come from?"

She repeated the question, louder this time.

"I'm a felon, remember? I can't carry."

"For the third and final time, are...you...armed?"

Her steely expression snapped him to the piss-your-pants reality that his life depended on answering quickly and correctly. Her eyes begged for forgiveness for what she was about to do.

He whispered, "No."

She opened a drawer and pulled out a Glock. Aimed it at his chest. "Lie on the floor. Face down. Arms behind your back. Wrists together. Don't move and don't say a word."

He made it to one knee before all hell broke loose.

# CHAPTER THIRTY-EIGHT

A syringe lay on the table, its two-inch needle aimed at Cash. A crystalline tear dangled from the tip. Same size as the sweat beads that dotted his forehead.

Marty Shafer twirled the syringe in a deadly game of spin the needle. It came to rest with the business end pointing at Cash.

Cash resisted the temptation to sweep the syringe to the floor and the even stronger compulsion to speak. Neither would be a smart move. Not on Shafer's turf. Interrogation room number one, at the busy intersection of Snitch Street and Liar's Lane.

Cash was hardly a stranger here, but in his past life as a prosecutor, he'd been on Shafer's side of the table. The ten-by-twelve-foot hotbox had all the personality of an empty storage unit. No windows. Nothing on the gray walls.

Shafer nudged the needle closer to Cash. "Know what this is?"

"I'm sure you're about to tell me." *Damn.* Vow of silence already broken. Better call in Goldberg before it's too late.

"It's your one-way ticket to hell." Shafer's threat hung in the dead air. "Moore and I don't see eye-to-eye on much, but we agree on seeking the death penalty for you. So now we're down to fighting over who gets the privilege of sticking you with the needle."

Breath leaked from Cash's lungs. Shafer's threat could mean only one thing. Taylor Donovan's body had turned up.

One more corpse on his conscience. Another lost lamb he'd failed to save. Joining a long line of ghosts haunting him. Starting with his mother, running through Martin Biddle, and ending with Taylor.

He should've been braced for the news. No surprise that Benanti had beaten him to the girl. Nor that Cash would be marked for the fall. The real mystery was why the feds saw him as a suspect, given his lack of motive to kill Taylor.

Cash let his last thought fly. "What's my motive?"

Shafer cracked a smile so galling that Gandhi would've slapped it off. "Come on, McCahill, you know we don't have to prove motive for a conviction."

"I've tried two hundred cases, and every juror in every trial has wanted to hear a motive. They'll sure as hell demand a rock solid one before sending someone to his death."

"You should focus on your motive to confess." Shafer slid a single page across the table. A waiver of rights form. Fine print that forfeited the right to counsel and every other fig leaf of protection under the Constitution.

Cash called it the fuck-me form, and he could recite the boilerplate in his sleep. He pushed the sheet back. Not eager to sign his own death warrant.

"Cop to the murder," Shafer said, "and we won't seek the death penalty. But the deal comes off the table in two minutes."

In ordinary circumstances a shot at dodging the needle would've given Cash pause, but Big Black lurked in the background. A return to prison meant certain death. Behind bars,

Cash might run and hide for a day or two, a week at most. But then he'd face an execution far more brutal than anything the feds could dish out.

The image of Martin Biddle at the end of a rope returned. Cash shuddered it away.

"I want to talk to my lawyer, Gary Goldberg."

Shafer leaned back. "You just made the biggest mistake of your life."

"Don't underestimate me. My life's a mashup of monster mistakes. This one won't even make the weekly top ten list." Cash's bravado failed to calm his racing heart. "And I'm still waiting to hear my motive to kill Taylor."

Shafer rocketed forward. "Taylor! Taylor Donovan? Who the hell said anything about her? We're charging you with killing Larry Benanti."

Cash recoiled. "What? Benanti's dead?"

"As if you didn't know."

Cash blurted out the first thing that popped into his head and the last thing he should've said. "Whoever did it deserves a medal, not the needle."

"Glad I got that on tape," Shafer said. "It'll play well at your murder trial." The tape kept running. "Even if you won't cop to killing Benanti, sounds like you're ready to come clean about killing Taylor."

Cash tensed. Took a minute to unclench his throat. "Have you found her body?"

"Not yet," Shafer said, "but when we do, proving your motive will be a piece of cake."

Cash locked onto Shafer's eyes, searching for a sign he was bluffing. Instead, he picked up a vibe that the agent had said too much.

* * *

Cash's interrogation migrated from the holding cell to the large conference room at the U.S. Attorney's office. Divided evenly between prosecutors and agents, the feds crowded along one side of a long wooden table, with Moore and Jenna Powell seated in the middle. The royal couple in charge. Pecking order in place.

Maggie Burns slouched at the end of the table, trying with mixed success to dodge eye contact with everyone. Collaring Cash must've returned her to the fold.

Goldberg broke the uneasy silence. "Whatever damn fool thing my client might've said before I got here will be tossed out by the judge."

"That's not the law," Moore said.

"Well, anything Cash said after asking for me gets quashed."

Cash smiled. Leave it to the old fart to nail the law on his second try. That is, if the judge decided to apply the law.

Big if.

"We simply made your client a reasonable offer," Moore said. "Confess to killing Benanti, and he gets life instead of death."

Cash fidgeted, drawing a kick to the shin from Goldberg. A reminder not to react to the offer. Not that he would've jumped at it anyway. In the federal system, life imprisonment meant just that. No parole. No time off for good behavior. No early release.

He'd leave prison in a wooden box. And with Big Black on ice, that'd be sooner rather than later.

"Here's my counter-offer," Goldberg said. "Release my client and do your damn job by finding the real killer. Shouldn't be more than ten thousand suspects to start with."

"A lot of suspects," Shafer said, "but none as sloppy as your boy. Our case couldn't be stronger if McCahill had signed a confession in Benanti's blood."

Moore cleared his throat, reminding his minions that the floor belonged to him. "About Benanti's blood, traces of it were found in Taylor Donovan's apartment, mixed with your client's. Plus, both men left a mess of prints there."

Goldberg rocked back in his chair. "So what? So both happened to be in Taylor's apartment, at the same time or not. Good bet that the Macy's Day Parade passed through that fuck pad, along with rivers of blood, sweat, and tears."

"I get the sweat and tears part," Moore said, "but blood?"

With no quick comeback, Goldberg did what he did best. Dodge a question by tossing out another. "What about motive? Why would Cash kill the golden goose? He'd made millions off Benanti and stood to make millions more. Only a matter of time before Benanti would've been indicted again."

The U.S. Attorney's shit-eating smile went from being merely annoying to full-blown infuriating. "You're seriously asking why someone would kill the person whose testimony helped send him to prison? How many days did Cash spend at Seagoville? Seven hundred, more or less. That's seven hundred reasons for him to kill Benanti, more or less."

"What I don't understand is why a murder investigation is being handled by the feds and not the local D.A." Goldberg sounded genuinely stumped. "Especially when the victim's a dirtbag like Benanti."

Moore and Shafer exchanged looks, one frown feeding off the other. Neither rushed to respond.

Moore broke the stalemate. "We're not at liberty to discuss that."

Cash leaned forward, hitting on the answer but trusting his lawyer to reach the same conclusion.

"Holy shit! Benanti was a snitch," Goldberg said. "Well, I'll be damned. You finally turned the bastard. Now the question becomes who he was rolling over on."

"Even if that were the case," Moore said, "it doesn't concern you or your client."

"Sure, it does." Goldberg's turn to flash a fuck-you smile. "You've just given the jury someone with a real motive to kill Benanti." He turned to Cash. "Let's go, son. They don't have the goods to book you today. That's why they're desperate for a confession."

Goldberg rose. Cash didn't. "I need to speak with Agent Burns, alone."

"Not a good idea," Goldberg said.

Moore looked crushed. "For once, I agree with your counsel."

"Five minutes is all I need." Cash's tone made clear he wasn't asking permission.

Maggie turned to Moore. "It'll be okay."

After the U.S. Attorney led his entourage out, Goldberg said to Cash, "For once in your train wreck of a life, think with the right head. She's a fed first and foremost. Never forget that. Five minutes, then you two are done."

Cash burned the first minute staring at Maggie, praying she'd crack first. She didn't. "Kept my promise to get your job back." He forced a smile. "All it took was for you to bring me in, dead or alive."

"It wasn't like that." Her voice, barely a whisper.

"Sure felt like it, what with my wrists cuffed behind my back and your knee grinding into my spine."

"There was an APB out on you. Had every trigger-happy cop and agent in the city combing the streets for a killer lawyer on the loose."

"But why did you have to be the one to take me down?"

"Don't try to flip this on me." A flash of anger amped her voice. "I didn't ask you to come to my apartment, and I begged you to go away. But you had to treat me like one of your booty calls."

"It wasn't like that." Cash sounded defensive.

"Sure felt like it." The anger had drained from her voice, replaced by a world of hurt. "Why did you have to come to my apartment?"

Cash paused. Not because he couldn't come up with a good reason but because too many jammed his mind. He finally settled on the safest one. "I felt guilty about your suspension and needed to make sure you were okay." Time to regain the upper hand. "Feeling a little less guilty now."

"I'd advise you to steer clear of the word guilty," she said, "while you're in this room."

Good point. "By the way, I'm not guilty. Not of killing Benanti anyway. Didn't know he was dead until Shafer told me."

"You shouldn't be discussing this with me."

"But I need you to know that—"

A banging on the door interrupted Cash. He had more to say.

"Your five minutes is up," Goldberg shouted through the door. "Make yourselves decent." He barged in.

On her way out, Maggie slipped a note to Cash. She had more to say as well.

# CHAPTER THIRTY-NINE

A flood of bad memories froze Cash in the lobby of the Ritz. First time to set foot there since his arrest three years ago.

He took in the action at the bar. Make that, the inaction. It was dead tonight. Of the four lookers on display, Cash knew three.

Karla and Kristi, high-end hookers and former clients, were working in tandem. Their fee structure rivaled Cash's back in the day. Whenever they got busted, they invariably tendered their special skills as payment for his.

Professional courtesy.

Time after time he'd passed on their offers, for reasons never explained to them. Everyone has a line not to cross, and Cash had two. Don't sleep with prostitutes, and above all, never represent pimps.

The third familiar face at the bar, FBI agent Maggie Burns, had arrested him twice. Tonight, she was fending off a bald businessman, who was about four inches shorter and a hundred pounds heavier than she.

Hard to blame Baldy for pegging Maggie as a pro. A hooker could work a high-end hotel only if she didn't come off as one, and Maggie looked like anything but. She could've been a business exec, banker, corporate lawyer, trophy wife—any or all of the above.

As Cash approached, Maggie whipped out her FBI badge and dropped it on the bar. A miracle the shock didn't send Baldy into cardiac arrest. He backtracked faster than a politician from his promises.

Cash took Baldy's place on the barstool. "There's a nicer way to say you're not open for business."

She snickered. "Like I'm supposed to feel sorry for a lying, cheating scumbag of a spouse. Screw that shit. My way might scare him straight."

"For a half-hour or so." Cash ordered a scotch and soda and turned to her. "What'll you have?"

"A seven and seven."

"What's that?"

"Diet 7-Up with a dash of real 7-Up." She patted her left side, where a shoulder holster hugged her ribs. "Can't drink when carrying."

"Imagine Baldy's surprise if he'd gotten your jacket off."

"He was never going to get that far," she said.

"What about me? How far will I get tonight?"

Her fleeting smile sent mixed signals. "A little farther than Baldy. Not as far as you'd like."

He took out the note she'd slipped to him earlier that day and laid it on the bar. "You gave me the place and time but forgot to put down our room number."

"You're more delusional than the loser I just chased off."

"A guy's gotta dream." He sipped the scotch. "If we're not checking in, what are we doing here? My last visit ended rather badly, with me in handcuffs, dragged before the cameras like *El Chapo*. Has kind of put me off this place."

Her expression got darker. "About the last time...."

She slid off the barstool, drink in hand, and led Cash to the lobby. She stopped midway between the bar and the reception desk and turned to him. "There's something you need to know about that night."

"If you're trying to seduce me, bringing up the worst night of my life isn't helping."

"Worst night of my life too." She looked away. "I was the one who searched Yvonne Strauss before she made contact with you."

The drink soured in his mouth. "Are you trying to tell me you didn't really search her?"

"On the contrary, I searched every inch of her. Full cavity. Shoes. Purse. Hair. Patted down every item of clothing. She couldn't have smuggled a breath mint in here."

"Then what's the problem?"

"When we got here, she had a panic attack. First time undercover. Nothing unusual about freaking out. Said she needed to go to the bathroom to calm her nerves."

"Did you go into the bathroom with her?"

She shook her head. "I had an issue with the recording equipment. I had to...." Her voice trailed off.

"After she left the bathroom, did you search her again?"

No response. Cash had his answer.

The revelation gut-punched him. He backed away from her and landed in a chair at the outer orbit of the bar.

For three years the mystery of how ten thousand dollars had materialized in Juror Number Ten's purse had dogged him. Tying up the loose end should've brought peace.

It didn't.

The waitress beat Maggie to Cash's table. He ordered two scotch and sodas. Stayed silent until the drinks came, then pushed one toward Maggie. "It won't be the first rule you've broken."

"I don't drink scotch."

"It's never too late to pick up a bad habit."

The first sip sent her into spasms of coughing and brought tears to her eyes.

"Your 302." His voice dropped to a whisper. "It didn't say anything about the bathroom break."

"My first draft did. It got edited out."

"By whom?"

"Doesn't matter," she said. "I was the one who let it happen. The one who signed off on the altered 302."

"It was Moore, wasn't it? The chickenshit was so afraid of losing that he crossed the line."

"I was working up my courage to tell you the whole truth when you signed the plea papers." Their eyes met briefly, before hers darted away. "Everyone had been certain you'd never plead. Said you were guilty but would never cop to it. I figured that if you pled guilty because you were guilty, then no harm, no foul from my screw up."

"You mean," he said, "from your cover-up."

"You were good for it, weren't you?"

He shook his head. "Tell me it was Moore."

She shook hers.

"Why tell me this now?" he said.

"I've been trying to tell you for three years."

"I spent two of those years in a federal pen about fifteen miles from here. Wouldn't have been hard to find me if you'd been looking."

"It wasn't a matter of finding you," she said, "but of finding the courage to kiss my job goodbye."

"What changed? You or the job?"

"Both." She slid a hand atop his. "I think you've changed too."

He pulled his hand away. "Right. I'm not as trusting as I used to be."

# CHAPTER FORTY

ash tapped the spotter's shoulder and took his place by the bench, looming over Tom Moore. Eucalyptus-scented towels made the Equinox Fitness Club smell more like a florist shop than a gym. More pickup lines than pushups in process. Too frou-frou for Cash's taste.

Seven reps into his third set of bench presses, Moore was struggling. Eyes bulging. Arms wobbling. Joints popping. A two-hundred-pound barbell hovered inches above his chest.

"Spot," he hissed through clenched teeth.

Cash looked around the room. A dozen potential witnesses were pining over their reflections in the floor-to-ceiling mirrors. He could probably get away with pressing down on the bar and putting a permanent dent in Moore's chest.

Cash shelved his revenge fantasies, for now. He needed answers first, so he lifted the bar and eased it onto a rack.

Moore's arms dropped like rags, his knuckles brushing the floor. Too spent to move. Color crept back into his face, and his breathing came under control.

"You trying to kill me?" Moore wheezed between words.

"The way I see it, I just saved your sorry ass." Cash kept one hand on the racked barbell. "And now I'm going to spare you the disgrace you so richly deserve. Tomorrow you'll resign as U.S. Attorney and announce that you will *not* run for governor."

"Why would I do that?"

"To avoid being fired and disbarred, along with all the bad press that would entail." Cash heaved the barbell from the rack and held it over the prosecutor's head.

Moore's hands flew to the bar. "Hey, what do you think you're doing?"

"Got it?" Cash didn't wait for an answer before letting go.

Within seconds, Moore's arms began to shake. A tremor turned into trembling. He mouthed the word *help*.

Cash leaned over, making his smile the last thing Moore would see. "I know what happened the night of my arrest. The juror went into the bathroom, unescorted and out of sight."

Moore's arms bowed to right angles, and the bar brushed his collapsing chest. He panted like a dog in heat and flipped his head from side to side. Eyes searching for a savior. Lips contorted by fear. Pleas caught in his throat.

"I also know about the original 302," Cash said, "and how you deleted the part about the bathroom detour."

Moore's nostrils flared. Staccato breaths sprayed saliva.

"Resign or I go public with the bombshell. Give you a taste of how it feels to be a pariah."

"Mistake." The word, more mouthed than whispered, spent the last smidgen of Moore's strength.

The bar touched down, biting into his chest. Not deep. Not long. But deep and long enough to leave a lasting impression.

Cash curled the barbell an inch or so. High enough for Moore to gasp for air but not slither free.

"I can hold this maybe a minute." Cash loosened his grip on the bar. "So you've got a short window to convince me I've made a mistake."

"Not...here," Moore wheezed.

"You're stalling." Cash lowered the bar until it touched torso.

Moore squirmed like a bug on a pin, his head jerking toward the locker room. Wet eyes begging for mercy.

Cash did a full curl. Two minutes later he and Moore were alone in the steam room, wearing only the towels around their waists.

"Am I sweating my balls off to keep our conversation private," Cash said, "or to make sure I'm not wearing a wire?"

"Both."

"I'm still waiting to hear why I shouldn't force you to resign and drop your shot at higher office."

"I can give you three reasons." Moore ladled water over glowing coils. Steam billowed into a wall between them. "For starters, have you thought through how it'll look if you prove your innocence to the charge of bribing the juror?"

"Yeah, it'll look like you sent an innocent man to prison."

"With an assist from Benanti, who came forward and agreed to testify against you, if the case went to trial. In return, he got credit for your guilty plea and a pass on the tax charge. Clear yourself of bribery, and you create a helluva motive on your part to kill him. Digging up the past puts you on the fast track to death row."

Moore watered the hissing coils. The men retreated to their corners, like sweat-shiny boxers between rounds.

"I can fade that heat," Cash said.

"What about Maggie Burns? Can she fade it too? The Bureau will know she leaked the original 302. How do you think the SAC will react?"

"Unlike you, she deserves credit for coming clean."

A laugh broke through the fog. "Right, because the Bureau has such a rich tradition of rewarding whistleblowers who embarrass the agency. Her reward will be a one-way ticket to the Bismarck office."

"Maggie made the only choice she can live with."

Moore stood and rewrapped the towel around his waist. "She won't be the only one to suffer if you go forward with this."

"If you're talking about Eva—"

Moore cut him off. "I'm not talking about her. Not yet anyway. If I go down, it won't be alone. In fact, there's a good chance I don't take a hit at all. Computer records will show that Maggie sent her original 302 not to me but to Jenna, and there's no forensic evidence that either shared the draft with me. That's called plausible deniability."

"And who says chivalry is dead?"

"You drop the bombshell," Moore said, "and the bodies start piling up. Maggie and Jenna for sure, and we both know Eva's vulnerability. Oh, and one last thing to consider, if you're foolish enough to toss Jenna in the grease. Her father owns the state bar, and he'll make damn sure you never get your precious license back."

When the wall of steam parted, Moore was gone.

# CHAPTER FORTY-ONE

"**W**hat's your problem?" Eva's voice shot to glass-shattering shrill.

Cash shrugged. "No problems on my end." *Other than a secretary who's about to lose her shit.*

He leaned back in Goldberg's chair and rested his loafers on the desk. A half-century of cigar smoke fogged the old fart's office. "I simply decided not to file a *Brady* motion."

"You mean not to file one today," she said.

"Not ever."

She sprang to her feet. "Why the hell not?"

"You can count on the fingers of one hand the *Brady* motions that've paid off. The government will never agree to grant me a new trial, and Tapia's the last judge on the planet who'd spot me a do-over."

"You don't know that until you try," she said. "Besides, win or lose, the motion kills Moore's bid for office. That's reason enough to file it."

"My motion, my decision."

"You bitch and moan about not having a license. Yet when it's practically in your grasp, you run away from it." Her voice softened, more pain than anger seeping through. "Have you lost your fire to try cases?"

"You know better than that. The courtroom's my entire world. Everywhere else, I'm just passing through."

"Then it's Maggie, isn't it?" She made the name sound like a dirty word. "You're protecting her."

An excellent time to exercise his right to remain silent. Eva had a nose for half-truths, and the whole truth wasn't an option.

"Fuck that bitch," Eva said.

*Been there, done that.*

"She hid the ball from us." Her voice revved to rant pitch. "Even worse, kept her mouth shut while you were locked up. She should be behind bars."

Goldberg limped into the office and slammed the door behind him. Shot Cash a cross look. "What did I tell you about sitting at my desk?"

Cash rocketed to his feet. "Just keeping it warm for you, old man."

"Will you two children dial it down?" Goldberg shook his head. "I could hear you out in the hallway." He heaved the leather briefcase toward the couch. It fell short. Judging from its wear and tear, not for the first time.

"We have two potential clients cooling their heels at reception," Goldberg said. "Given our financial straits, we can't afford to scare them off. So for the next hour or so, can we at least act like we're on the same team?"

Eva pointed at Cash. "But this *tontito* refuses to—"

Goldberg cut her off. "Maybe I didn't make myself clear. We have potential *paying* clients outside. Eva, greet our guests and find out which one has the deeper pockets. That's who we'll meet with first."

\* \* \*

Ten minutes later Eva returned with a rundown. "We have a veteran cop who wants to meet with the team," she said, "and a grieving widow who asked to see Cash. It's a toss-up as to who goes first."

"Unless we're talking crooked cop," Cash said, "he'll be a low-pay, slow-pay client."

Eva eased into her chair. "He's more stupid than crooked."

"Hardly narrows the field," Cash said.

"How good-looking is the widow?" Goldy said.

"On a scale of one to ten," Eva said, "a twelve."

Goldy slapped the desk, ready to make his ruling. "Eva, babysit Cash while he meets with the widow, and keep him from making a damn fool of himself. The dumb cop can cool his heels."

\* \* \*

Pale and petite, Bettina Biddle locked a deceptively strong grip on Cash's hand. The faintest traces of crow's feet fanned from the corners of her gray eyes.

Cash chalked up the crow's feet to the loss of a husband, first to prison and then to the noose, to the day-to-day grind of single motherhood, and to the question that would haunt her for the rest of her days: *Could I have done something to prevent the suicide?*

The same question dogged Cash. He broke her hold on him, the physical one anyway, and retreated behind the desk. He introduced Eva as his paralegal. As if a paralegal had his own paralegal.

Bettina sat. "You left Marty's funeral before I had a chance to thank you for coming."

Busted. "I didn't want to bother you."

"I also wanted to thank you for being Marty's friend in prison. His only friend there." Bettina's Deep South roots softened her voice. "He looked up to you and believed that your brief would set him free."

Cash winced. "I wish I had filed it sooner."

"The brief is why I'm here." She looked out the window. "I visited Marty the day before his death, and he was so upbeat about his chances on appeal, especially with you as his lawyer."

Cash thought of reminding her that he didn't have a law license, then or now. To the outside world, it was Goldy's brief. He decided not to bring it up.

"Marty didn't commit suicide," she said. "He wouldn't do that to the girls...or me. He was murdered, and I want to hire you to prove it."

Cash rocked back in his chair. "Missus Biddle, this is a matter for the authorities to handle. You should take your suspicions to the—"

Bettina cut him off. "The Justice Department ruled Marty's death a suicide and closed the investigation. You have to get it reopened."

"This isn't what I do." He couldn't look her in the eye. "I'm sorry, but I can't help you."

"Can't or won't?" Bettina said.

"Either way, same result." Cash braced for waterworks from the widow. None came. She was tougher than she looked. That or she was cried out.

He opened a desk drawer and pulled out the photo Biddle had kept in his cell, the one of Bettina and the twins. "Marty slept with this every night under his pillow. He'd want you to have it." He held out the photo to her.

"You keep it," Bettina said, "to remind you that two girls will grow up thinking their father killed himself."

Low blow. And not the last one to be landed. No sooner had Bettina left the office than Eva turned on Cash. "Get her back in here. Tell her we've reconsidered and will take the case."

"She doesn't have a case," Cash said.

Eva raised her voice above his. "Then tell her we'll look into her husband's death."

Cash matched her decibel level. "I had a front row seat for what Biddle went through behind bars. I understand why he did what he did."

"Then get off your butt and do something about it," she said. "I vote we take her on as a client."

"Being a sucker for lost causes, you always vote that way. But the debate's over. Bring in the cop, and let's hope he was crooked enough to afford us."

"I'll get the cop," she said, "but you're crazy if you think the debate's over."

* * *

Cash had expected Bettina Biddle to rain tears at his rejection. She never did.

The cop more than made up for it, breaking down at the threshold of Goldberg's office. He blubbered about the prospect of losing his stripes, his job, his marriage, even his freedom.

It took Cash less than five minutes to confirm Eva's diagnosis that Sergeant Melvin J. Jacobs suffered from stage four stupidity. A miracle he could remember to breathe.

The *J* stood for Jackoff. While James appeared on his birth certificate, he'd always be Jackoff to the force. The brothers in blue had saddled him with the nickname, and it had stuck throughout a twenty-two-year slog of a career.

As a rookie he'd been sent to bust a porn theatre on Harry Hines Boulevard, where Dallas' perviest pervs huddled for a midnight circle jerk. When backups arrived, they found Melvin on the back row, pants down, knob polished.

Hence, the handle and the birth of the legend of Jackoff Jacobs.

Three times over his rollercoaster career, he'd reached the not-so-lofty rank of sergeant by dint of seniority, not by sweat and certainly not by savvy. Twice he'd been busted back to patrol for bullshit infractions.

"A third strike," Jackoff whined, "and I'm out of a job and a marriage."

Hard for Cash to stomach the sobbing six-footer. Eva handed the cop a tissue and patted his back. She had a soft spot for children, animals, and idiots, and Jackoff hit the trifecta.

Eva automatically fell into the give-a-sucker-a-break column. One more vote, and Jackoff would make the client roll.

A short and shrinking list.

Goldberg cleared his throat. "Sounds like you need an employment lawyer, not a criminal attorney like me."

More waterworks from the cop. "This time the brass is playing hardball. If I don't resign by Monday and forfeit my pension, they'll go to the grand jury and get me indicted."

"For what?" Cash said. "I still haven't heard what you did wrong. If they plan to charge every fuckup on the force, we'll be down to six cops patrolling the city."

"They claim I filed a false official report about surveilling a drug house."

"Did you?" Cash never expected to hear the truth from a client, not in the first interview anyway. Still, they might as well get an early start at exposing the accused's inevitable lies, excuses, and evasions.

"You have to shoot straight with us," Goldberg said. "Even though we haven't agreed to take your case, anything you say today falls under the attorney-client privilege. Understand?"

Jackoff nodded.

"Are you good for it?" Cash said.

The cop kept nodding.

Cash leaned forward in his seat. It was almost unprecedented for someone to come clean so quickly. The rare burst of honesty earned his vote.

"How could the brass know you weren't where your report said you were?" Cash said.

"That's what really pisses me off." A flash of anger made Jackoff sound more like a fighter than a victim. "There was a goddam tracker in my car that put me a mile from the drug house. But only for an hour...maybe two."

Cash played a hunch. "Did your patrol car happen to be parked outside the nearest bar?"

Another nod.

"There's a tracker in every police car," Goldberg said. "After more than two decades on the force, how could you not know that?"

*Yep, stage four stupidity.*

Jackoff blushed. "It slipped my mind. When something's there all the time, you tune it out."

Cash stood abruptly. "Exactly." Said more to himself than the others. "It's been in front of us the whole time."

He rushed from the office. Life's funny that way. Leave it to a lazy-ass cop who hadn't cleared a case in his career to hit on the key to cracking the biggest one in Cash's life.

# CHAPTER FORTY-TWO

Mickey Dillon, a.k.a. Mick the Quick, drooled at the sight of line after line of luxury cars in the underground garage. Way too much temptation for a car freak like Mick. Benzes, Beamers, Jags, and Porsches practically begged to be boosted, with Taylor Donovan's silver Carrera high on the list.

Cash patted the soft top of her six-figure convertible. "How quickly can you strip her down and find the secret prize hidden inside?"

"Once we get her back to my chop shop," Mick said, "five to six minutes, no sweat."

Cash had other ideas. "Job gets done here."

Hyper by nature, Mick went all twitchy. "I operate only on my turf."

"You need to be more flexible," Cash said. "There's more than one way to skin a cat, or in this case, a car."

"Too risky to do the job here. Too many witnesses."

"The Porsche stays put. We can't afford to give the cops an excuse to bust us for auto theft."

"And you think it'll look less suspicious for me to tear apart a car that cost more than my house?"

Cash shrugged, as if they had nothing to fear from the police.

"If 5-O comes down on me," Mick said, "that's strike three, and I'm fucked for life."

With the career criminal about to bolt, Cash previewed his cover story for the cops, if they showed. "It's called hiding in plain sight. How can anyone suspect us of being up to no good when you're working on a car in the open? On the off chance anyone raises questions, you're doing this at the owner's request, and she's not around to contradict it."

Mick blinked rapid-fire. Hard to tell which beat faster. His eyelids or his heart. "I don't know."

"If I wasn't one hundred percent sure that I could talk our way out of trouble, would I be here with you? Would I risk a return trip to prison and losing my law license forever?"

Cash stopped short of the whole truth. Didn't mention that he'd sent Eva back to the office, kicking and screaming. Just in case.

Mick cracked his knuckles, warming up to do his thing. "You swear that this job clears my debt to Goldberg and that you'll spot me a freebie the next time the cops hassle me."

"I'm a lawyer," Cash said with a straight face, "and you have my word on it."

"I'd like it in writing."

Cash ignored the request and tapped his watch. "Your six minutes start now."

It took Mick less than thirty seconds to jimmy open the driver's door. First break of the day, no alarm. Cash breathed easier. Sure, there could be a silent alarm, but at least nothing to draw an immediate crowd.

Eight minutes later the dashboard lay across the floor, and a jigsaw puzzle of parts filled both bucket-seats. "Bingo." Mick flipped a coin to Cash. "Missed this sucker on the first sweep."

Cash lifted it to eye-level. "This tracking device looks exactly like a quarter."

"That's because it is a quarter," Mick said. "No tracker in there."

"You sure? Check again."

"I stripped this baby down to the frame. A Tic-Tac couldn't get past me."

Cash rubbed his chin. Another brilliant theory shot to hell. "Benanti's such a control freak that I would've bet the family farm he'd plant a tracker in Taylor's car."

"You don't have a family farm," Mick said. "Matter of fact, you don't have a family."

*Ouch.*

"But so we're straight," Mick said, "my debt's gone, and you owe me a freebie, right?"

"Did you get that in writing?" Cash said.

"Fucking crooked mouthpiece!" Mick kicked the front tire of the Porsche and howled in pain while hopping around on the other foot. "I'd trust a rattlesnake before—"

Cash cut him off. "Chill. I was pricking with you. Put the car back together, and let's get out of here. You've got your deal." He shook his head. "Still hard to believe Benanti didn't tag her car."

Mick gingerly put weight on his kicking foot and winced. "Like you said, there's more than one way to skin a cat. More than one way to bell one too."

# CHAPTER FORTY-THREE

"Congratulations," Cash said to Goldberg, "on being the proud owner of the second ugliest mutt I've had the misfortune of laying eyes on."

The one-eyed dog dragged the old man down the Katy Trail, lunging and yapping at every living creature in its path. The leash slacked and tightened on the start-and-stop, zig-zaggy course. The pet, like the owner, limped badly.

"Better not let Eva hear you diss my new best friend," Goldberg said. "She rescued him from the pound last month."

"Figures, since she has the butt-ugliest dog I've ever seen."

Goldberg struggled to keep pace. "Our secretary labors under the delusion that walking a dog will lengthen my life."

"More likely to land you in an early grave." Cash took the leash and jerked the dog to a stop. "What's his name?"

"Beavis, after my favorite character."

"Should've named him Butt-Head, after mine."

Cash scrolled through pics on his iPhone, freezing on a frame of Mick the Quick, surrounded by Porsche parts in an underground garage. "Recognize this pillar of the community?"

"Sure. Mickey Dillon. That thief owes me money."

Cash pocketed the phone. "Not anymore. He performed a service for the cause of justice that cleared his debt."

"Wonderful," Goldberg said with sarcasm to spare. "It's not like we need the money."

"You were never going to collect from that deadbeat anyway."

Goldberg silently conceded the point.

"I had Mick search Taylor's Porsche for a tracking device, but he came up empty."

"Either Mick's slipping," Goldberg said, "or the dearly departed Benanti wasn't the control freak you imagined him to be."

"There's a third alternative. Benanti might've been an even bigger control freak than I thought." Cash stooped to pet Beavis but pulled back when the dog growled. "I ever tell you about my first case for him?"

"Was that before or after you sold your soul to the devil?" Goldberg said.

"Don't look down your nose at me, old man, not with your rogues' gallery of clients. When I met Benanti fifteen years ago, he was still on wife number two and had a different business model. He started out in the loan-for-car-title racket, making payday loans to sad sacks who couldn't hack bank financing. He charged exorbitant interest rates and pocketed the pink slips as collateral."

"Sounds legit," Goldberg said, "more or less."

"Semi-legit but a dicey way to make a buck. The borrowers kept falling behind on their payments and taking off with the wheels. That meant no money coming in and no clue where the collateral was. Often it cost more to track down the deadbeats than remained outstanding on the loans. Even when Benanti's bloodhounds managed to find a borrower, the car could be six states away."

"Is your point that Benanti wasn't an evil genius," Goldberg said, "but a shitty businessman?"

"Not at all. He became the first to make the business profitable, by installing GPS trackers in the cars and making the borrowers pay for the privilege of being surveilled twenty-four seven. All of a sudden, seizing the collateral post-default became quick, cheap, and easy."

"Still sounds legit," Goldberg said.

"The loan-for-title operation evolved into the used car business, which again started out okay. He had a fleet of repossessed cars to sell for a small profit, but the real money rolled in when he began moving stolen cars for Mexican cartels."

"So that's where he crossed the line," Goldberg said.

Cash nodded. "And not for the last time. About ten years ago, he dumped wife number two for Mariposa, whose real name is buried in dead files in Nevada. That's when they graduated from moving stolen cars to human trafficking."

"Whoa!" Goldberg sounded skeptical. "That's a helluva leap."

"Not really. By then the cartels were dealing in drugs, weapons, hot cars, hotter tail, whatever turned a profit. Once he got in bed with the cartels, he became their bitch."

"A well-paid bitch," Goldberg said.

"He made decent money in the loan-for-title business, fuck-you money in stolen cars, and a killing from the flesh trade. He opened the flagship *Metamorphosis* in 2010 in North Dallas, and the chain of clubs spread like the clap across the southwest."

Goldberg frowned. "So Benanti's a greedy bastard who fell in with greedier bastards. What's your excuse for representing him all those years?"

"Once you're on board with Benanti, you don't quit him. He dumps you, but only after he's done with you and usually into an open grave. Plus, he's nowhere near the top of the food chain. When he got into business with bad guys south of the border, he found himself riding a tiger. He couldn't dismount without being eaten."

"My heart bleeds for him," Goldberg said.

"Save your sympathy for me. Once I won my first case for Benanti, years before he got into trafficking drugs and flesh, I found myself riding a tiger atop a bigger tiger."

"That explains something that's bugged me for a long time," Goldberg said, "which is why someone who claims to hate pimps as much as you do would whore himself out to the king of pimps."

Cash tightened his grip on the leash. "I'm trying to find a way out, but not even Benanti's death gets me off the hook. Like I said, he answered to higher powers."

Goldy took back the leash. "Benanti's ties to traffickers present a whole world of suspects with a motive to silence him. Might lead us to his killer and answer a lot of questions."

"While raising fresh ones," Cash said. "For starters, if I read Benanti right, we didn't find a tracker in Taylor's car because he didn't need one there."

"What are you saying?"

"I'll show you." Cash pointed to a black Labrador bounding toward them. "See the show dog?"

"You look at the Lab," Goldberg said, "while I check out the owner."

"Get real, old man. She's young enough to be your granddaughter."

Cash flagged down a brunette in a silver jogging suit. When she stopped, the Lab heeled.

"Beautiful dog," Cash said.

"Thanks." Her perfect smile was short-lived. "And your dog is...interesting."

"I notice you don't have a leash," Cash said.

"No need." She patted the pet. "Bonnie responds to my voice commands."

"But aren't you worried that a prize like her will get lost or snatched?"

"Not while I have this." She pulled out her iPhone. "An app shows me where she is at all times."

"The tracking device," Cash said, "is it on her collar?"

"It's *in* her."

Cash let the *ah-ha* moment sink in for Goldberg before saying to the jogger, "Don't let us hold you up."

Goldberg tendered her a business card. "You jog here often?"

Cash intercepted the card. "Please ignore my father. It's time for me to get him back to the rest home."

The brunette shot them a quizzical look, then trotted away with Bonnie.

"Don't ever cock block me like that again." Goldberg sounded serious.

"Like you had a shot." He handed the card back to Goldberg. "Keep it in your pants. Now what did we learn here?"

"Are you thinking what I'm thinking?" Goldberg said.

Cash nodded.

"But that doesn't make sense." Goldberg stroked his salt-and-pepper stubble. "If Taylor knew Benanti could follow her every move, why would she come to our office?" He stopped stroking. "Unless she just got careless."

"I'm not buying that," Cash said. "She intended for Benanti to know about her visit to us. See you later."

"Where are you going?" Goldberg said.

"To find out what else Taylor has been lying about."

# CHAPTER FORTY-FOUR

The pool sweep glided through cobalt waters like a sting-ray. A tentacle broke the surface, the lash of water flogging Margot Donovan but leaving Cash unscathed.

Sunning on a deck chair, Margot didn't flinch. Water beaded atop the oily sheen of skin, both bronzer and tauter than natural. She gave off the vibe of a nonsmiler. Then again, it'd probably take a crowbar to lift her Botox-bloated lips.

For all Cash knew, she didn't have much to smile about, despite the trappings of wealth. Perhaps because of them.

Chanel sunglasses blocked Cash from reading her eyes. Not that his eyes would've lingered on hers. The flesh on display in a string bikini demanded his full attention.

"I've seen that look before," she said.

"What look?" Acting as if he hadn't been caught staring.

"The expression that says I'm not what you expected to find, which means you've been talking to Taylor."

"Guilty as charged." Cash removed his blazer, sweat-stained a deeper shade of blue, and loosened the red tie. A hot day just got hotter.

Even in a backyard boasting a lap pool, a tennis court, and a dog run, he couldn't shake a sense of claustrophobia. The twenty-foot privacy fence closed in on them. Palm trees loomed, as evenly spaced as prison bars. Bug zappers rained death from the sky.

"You braced for an encounter with the evil stepmom, and now you're having doubts about Taylor's description."

*I'm having doubts about Taylor, period.*

"Well, you're certainly younger than I expected," he said. "Can't be more than ten years older than your stepdaughter."

"Nine to be exact, but who's counting?"

He sat on the edge of her deck chair. "Evidently Taylor is."

"What freaked her out was the gap between her father and me." She took a sip from a perspiring glass. Looked like lemonade, probably spiked. "Don't strain yourself trying to do the math. Steve was thirty-one years older."

He didn't speak his mind. *Old enough to be your father.*

"You don't approve." Her tone threatened to kill the conversation.

"Not my place to pass judgment." His delivery drained a good deal of tension from the exchange. "How long were you and Steve married?"

She sat up in the chair. "Three of the best years of my life. Of his too. Until his heart gave out."

Again, Cash kept his thoughts to himself. *Tough for an old warhorse to keep pace with a young filly.*

"Fair or not," he said, "Taylor blames you for putting her father in an early grave."

"Of course she does. Me, I think the stress of a dysfunctional family did him in." She took another sip. "Despite what you've heard, I didn't marry Steve for his money. I loved him from day one, and not an hour goes by that I don't miss him."

"Like the saying goes, one door closes, another opens. A beautiful woman living in a ten-million-dollar mansion.

Can't imagine you'll be lonely long." It came out harsher than intended.

"Even a mansion," she said, "can serve as a prison."

Cash laughed. "Lady, I've seen prison from the inside. Mine didn't have a chandelier the size of an Escalade. Or a TV in every room. Plus a theater that seats thirty, a private gym, and a wine cellar that puts Fearing's to shame."

"What sharp eyes you have. You picked up all that while walking from the front door to here?"

"I might've wandered a few feet from the foyer, after your butler left to see if you'd receive me."

"Miles isn't my butler. More like my guard. Taylor hired him to be her eyes and ears."

"Simple fix. Fire Miles and hire your own man."

Her turn to laugh. "That's not how it works. I live in this house on a monthly stipend, only as long as I remain unmarried and faithful to a ghost. The bulk of Steve's estate went to Taylor and her brother, as will the house when I fuck, marry, or die, whichever comes first."

He stockpiled more whoppers to add to the growing list of Taylor's lies. Like the claim of sudden poverty following her father's death. Bullshit. Or the description of a gold-digging stepmom with tight control of the purse strings. More B.S.

"What about the brother?" Cash said. "What's he like?"

"Oh, Ricky's okay when left alone. Problem is, Taylor won't let him be. She's pushing him into law school, grooming him for something way over his head."

"What does she have in mind for him?" Cash said.

"Don't know. Doubt Ricky does either."

Cash had an idea, one that cast Ricky in a new light. Putting him on a fast and fatal track to becoming a cog in Mariposa's machine.

"Whatever she has planned," Margot said, "it won't end well for the boy."

"How will it end for you? Can't be healthy to stay cooped up here. You're young, attractive. Why not leave this place and see what the world has to offer?"

She stared at him as if he had crash-landed from another planet. "You don't get it. There's no place for me to run. Nowhere to hide."

Cash smiled. "Funny, but Taylor once said the same thing to me."

Margot rolled onto her stomach, exposing a tattoo on her right buttock. A blue butterfly, the size of a silver dollar. Same design, color, and spot as Taylor's ink.

His cell phone chirped. It was Goldberg. He took the call anyway.

"Is Eva with you?" The old man sounded panicky.

"No," Cash said, "I thought she was with you."

"She didn't show for work today, and she's not answering her cell phone. I called her apartment, but Paula said she'd left for the office hours ago."

"I'm on my way, and don't worry." Cash proved no more successful than his boss at draining the fear from his voice. "When she does turn up, I'll wring her little neck."

Cash killed the call. He had a neck to wring, all right, but it wouldn't be Eva's.

# CHAPTER FORTY-FIVE

Nothing draws vultures like a fresh carcass.

TV vans jammed the lots ringing the courthouse, forcing Cash to park on the street and risk a tow. By the time he hauled ass to the third floor of the federal building, an SRO crowd packed the media room and spilled into the hallway.

U.S. Attorney Tom Moore's voice blared from speakers planted throughout the floor. Not a bureaucrat or cockroach could escape the sound of the fat man singing the blues.

Cash knifed through the crowd, catching glimpses of Moore and the drift of his swan song. Alone at the podium, Moore stared into a bouquet of mics. "I come before you with a heavy heart." His tone plumbed new depths of self-pity. "This is the last time I'll address you as *the* United States Attorney for North Texas."

He paused for the masses to grieve. Only the crowd didn't respond. Not a wet eye among the lot. Not even a lone gasp of despair.

Moore soldiered on. "Despite the urging of thousands of Texans, including many of you gathered here, I have decided not to run for governor." His voice broke. "It's time for me to step away from the public stage."

Not that he took his own cue to leave the actual stage. Instead, he gripped the podium like a drowning man clutching driftwood. "I'm stepping down from my post immediately."

Cash silently cheered. The money men in the party must've cut off the spigot. No dough, no go.

The biggest tipoff to Moore's sudden fall from grace, no Jenna Powell at his side or even in the room. Good old Jenna. She stood by her man, win or tie. Ten to one her father had already rounded up a new candidate, for not only the ticket, but also her hand.

Wading toward the podium, Cash bumped into Sandy Robinson, his probation officer. The last person he wanted to see. Her expression said the feeling was mutual.

"You here to slip another knife into our fallen Caesar?" she whispered.

"Just trying to figure out which way the wind's blowing," Cash said. "What's the scoop on Moore's exit?"

Sandy shook her head.

"Who's taking his place as top dog?"

"No one who'll lift a finger to help you."

He goaded her with a we'll-see-about-that smile before elbowing a path through reporters, there to lap up the blood of fresh kill.

Troy Dunbar, the junkyard dog at Channel 8, took the first bite. "Is your resignation and decision not to run for office tied to the botched Benanti investigation?"

Cash caught the early signs of panic at the podium. A flash of color mottled Moore's cheeks. His knuckles whitened.

"I'm not taking questions this afternoon." A chorus of groans greeted Moore's announcement and rattled him into reversing field.

Bad decision.

"There's no truth to any of that," Moore said. "I can't comment on an ongoing investigation beyond saying that the Benanti matter is not over."

"How can it be ongoing," Dunbar said, "when the target is dead?"

"Did the Justice Department open an ethics investigation on you?" Marty Cohen of Channel 4 shouted. "And did you agree to resign in return for the department dropping that investigation?"

The floodgates thrown open, the press piled on, surging forward and shouting over each other. Reporters who had kissed Moore's ass for four years were kicking it now.

Moore had no one to turn to and no way to respond that didn't make things worse. His lips quivered, eyes darted toward the nearest exit—signs he was about to run like a rabbit.

From his years in the office, Cash knew the fastest escape route. Moore would slip through the door behind him. Scamper down a side corridor. Enter his corner office through the back way.

Cash bailed from the press room and sprinted down the corridor, beating his nemesis to the back door.

"Get out of my way." Moore shoved Cash aside.

Cash pushed back.

Moore hit the wall, the startled look on his face giving way to a cold glare. "You struck a fed, asshole. That'll tack two years onto your sentence."

"You just resigned in front of fifty reporters, dumbass. That means I can beat the shit out of you, no consequence. Welcome to the real world."

"Leave me alone." Moore's chest deflated, as far as his bulk allowed. A tear snaked down his cheek. "Some lousy S.O.B. leaked my resignation, and the bastards came loaded for bear."

Cash couldn't muster any sympathy, not that he tried all that hard. After all, the whiner had leaked Cash's guilty plea and scores like it. The leak-like-a-sieve strategy had kept the media off Moore's back, until today.

"Live by the leak," Cash said, "die by the leak." He stiff-armed Moore against the wall. "Tell me where you're holding Eva, or the beatdown of your life begins in five seconds."

"Eva?"

"Don't play dumb." He pressed on Moore's sternum. "You know who she is. Three years ago you threatened to deport her, unless I pled guilty to the bullshit bribery charge."

Cash gave a final shove before easing off. Moore gasped for breath, bracing his palms on his knees, staring at the floor. "No clue...where she is."

Cash didn't believe a word he said, but the pain and fear in his voice, well, they were real. "You used her as a pawn against me once. Why wouldn't I believe you'd do it again?"

Moore managed to stand almost upright. "What good would that do me now? We have a deal. I leave her alone, and you bury the *Brady* issue."

"When we struck that deal, you had a future. Now that you've got nothing to lose, maybe deporting Eva is your revenge on me."

"I'm down," Moore said, "but not out. And I'm not your problem now."

"Then who is?"

Moore looked past Cash and whispered, "Speak of the devil."

STING LIKE A BUTTERFLY

Cash turned to face Jenna Powell, walking toward him and carrying a box of law books. With her blonde hair in a ponytail, dressed in jeans and a T-shirt, she could've passed for an intern.

Cash couldn't resist a bitter smile. "Didn't wait long to move in, did you? Moore's body isn't cold yet."

Her smile killed his. "Let the dead bury the dead." She turned to Moore. "I'll take those keys now."

He silently surrendered them and trudged away.

"That was cold," Cash said, "even for you."

"He disgraced the office."

"From what I hear, he wasn't the only one."

She tightened her hold on the box. "This is a restricted area, and you don't have a pass. For old time's sake, I'll give you a ten-second head start before calling security."

"We have to talk."

"Make an appointment with my secretary."

"You have an opening now." He took the keys from her, unlocked the door, and followed her into the corner office. "I see you've already made yourself at home." Her diplomas hung on the wall. B.A. from Holyoke (*summa cum laude*) and J.D. from SMU (*magna cum laude*).

"This isn't helping get your license back," she said.

"Glad you brought up my license. Being the boss means you've run out of excuses for not coming through for me."

She sat behind the desk and ran her palms across the arm-rests. "It's not that simple. Because of our past relationship, the press would crucify me if my first act in office was to help you."

"Then let Eva go, and you can forget about my license. You won't have to burn any capital on me."

"What makes you think we have her?"

251

Cash couldn't bring himself to say what he was thinking. *Because the alternative is too terrible to face.*

"Do you?"

"No one from my office played any role in her disappearance." She sounded like a lawyer. "I can't say any more."

"You already have."

# CHAPTER FORTY-SIX

I t took Cash two hours and two hundred dollars to spring his car from the pound. The fine hurt. The lost time, more so.

When he circled back to the federal courthouse, it was dark as a tomb. Even drones with no lives, like Shafer, had left the building.

Not that tracking down the agent would prove all that tough. The pariah had only a few safe holes to crawl into.

Cash's first stop, Shafer's shotgun-style house in Garland, a blue-collar suburb of white-collar-worshipping Dallas. The six houses crammed onto the block bore signs of mass assembly by the same starter home builder. A single porch light flickered at Shafer's place, less as a welcome beacon than a feeble attempt to ward off trespassers.

Cash pictured a solitary wretch inside, brooding over the ones who had gotten away. Not only the tax cheats who had lived large and laughed last, but also the ex-wives who had lived small and left first.

He checked the one-car garage. The absence of a dented-and-dinged Volvo inside meant the agent wasn't home, which left Cash with two choices—wait for Shafer's return, or hit the handful of watering holes for the most predictable animals on the planet: law enforcers.

The badge-and-beer tour began and ended at the oldest cop bar in the city. Alvarez's Hole in the Wall, a.k.a. The A-Hole, was a dimly-lit dive contagious to anything cloth, crystal, classy, or low cal.

The bar catered to badasses and burnouts of every stripe, with a pecking order that put beat cops atop the heap and feds several rungs below. Even among feds, IRS agents scraped bottom.

No surprise to find Shafer drinking alone at the bar and binging on peanuts. A moat of shells ringed the legs of his stool.

An untouchable. The lowest of the low.

Okay, maybe not the absolute dregs. Cash's entrance dropped the decibel level in the packed bar to tombstone silence. His mere presence healed the rift between locals and feds, banding everyone against the most hated creature on the planet: a criminal defense lawyer.

Cash didn't make it three steps inside the building before a burly cop with gin-and-garlic breath stiff-armed him against a wall. Cash recognized the attacker, a loose cannon in Vice called Rambone, with a history of excessive force charges. Most had been dropped after witnesses recanted, but two had drawn suspensions.

"Can't you read, dumbshit?" Rambone pointed to a sign hanging over the door:

NO ASSHOLES ALLOWED.

"That means you," he said.

"I'm here to meet a friend." Cash waved to Shafer, who made a point of not waving back.

"Any friend of yours is no friend of ours." Rambone clenched his fists, pumping life into the twin python tattoos on his Popeye forearms.

Shafer slid off the stool and tapped Rambone on the shoulder. "Let me take this fool off your hands."

"He a friend of yours?" The cop's tone made it clear he'd better not be.

"Hell no, and he was just leaving." Shafer grabbed Cash by the arm and hustled him toward the exit. "Better get you out of here before the cops sort out who gets to whip your ass first."

The threat of rain hung over the night. Shafer and Cash ducked into a place two doors down the block, a combination coffee shop and tattoo parlor called Ink 'N Drink.

Pick your poison.

Cash went with two coffees. Hold the tatts.

They took the farthest table from the door. Shafer kept his back to the wall, eyes on the entrance. A law enforcement thing.

"Why do you go to that cop bar anyway?" Cash said. "They hate you almost as much as they do me."

Shafer smiled. "Answered your own question when you said *almost*. It's a relief to an IRS agent to go anywhere he's not the most hated."

Cash cut short the small talk and went straight for the jugular. "How long have you been on Benanti's payroll?"

The smile faded from the agent's face, eclipsed by a look that would've curdled the cream in Cash's coffee. Except for the fact it had already gone bad.

"If I were really in Benanti's pocket, you wouldn't have to ask. You were his mouthpiece."

"I represented the scum on and off for fifteen years, more off than on, but I wasn't privy to all the crooked cops and agents in his stable. He kept information siloed. Shared only what he wanted you to know."

"So you think I chased him all those years for my health?"

"You never caught him," Cash said.

"I have you to thank for that. We had him on the ropes until you got caught bribing a juror. At that point Moore made it all about you. He thought we could flip you, but I knew better. You'd be way more frightened of Benanti than of prison."

A goth girl with a glassy stare floated into Ink 'N Drink. High on something. Floral tatts sleeved all four limbs.

Shafer's eyes followed her until she disappeared behind a black curtain separating the two sides of the shop. He turned back to Cash. "A lot of good folks failed to take down Benanti. You can't seriously suspect all of us. That's being paranoid."

"Even taking into account the general incompetence of government work, you go to the front of the lineup. I offer to bring Taylor Donovan to you, and the next thing I know, she's gone. Probably dead. Did you have something to do with her disappearance?"

Shafer stiffened. "Did you?"

"She was my client. Why would I want to get rid of her?"

The agent's lips turned white from the strain of holding back. The pressure finally proved too much. "To keep her from snitching you out."

"That's crazy," Cash said.

"She came to see me once, alone."

Cash pushed back from the table. "Wait a goddam second! You can't talk to Taylor without me. That violates every—"

Shafer cut him off. "I can if she's offering to testify against not just Benanti, but also you. You're always going on about motive. Well, she was ready to dime you out. There's your motive for murder."

Cash's insides churned. His brain fired wildly in all directions. If Shafer was telling the truth about Taylor, Cash would be the main suspect in her murder. If Shafer was lying, he'd done a helluva frame job on Cash.

Someone was lying. Shafer. Taylor. Maybe both.

"So right now," the agent said, "you look good for two murders. With Benanti, we have a body and a motive. With Taylor, we have a motive but no body. Just a matter of time until we rack up two dead bodies with two solid motives, both leading straight to you."

Cash retreated into the silence of the damned.

"Only problem," Shafer said, "is that I can't decide whether Taylor was a righteous snitch or a dirty mole."

Cash grasped for the lifeline. "What do you mean?"

"When she came to see me, we already had someone inside Benanti's organization."

"Who?"

"Nice try," Shafer said, "but you're not nearly as subtle as Taylor proved to be. I have a nagging suspicion she came out of the cold, not to turn on you but to gather intel for Benanti. I keep going over what we talked about in my head. Worried sick that I let something slip that cost a life."

"Your mole?"

Shafer nodded. "I suspect you're here tonight for the same reason. Makes me fear that something I say will get someone else killed."

"That was how Benanti kept his edge all those years. He bought so many souls that you began to suspect everyone. I assumed you were dirty, and you thought the same of me."

"Still do," Shafer said.

"Gotta trust someone sometime," Cash said, "and I'm willing to take you off my shit list, for the time being."

Goth Girl emerged from behind the curtain, followed by a goateed tattoo artist with no visible ink. They walked along a series of color photographs on the walls. A gallery of tattooed human flesh. Arms, legs, tits, abs, fingers, toes, soles, thighs, eyelids, cheeks, whatever.

They passed by a photo of a blue butterfly tattoo on a buttock. Three photos down, they stopped. Goth pointed to a picture of a thorny rose bush. More thorn than rose.

Goth and Goatee disappeared behind the curtain again.

Cash rose.

"Where are you going?" Shafer said.

"Chasing butterflies."

# CHAPTER FORTY-SEVEN

A pale ass greeted Cash behind the black curtain.

Goth Girl lay stomach down on a padded table. Briefs bunched at her ankles. Flip-flops and shorts on the floor.

A goateed artist hovered over her. Tatt gun in one hand. Cig in the other.

Goth Girl turned her face toward Cash. He counted seven silver rings, one in her nose and three on each lobe. No telling how many remained out of sight.

She rolled onto her left hip and hiked in the air her right cheek, which served as tonight's canvas. It was the right buttock but the wrong tattoo. Not a blue butterfly but more flowers for the garden of flesh.

Cash cleared his throat, and Goatee turned around. "Hey, dude, you can't be back here." The threat would've carried more weight if the speaker did. At maybe five-six and 130 pounds, he looked as if he followed a strict regimen of no natural light, no health food, and absolutely no exercise. "If you want an ink job, make an appointment."

Goth Girl craned her neck for a better view of Cash. "Let the peeper stay, long as he's willing to pay for the show." A lisp made her sound even younger than she looked.

"How old are you?" Cash said to the girl.

Her smile revealed a silver tongue stud. Mystery of the lisp, solved. "Past the age of consent."

"Not where I was going with the question," Cash said, "but if that's true, you should know better." He grabbed Goatee's wrist and wrested away the gun. "And what's your name, Rembrandt?"

"Andre."

"Okay, we'll go with Andre for now." Betting it had been Andrew or even Andy before the body art boom hit Deep Ellum. Cash turned back to the girl. "Has Andre done the rest of you?"

"Yes."

"Why him? There are a dozen tattoo shops in Deep Ellum."

She sat on the edge of the table, facing Cash and exposing a landing strip and two more rings. Her panties slipped past her feet and floated to the floor, leaving her nude but for a T-shirt and the tatts.

Cash threw her a towel. "Cover yourself and tell me why you keep coming back to this guy."

"He's the best." Her feet dangled above the floor, swinging in small scissor kicks. Toenails painted black as onyx. "For an awesome tatt, he's your man."

"I'm here for information, but it sounds like he's still the man." Cash dragged Andre outside the curtain to the coffee shop side and stopped at the photo of the buttock with the blue butterfly tattoo. "That your handiwork?"

Andre nodded warily. He didn't blink fast enough to dam the flow of tears.

Cash pulled a photo of Taylor Donovan from his pocket. "You ink her?"

"My client list is confidential." Came off closer to a plea than a statement of principle.

Cash laughed. "That's my line, asshole."

Shafer had split, sticking Cash with the bill. Also leaving no witnesses to what was about to go down. Other than Goth Girl, of course, but that walking billboard for bad judgment carried less credibility than Andre.

He bent back Andre's right hand until he dropped to his knees and screamed in pain. His eyes gushed.

"When I break both your wrists, you won't have to worry about keeping your clients confidential, since you'll have no more clients."

Andre held out for a nanosecond before spilling his guts, literally and figuratively.

* * *

"Stop knocking on my damn door," Shafer shouted from inside his dark house.

Cash's fist froze between knocks. "Let me in."

"The only reason I'd open the door is to make sure I don't miss with my trusty Glock. Could always claim I thought you were a burglar. It's not like the cops would lose sleep over your timely demise. Might even score me free drinks for life at the A-Hole."

"Exactly what would I be here to boost? Your menagerie of animal figurines above the fireplace?" A wild stab that a loner like Shafer collected knick-knacks that no self-respecting granny would allow in her trailer.

"No way I'm letting you in. If you want to talk, call my office for an appointment. I might have an opening two years from never."

"Did your dead snitch have a butterfly tattoo on her ass?" Cash said.

A full minute of silence passed. The click of a deadbolt signaled that Shafer had been hooked. Cash turned the knob and pushed. The door creaked open to reveal an empty entryway.

The first look inside Shafer's house confirmed his worst suspicions about the agent. Not the part about him being dirty, still an open question. But the deeper, darker secret of the glass menagerie on the mantle.

"What do you know about a butterfly tattoo?" Shafer's voice came from the next room, drawing Cash deeper into the darkness.

A lone light over the kitchen table shone on a mat. On closer inspection, not a mat but a manila folder. Shafer opened it and laid out six full-color blowups. Five of a woman in a net dangling from the limb of a massive oak tree. Naked. Curled in a fetal ball. Suspended between heaven and earth. Helpless as a trapped butterfly.

The sixth shot showed three objects laid out on the ground below her. A knife, water bottle, and cell phone. Placed just beyond her reach.

Cash couldn't I.D. her. In the shape she was in, her mother wouldn't be able to. Buzzards had feasted on her flesh. Shredded her skin. Left black holes where the eyes had been.

Cash struggled to speak. To ask if this was the agent's chickenshit way of saying Eva had turned up. On closer look, though, not Eva. Not even close. The victim was taller and paler than his missing sidekick.

Cash found his tongue. "Your snitch?"

Shafer bristled. "My *informant*."

"How did she die?"

"Slowly. Horribly. With more pain and suffering than...."
Shafer's voice trailed off. He looked away from the table. Away
from Cash. "C.O.D. was a combination of dehydration, expo-
sure, and shock."

"How long did she suffer?"

"Days." The agent pulled another photo from the folder
and dropped it on the table. A close-up of a blue butterfly tattoo on a black-and-blue buttock. The familiar tatt framed by
rope burns. "What do you know about this tattoo?"

"It's how Benanti marked his property," Cash said.

"It may be more than that." Shafer gathered up the photos
and slipped them back into the folder. "The autopsy report
noted that the tattoo covered a small scar left by an incision.
Know anything about that?"

The incision cleared up several mysteries. Like how Benanti
had tracked down Shafer's dead informant. Also, what Taylor's
motives had been when she visited first Goldy and later Shafer.
If Benanti had been able to follow her movements all along and
she had known it, she was a spy, not a snitch.

One question it didn't answer—whether Shafer was bent,
straight, or something in between. Ally, enemy, or alloy. If he
was telling the truth about Taylor reaching out to him, she had
played both the agent and Cash. But if Shafer was lying about
that, he had set up Cash for a murder rap.

Cash counted on his gut to sort it out.

Shafer didn't wait. "What can you tell me about the incision?"

Still on the fence, Cash leaned toward treating him as an
ally. Not so much out of trust, but because he had no one else
to turn to. "It's how Benanti kept tabs on his property."

"What do you mean?"

"The tattoo marks the spot where Benanti had a tracking device implanted in his girls. Someone must've removed your informant's tracker before leaving her to die."

Shafer nodded. "How long has your secretary been missing?"

"My *assistant*." Cash's turn to correct the record. "Thirty-six hours."

"I don't have to tell you that the odds of finding her alive—"

Cash cut him off. "Right, you don't have to tell me. I'm working as fast as I can, and I won't stop until I find her."

"Work faster," Shafer said. "Mariposa Benanti is putting the finishing touches on an airtight case that you killed her husband. She's almost done, meaning you're almost done too. Your days on the street are numbered."

# CHAPTER FORTY-EIGHT

Another bare ass on a padded table tempted Cash. That made two in two days. He must be living right.

A piano solo poured from speakers mounted in the ceiling. The tinkling of keys simulated gentle rainfall. Took only a few bars for Cash to name the song: *Laura.*

The theme from the classic noir film. As if he could forget the song or the siren on the table.

A dim bulb threw off enough light for Cash to make out Laura's faded tattoo. A blue butterfly on the right cheek. No doubt marking the spot where a device had been implanted. Open question whether, with Benanti gone, anyone still bothered to track her.

Laura had the taut body of a cross-trainer. Judged solely by the flesh on display, she could be anywhere from twenty-five to fifty-five.

But Cash had a bead on her true age, having known her from the early days of Benanti's evolving empire. She had been the crime boss's wife during his descent from sleazy car dealer to ruthless flesh peddler. Back when Cash had first appeared on Benanti's radar. Or more accurately, walked into his web.

Like Cash, a fresh-off-the-plane looker named Laura Wade had found herself trapped in Benanti's world. After a five-year run as wife number two, she lost out to Mariposa. That put Laura at the upper end of the age range.

A shirtless Latino kneaded her calves. A cocky smirk and a six-pack suggested that he scored the hat trick: masseuse, trainer, and boy toy. Not necessarily in that order.

Cash's first challenge, lose the witness. "Missus Benanti and I would like to be alone."

No response from Six-Pack. Not even to acknowledge Cash's presence. His fingers climbed past Laura's thighs and squeezed her buttocks, the pressure stirring the butterfly to spread its wings.

"I go by Miss Wade now. Maiden name."

Probably not by choice. Mariposa had a wicked territorial streak. She'd make damn sure there was only one Missus Benanti in the mix.

She patted Six-Pack's rump. "Meet me in the gym in ten minutes."

On the way out, Six-Pack shoulder bumped Cash, a warning to watch his step.

Cash turned up the lights. The rubdown room was Spartan and small. Not much larger than his once and future cell at Seagoville. Barely enough space for the massage table, a wooden chair, and a rolling tray covered with lotions and oils. His and her terry cloth robes hung from hooks on the wall.

"You might not remember me," Cash said, "but—"

She cut him off. "I remember you." Her tone made clear it wasn't in a fond way. "You were Larry's mouthpiece."

"Ancient history," Cash said. "We had a parting of the ways a few years back."

"Didn't you try to fix his jury?" She didn't wait for a response. "So why aren't you in prison?"

"Got out on good behavior," he lied.

"Doubt that." She sounded older and more cynical by the word. "I recall you were a very bad boy."

"And I tried so hard to be on my best behavior around you."

She laughed. "You hit on me more times than I can remember. A miracle we didn't wind up in an early grave together. That was back when Larry actually gave a shit about me. I hear you made a play on my replacement too."

Guilty as charged. "She moved on me first."

"That gives you and me something in common," Laura said.

Hard for Cash to shake the image of Laura and Mariposa, lips together and limbs entwined. Not exactly news that Mariposa batted from both sides of the plate. Taylor Donovan had hinted at the same thing.

"I'm a changed man now."

"Doubt that too." Laura remained stomach down on the table. "Only two things can keep someone like you in line: fear and fatigue. So are you afraid or tired?"

"I'm tired of playing games with you, and I'm scared shitless of Mariposa. She's trying to pin Larry's murder on me."

"If she wants you out of the way, you're already gone." The voice of experience.

"No one has a better motive for offing Benanti," Cash said, "than the ex-wife who got dumped for a younger model."

"If you're in the market for a fall girl, keep looking. I've been a prisoner here for ten years. Welcome to my private hell."

"You wouldn't be stupid enough to do the hit yourself," he said. "Contract killers come cheap in Texas."

"But don't they always turn out to be undercover cops?"

"Nine times out of ten, but maybe you got lucky and found a cop who really moonlights as a hit man. Plenty of precedent for that."

"For someone who's supposed to be street savvy, you really don't have a clue. When Mariposa took over, she wanted me dead, but Larry let me live...sort of. Long as I know my place and color inside the lines, I keep breathing. Set one foot outside the grounds, and I'm a goner. Now that Larry's dead...." She didn't have to finish the sentence.

"You call this living?" He dialed back the judgmental tone. "Why not take off and try your luck in the real world, like the rest of us?"

"Run or stay, it won't change the outcome. Soon as the dust settles on Larry's grave, Mariposa will find a way to put me in mine."

"Why make it easy for her? Haul ass out of here. Try a new city, maybe even a new country. Take a new identity. Get lost in the crowd."

"That's not so simple for me," she said.

His turn to laugh. "Is this the part where I'm supposed to feel sorry for a beautiful woman, because it's so hard for you to pass unnoticed?"

"Larry didn't let Mariposa kill me." She lifted her torso off the table and turned to face him. "But she got to leave her mark."

Cash stifled a gasp. Prayed that his poker face masked the shock. A purplish-pink scar formed a *B* on her forehead.

The Benanti brand.

# CHAPTER FORTY-NINE

The call woke Cash at three-thirty a.m. Not that he'd been sleeping all that soundly anyway. Not with Eva missing for two days.

A call at this hour had to be bad news. He braced himself.

"*Soy* Catalina Martinez." The mother's voice was raw, shaky. Like she'd been crying or drinking all night. Probably both. "I can't reach *mijita*."

When excited or emotional, Eva's mother concocted her own version of Spanglish. Cash calibrated how much to share with her. Too little bordered on callous. Too much threatened to push her over the edge.

"When was the last time you heard from her?" he said.

"*Más que una semana.* She calls *todos las noches, pero... pero....*" She lapsed into another round of crying.

To stave off a complete breakdown, Cash resorted to a lie. "She took a few days off work. Probably holed up somewhere with bad cell service."

"*Con su novio?*"

This time he took refuge in the truth, with a firm "no." But not the whole truth. Eva hadn't had a boyfriend since grade school. "Missus Martinez, I'll get in touch with her and make

269

sure she calls you. Now don't you worry." *Because I'm worrying enough for both of us.* "Did she send money this week?"

"*No importante. Quiero hablar con mijita.*" She launched into a tearful, halting prayer for her daughter's safety.

Cash caught the words *Dios* and *virgencita* sprinkled throughout. The rest of the prayer went over his head.

\* \* \*

Thursday night brought heavy traffic to the Ritz bar. Singles making last-call pitches for Friday night hookups. Marrieds cruising for a taste of freedom before weekend lockdowns in the burbs. Pros who looked like anything but.

Even after three years on ice, Cash managed to score his old table. The one with the best view of the talent teed up on bar stools.

Of the guests invited to the party, Jenna Powell showed first. Predictable. In law school she had always arrived early for class and taken the center seat of the front row. Hers was always the fastest hand in the air following a teacher's question. Cash had fallen for her anyway.

Maggie Burns of the FBI placed second, and Shafer of the IRS filled out the table. He made no effort to hide his displeasure at being there. A ruddy complexion and rumpled khakis marked him as out of his element and way out of his league.

The taxman broke the silence. "Can someone tell me what the hell we're doing here?"

"For starters," Cash said, "enjoying the city's best martini." He raised his glass for a toast. "To old and new friends."

Shafer didn't reach for his glass. "Count me out. I make it a point not to drink with felons or their lawyers, and you fall into both camps."

"Stick around," Cash said, "and maybe we'll solve a crime or two tonight."

Shafer's expression soured to disgust. He reached for the drink.

"First crime first," Cash said. "Since the gang's all here, let's start by reenacting the night I got busted for jury tampering."

"Why the hell would we do that?" Shafer said. "It's not like we get the satisfaction of sending you back for a second sentence, or even make you complete your first."

Cash caught the waitress's eye and circled his forefinger in the air. The universal signal for a fresh round of drinks. "Humor me anyway. After all, here's where Maggie dropped the ball."

Shafer leaned forward. "What are you talking about?"

"Actually, she screwed up twice." It came out harsher than Cash intended. "First, by letting the juror out of her sight for a bathroom break. Then by failing to search her when she came out."

"What?" Shafer stared at Maggie, then Jenna. Neither looked him in the eye.

That told Cash what he needed to know. Shafer had been in the dark about Maggie's screw-up and Jenna's cover-up. Bumped the agent a few notches higher on the trust-o-meter. Still a raging asshole, but possibly an honest one.

"Now that we're all on the same page," Cash said, "it's showtime."

"I don't know what you're hoping to accomplish." Maggie sounded weary, deflated. "You've already done the time."

A round of martinis arrived. Cash kept the tab open.

"Right. I did two years for a crime I didn't commit. The least you can do is play along for a few minutes." Cash took a sip. "So drink up and hit your marks. I'll stay here because this was my table on the fateful night." He pointed to Maggie. "Where were you stationed?"

"In the manager's office behind the reception desk, waiting for the cue to send out the juror."

"Take your post," Cash said.

Maggie hadn't touched her drink. "What exactly am I supposed to be looking for?"

"Put yourself back on that night and retrace your steps. Maybe something you see or hear will trigger a memory that'll help us figure out who passed the cash to Juror Number Ten."

Maggie shrugged and headed toward the reception area. She left the drink behind.

Cash turned to Shafer. "Where were you?"

"In the parking lot with the takedown team, waiting to slap the cuffs on you."

"Off you go."

"Jesus H. Christ." Shafer rose so violently that his chair toppled backward. He stormed halfway to the exit before doubling back to grab his glass, muttering to himself all the way out the door.

"Where was our newly-minted U.S. Attorney the night your office took me down?" Cash said.

Jenna ran her forefinger along the rim of the glass. "As far away from here as possible."

"Was that by choice?"

"I didn't want to be anywhere near the arrest, and Tom didn't want me here either."

"Guess he couldn't count on your loyalty, which is the one thing he and I have in common." He held up two fingers to the waitress, ordering two more drinks. "Stay here and keep me company. Help me ward off the hookers."

Jenna exercised her right to remain silent. Cash nursed his drink and searched for words to kickstart the conversation. Came up with nothing. Big relief when the exiles returned to the table.

"Anything to share?" Cash said.

Shafer snorted. "Total waste of time."

Maggie pushed away the drink. "Same here. Most likely the cash got passed to Yvonne in the restroom."

Cash nodded. "Hoped one of you might recall seeing someone enter or leave the hotel or even better, the bathroom... someone who looked suspicious or out of place."

"The accomplice was probably already in the restroom when we got here," Maggie said, "and waited to leave until after we'd cleared out."

"Any chance the Ritz has tapes showing who entered and left the hotel that night?" Cash said.

Maggie reclaimed her drink. "I ran down that lead. They keep tapes thirty days before reusing them. By the time I checked, the one for the night of your arrest had been taped over multiple times."

"Which means tonight has been a royal waste of time," Shafer said.

"Not necessarily," Cash said. "Never hurts to know who can be trusted." He looked at Jenna. "And who can't."

Shafer rose. "Trust this. I won't come running the next time you call." He took off.

"Sorry this didn't pan out," Jenna said, "but I'm bailing too." She left behind an untouched martini.

Cash turned to Maggie. "What about you? You got some-place else you have to be?"

"I'm exactly where I need to be." She opened her purse, took out a pair of handcuffs, and placed them on the table.

"I'm game if you are," he said. "Maybe we can get my old suite back."

"My boss has different plans for your sleeping arrange-ments. I have a warrant for your arrest for killing a federal wit-ness." She rummaged through her purse. "Damn. Must've left it in the car. If you're here when I get back, I'll have to take you in."

"And if I'm not here?" he said.

She winked. "Catch you later."

# CHAPTER FIFTY

First stop of the morning, Wells Fargo, where Cash wired three grand to cover Missus Martinez's allowance for the month, plus two months in advance. Possibly the last gift Eva's mother would receive.

Second stop, Eva's apartment, where he grilled Paula. She swore there'd been no breakup. No lovers' spat. Not even a cross word. Just a goodbye kiss before Eva left for the office and vanished.

"You've got to find her," Paula said to Cash on his way out. "Then you have to let her go."

Cash didn't push back. Not the time or place. Not sure there would ever be a time or place.

Next stop, Maggie's apartment, where he'd shake the tree to see what fell out. Arrest warrant be damned. He was running out of options.

The FBI agent opened the door the width of the security chain. Cash wedged his boot into the crack.

"What part of I-have-an-arrest-warrant-with-your-name-on-it did you not understand?" She sounded tired and looked even more so.

"I need a few more days on the outside."

"And I need to chill on my day off," she said. "Looks like we'll both be disappointed today."

"Mostly I need your help. Eva's missing."

Her brow furrowed. "Your secretary?"

He nodded.

"How long has she been gone?" Sounding less like a lover and more like the law.

"More than forty-eight hours."

"Call the police."

"Can't."

"Oh right. She's illegal. You two are racking up quite a felony scorecard. Must be well into double digits on the sentencing guidelines by now."

She unlatched the chain and stepped away from the door. Not exactly a warm welcome or even an invitation. He slipped inside before she could change her mind.

Her back to him, she cinched tighter a silk robe that fell to mid-thigh. Even barefoot, she seemed taller than he remembered.

"That's why you'll have to search for her on your own," he said, "and off the books."

She turned around to face him. "No, what I have to do is my job, which right now involves arresting you." She pulled out a pair of handcuffs from a drawer and tossed them at his feet. "Put them on."

"Or what? You going to shoot me?"

"Don't tempt me."

"If you were going to arrest me, you would've done it last night."

"I'm not the only one out there looking for you." Her tone softened.

"I know. That's why I can't go home or to Goldberg's office. I've got nowhere to hide but here."

"Seek sanctuary in a church," she said. "No one would look for you there. What you can't do is stay here. That's way too much heat for me to fade."

He couldn't argue with that. The last thing he wanted to do was take her down with him. He moved toward the door. Stopped and spoke without turning back to her. "Whatever happens to me, you've got to find Eva."

"I can't." She sounded apologetic.

"Then do me one small favor." He didn't need eyes in the back of his head to know he'd hooked her. She could deny him once, even twice, but not three times. "In an hour or so, you'll get a call from Ricky Donovan, asking if his sister's in the witness protection program."

"Why would he think that?"

"He'll have heard it from a reliable source."

"Meaning you," she said.

Cash nodded. "All you have to do is back me up."

"I won't lie to him."

"Not asking you to. Just tell him that you can neither confirm nor deny it. His imagination will do the rest."

\* \* \*

Clusters of students in preppy attire milled on the manicured lawn outside SMU's Underwood Law Library. Ricky Donovan worked the crowd like a politician at the Dallas Country Club, rubbing shoulders with scions of society. If the kid had any heartburn over his sister's disappearance, it didn't show.

Cash grabbed Ricky by the arm and dragged him away from the moneyed crowd. Plastic smile gone, Ricky dug in his heels and pulled free his arm. "I was in the middle of an important conversation."

"And now you're at the beginning of a more important one," Cash said.

"I doubt that." Ricky glanced over his shoulder at the life-changing connections left behind.

"Don't worry about them. There'll be plenty of time for ass-kissing after we've wrapped up here. Besides, back in my school days, all the best contacts came from keggers."

"Yeah, like I'd take career advice from a disbarred lawyer."

"I see my reputation precedes me." Cash paused for a couple straight out of an Abercrombie & Fitch ad to pass by. "If you manage to worm your way into law school, you'll have three years to suck up. Till then do what college seniors are meant to do. Raise hell and lower your GPA."

"FYI, I've already been admitted to next year's law school class with a full scholarship."

Cash whistled. "Early admission and a free ride to boot. Looks like someone pulled strings for you. Big sister maybe? By the way, have you heard from her?"

A pause before Ricky said, "Not since we last talked."

Cash smelled a lie but didn't call him on it. "Too bad because you won't be hearing from her...ever."

"What do you mean?"

"She went into the witness protection plan. That means new name, new identity, new occupation, and new city. Most of all, no contact with anyone from her past life, including you. Especially you."

"She wouldn't do that."

"She would to save her skin."

"How do you know this?" Ricky sounded shaky.

"I got her into WITSEC."

Ricky's cocky façade crumbled. "If that was true, why would you tell me?"

"You shouldn't spend the rest of your life waiting for a call that'll never come." Memories of his missing mother gave Cash pause. "I know how that feels."

"I don't believe you."

"Don't blame you. We don't know each other all that well, and I just dropped a bombshell on you." He handed a business card to Ricky. Not his card. "Call this agent, and she'll confirm it."

Ricky stared at the card. "Are you saying that if I call Agent Burns, she'll tell me that my sister's in the program?"

"Of course not. She can't say where Taylor is, but she can tell you without telling you."

"How?"

"Just call that number," Cash said, "and ask where your sister is."

"And what will she say?"

"What sister?"

# CHAPTER FIFTY-ONE

Cash measured his freedom in minutes. His life expectancy, in days.

Time to dust off the Hail Mary play. Roll out the disinformation on Taylor Donovan's disappearance while he still could. No telling when the net would drop over him. Given Mariposa's tentacles into law enforcement, he wasn't long for the outside world.

On back-to-back calls, he recycled the story about Taylor's acceptance into WITSEC to Shafer and Goldberg. The same line given to Ricky Donovan earlier.

If Shafer was on Benanti's payroll, the false rumor would smoke him out and send him running to the prosecutors to wheedle info on Taylor's whereabouts. No way was Goldberg in Benanti's pocket, but by now his phones could be tapped by cops, crooks, or both. The disinformation could've gone viral.

Both Shafer and Goldberg urged Cash to give himself up but for different reasons. The agent angled to take credit for the collar, while the mentor feared Cash would be beaten, shot, or worse.

Cash finally bowed to reality. He wasn't getting any closer to finding Eva or Taylor. And the longer he dodged arrest, the guiltier he looked. Besides, with no safe haven at hand, it was only a matter of time before he got picked up.

He agreed to surrender to Shafer, hoping to collect a chit in the process. But before doing so, he detoured to the federal courthouse to check another suspect off the list, Probation Officer Sandy Robinson. He counted on her Botox-bloated lips to spread the witness protection tale to Judge Tapia and her extended court family.

Federal judges love to bitch about their salaries, frozen for decades by a cold-hearted Congress. Hell, rookie lawyers at firms out-earn them, despite the reality that their hours on the bench and caseloads grow longer every year.

Maybe Tapia had set up a private, off-the-books bonus plan, funded by the Benantis. Not like she'd be the first judge on the take. Plenty of precedent for it.

As Cash took the Pearl Street exit off the North Dallas Tollway, a black van swooped in front of him and screeched to a stop. He braked hard but fender-bumped the van.

"What the fuck!" The airbag inflated, knocking Cash breathless and pinning him to the seat.

A second van closed fast from behind and kissed the back bumper of the Impala, now caught in a vise. Four goons poured from the vans and sprinted toward Cash. One stabbed the airbag, and another pulled him from the car. A gut punch cut short his protest.

Cash recognized the thug who had sunk the hard right into his core. Bobby the bodyguard. Mariposa's muscle and perhaps more.

All told, it took less than a minute to clear the vans and the Impala from the exit. A professional bump and snatch.

Given a choice between being kidnapped the hard or the easy way, Cash would've opted for the latter. Not that he got a choice. The injection in his arm would've done the trick in seconds, but a blow to the back of the head turned lights out immediately.

One more score to settle with Bobby. Someday.

\* \* \*

Cash came to with the taste of blood in his mouth. His blood. A close call as to which hurt worse: his head or gut.

His wrists and ankles were tied to a wooden chair, tight enough to cut off circulation. A blindfold kept him in the dark about where he was but not about who loomed over him.

Mariposa's perfume gave her away. Clive Christian's No. 1. At a thousand dollars an ounce, no one else in Cash's world could afford the liquid gold, but she had the bankroll to bathe in the stuff. The scent cut through his blood-clogged nostrils.

"What took you so long to find me?" The effort of speaking sent Cash's migraine to stage four. His head definitely hurt worse.

"I'm a busy woman," Mariposa said, "with more important matters on my plate."

"Yeah, I'm sure that running your dead husband's criminal enterprise is a fulltime job."

"You've got five minutes to make your last closing argument before I turn you over to my boys."

"First, indulge my curiosity." He strained to sound more curious than desperate. "Who tipped you off that I'd put Taylor into witness protection?"

"Be quicker to list who didn't." The scent of perfume grew stronger. "But if you're hoping to get my confession on tape, don't bother. We found the device in your shoe. Also the one stitched into the cuff of your pants."

He let out a loud sigh. "The best-laid plans...."

"I wouldn't use *best-laid* to describe you or your plan." She paused for the putdown to sink in. "So what's your backup play?"

"To offer you a trade. Taylor for Eva."

"Doesn't betraying a client violate your so-called ethics?" She made *ethics* sound like a dirty word.

"Desperate times, desperate measures."

"Even if I want to get my hands on Taylor, what's to stop me from torturing you until you give up her new identity and location? That way I have both Eva and Taylor to play with."

"Since the only thing keeping me alive is knowledge of Taylor's whereabouts, I'll choose death over telling you where she is. Unless, of course, you let Eva go."

"You underestimate Bobby's skill at inflicting pain," Mariposa said, "and overestimate your ability to withstand it. But to save time, I'll trade the brown one for the blonde. Tell me where Taylor is and what name she's using."

"You know how this works. Proof of life first."

"Hmmm, that's a problem. While Eva is more alive than she's ever been, she's very busy at the moment. We're in the process of turning your little caterpillar into my beautiful butterfly."

"Drop the caterpillar-to-butterfly bullshit," he said. "I heard that crap from your late husband, and it doesn't play any better coming from you. Still boils down to an excuse to treat women as less than human." He cut to the bottom line. "No Eva, no Taylor."

"We'll see about that," she said.

He tensed, bracing for a blow. Or worse.

A second perfume wafted into the room. Stronger than Mariposa's brand. Less subtle but no less intoxicating.

Cash's blindfold came off. He blinked once, twice before Taylor came into focus, standing next to Mariposa.

# CHAPTER FIFTY-TWO

Mariposa pulled Taylor closer and said to Cash, "Looks like you're a salesman without portfolio."

Taylor laughed. "Or a lawyer without his briefs."

Mariposa's black boots and skinny jeans made her legs look a mile long. She had a good four inches on Taylor, who must've come straight from the pool. Her hair was wet, and she wore a terry cloth robe. Water prints from her bare feet marked the wooden floor.

The three of them shared a familiar room, but Bobby and the backup crew would be close by, waiting for their turn to crash the party.

"How about untying me," Cash said, "or at least loosening the ropes." His hands and feet were numb.

Taylor stepped forward, cupped Cash's chin in her palm, and forced him to look her in the eye. "Good to know that I would've made a fatal mistake, if I'd been foolish enough to put my life in your hands."

Her slap scrambled his vision. It cleared to reveal what Taylor was now and had always been. A plant by the Benantis to ferret out intel from Cash and the feds.

He looked around. The soundproof study on the second floor of the mansion had served as the war room during

Benanti's third and final trial. The one aborted by Cash's arrest for jury tampering.

A pyramid of cardboard boxes was stacked against the west wall. Pages, yellow with age, plastered the east wall, each with a detailed outline of the cross-examination of a government witness. Cash had spilled blood, sweat, and tears in this room.

Evidently not for the last time.

Fresh blood pooled in his mouth. "You're wrong about me." He spat before going on. "If I'd really known where you were, I would've taken that secret to the grave." He winced at his poor choice of words.

Leave it to Mariposa to seize on the slip. "Speaking of graves, you seem to have dug one large enough for you and your secretary."

"Let Eva go. She's of no use to you."

"That's where you're wrong," Mariposa said. "She's finally being put to her highest and best use. You have no idea how many men are hell-bent on *curing* lesbians with a hard fuck, a harder beating, maybe both." She squeezed Taylor's hand. "And what they'll pay for the privilege."

Cash struggled against the ropes and lost. He was down to his last weapon: his tongue. "Makes me want to surrender my guy card."

"You're probably wondering why you're still alive," Mariposa said.

The thought had crossed his mind. He left it there.

"You've still got a small part to play, a final few lines to deliver." She let go of Taylor's hand. "While we did a good job of framing you for Larry's murder, one or two skeptics remain unconvinced of your guilt."

Cash couldn't resist a fleeting smile over the tiny triumph. Like the heady rush at trial of knowing he'd swayed at least one juror. If he had only one true believer, he bet on Eva.

If two, Eva and Goldy.

"Your job," Mariposa said, "is to be so damn convincing in your confession that even your mother will accept your guilt."

"My mother's long gone."

"Explains a lot," Mariposa said.

Cash tensed against the ropes. A rising tide of bile burned his chest and throat.

Mariposa opened the door, and Bobby stepped inside, gun in hand. On a closer look, not a gun but a recorder. Cash's relief was temporary.

"Time to record for posterity how you killed Larry," the widow said, "and why."

"Start the ball rolling by telling me how and why I did it," Cash said. "Then fill me in on why I'd make a false confession to get you off the hook."

Mariposa took the recorder from Bobby and sent him from the room. On his way out, he gave Cash a smile that said *see you soon, sucker*.

"The why part is easy," Mariposa said. "You blamed Larry for putting you in prison on false charges."

"Why wouldn't I blame you as well?"

"Good point," she said, "which is why your confession will make clear that I had nothing to do with bribing the juror or killing my husband."

"Why did you kill him?" he said.

"You don't need to know that for your confession."

"Throw me a bone. I don't have a recorder on me, and my word's not worth shit to the feds."

Mariposa and Taylor exchanged a look, then a shrug.

"The people my husband worked for got nervous. Poor fool never made it to the top of the food chain and never would. His third indictment turned out to be the third strike."

"But I got him off the first two times and would've won the third trial, if everyone had left well enough alone."

"The boss of bosses didn't share your confidence, and she sure as hell didn't trust Larry to keep his mouth shut facing life behind bars. So she gave me a choice. Share Larry's fate like a good wife, or take over his territory and get on with my life."

"Should've tipped off your hubby when you changed the wedding vows to *until the threat of death do us part*."

Mariposa snickered. "Like you wouldn't have done the same."

"Who's the boss lady?" he said.

"That's way above your pay grade."

"Just asking. Sounds like she might need a good lawyer someday."

Mariposa's smile widened. "I'm sure she can afford one with a valid license."

"Okay, I've got the why down. So how does the script have me killing Benanti?"

"The good news," Mariposa said, "is that we're giving you a shot at beating the charge, or at least pleading it down to manslaughter. You and Larry argued at Taylor's place."

"Over what?" Cash said.

"Over her, me, money, all of the above. Doesn't really matter." Mariposa fiddled with the recorder. "He pulled a knife. You fought back. Took the knife away and stabbed him during the struggle. Explains your prints on the murder weapon and your blood at the scene. Most important to you, it takes the death penalty off the table."

Cash didn't mention that his return to prison would put the death penalty back on the table. "One last question. Why would I give you a get-out-of-jail-free card by making this bullshit confession?"

"For a chance to stay alive," she said.

He pretended to weigh the offer before countering. "Not good enough. But here's what I'll do. Trade my confession for Eva's freedom."

"That's not possible." Her fingernail clicked against the metallic recorder. A nervous tic or a tip-off of how badly she wanted his confession on tape.

Cash bet on the latter. "Bring Eva to me, and I'll say whatever you want."

Taylor grabbed Mariposa's arm. "Too risky. I say we kill him and make sure the body's never found. Everyone will assume he fled. Makes him look guilty as hell. Then we don't need his confession."

Mariposa broke her lover's grip. "I can't bring Eva back here, but I'll give you a choice. Record your confession now, and you can walk out the door a free man, at least until the feds pick you up."

She paused, giving him a chance to jump at her first and best offer. When he didn't, she went on. "Or you can take Eva's journey south and enjoy a brief reunion with her, before she gets back to work and you make a deathbed confession."

"How can I pass up an all-expense-paid vacation to Mexico?" He studied the reaction to *Mexico*. Mariposa had none, confirming his suspicion.

"It'll be a working vacation," Mariposa said.

"Should I book round-trip or one-way?"

Mariposa smiled. "I'll make the travel arrangements."

"I have to tie up a few loose ends first," Cash said.

Mariposa slipped the recorder into her pocket. "Wheels up tomorrow at noon at Love Field. If you're not there, I'll bring Eva back to you. One limb at a time."

# CHAPTER FIFTY-THREE

"A funny thing happened on the way to the courthouse," Cash said.

Maggie Burns looked antsy at Ink 'N Drink, where her tatt-free flesh screamed "NARC!" to the patrons of the coffee shop/tattoo parlor. "Let's go to Alvarez's down the block."

Cash balked. "I survived one visit to that cop hangout. Not eager to tempt fate again."

"You should've self-surrendered, like you promised."

"I was on my way to do that, when Mariposa had me swept off the street."

"What's your excuse now?"

"I'll turn myself in after bringing Eva back from Mexico."

Maggie's jaw dropped. "You don't really think you're going to Mexico."

"Why not?"

"For starters, you don't have a passport or permission from the court to leave the district, much less the country."

He sipped what passed for coffee. "You can get my passport from the clerk. Just don't tell Tapia where I'm going or why. I don't trust her or her staff."

Maggie's frown deepened. "The only way this could possibly happen is if it's done strictly by the book. That means getting the green light from my boss and Tapia. Our trip to Santa Fe almost cost me my badge."

Cash had anticipated the roadblocks. "Then don't ask Tapia for permission. Tell her I'm going, period."

"That's not how it works with a federal judge."

"It will with Tapia because she's angling to move up to the appeals court. That means a background investigation by the Bureau. If this is pitched as my request, she'll turn it down. If it's something the Bureau wants, she'll sign off."

Maggie took a deep breath, let out a long exhale. "Give me a few days to run this up the flagpole."

"You've got a few hours. I leave for Mexico at noon tomorrow."

"That's crazy! Even if you could get into Mexico, how are you going to get out?"

A waitress approached with a coffee pot, her bare arms and legs walking billboards for the tattoo artist behind the black curtain. Cash waved her off. "That's where you come in."

"It would take weeks," she said, "maybe months to get the *federales* on board."

"Ready or not, I take off at noon."

"Mexico is a big country. How am I supposed to find you?"

"Follow the butterflies." He rose.

"Where do you think you're going?"

"To see a man about a butterfly net."

* * *

"I didn't think you'd show," Mariposa said.

"You really don't know me." Cash settled into the leather seat and fastened the belt. Only six of twelve seats in the Gulfstream 650 were taken. He and Mariposa sat across the aisle from each other, with Bobby and two more stooges on the back row.

An attendant offered him a flute of champagne. He shook his head, not ready to pick his poison.

"Let us celebrate the beginning of our final journey," Mariposa said, "with a drink." It came off as a command.

He took a sip, then another. His head began to spin. His eyes flicked in and out of focus. He tried to rise, but his legs turned to rubber.

The flute slipped from his hand, and he collapsed into the seat.

* * *

Cash woke in a strange bed, with a groggy sense of having been moved in the night, maybe more than once. A metallic aftertaste curdled his tongue, and his throat burned from cigarette smoke.

He tried to sit up, but a metal cuff tethered his right wrist to an iron bedpost. Not much slack there, but he managed to prop his back against the headboard.

His free hand rubbed the sleep from his eyes, then wished he hadn't. A bedside Bobby the bodyguard rocked in a wooden chair, whittling a sharp stick with a hunting knife.

Bobby stopped whittling. "Welcome to hell."

"I can live with that," Cash said, "long as I take you with me."

"Difference is, I can come and go as I please."

"Where am I?"

"Where you wanted to be."

Cash shook his head to clear the cobwebs. Didn't help. Only worsened his headache.

The room doglegged to the left, the door out of sight. The bed stank worse than Cash's prison bunk. Sweat, blood, and semen stained the yellow sheets.

The stench told Cash where he was. Not the exact location but the business he had fallen into. A whorehouse where bottom-bleeding hookers eked out a living on the rapid turnover of customers.

Cash cleared his throat. "Even if you manage to escape hell this time, you'll be back."

"Enjoy your final few words." Bobby rose from the rocker, knife in hand. "Soon as Mariposa gives me the green light, I start slicing and dicing." He touched the tip of the knife to his forefinger and fake-winced.

"Your boss has threatened me with castration before and failed to follow through."

"Your pecker's safe," Bobby said, "for now. We've got a whole new hell in store for you."

Cash refused to give Bobby the satisfaction of pushing for specifics. Just prayed for a quick end for himself and a quicker one for Eva.

Bobby figure-eighted the knife in the air. "Me, I wanted to chop you up piece by piece. Start with the fingers, then the toes, ears, eyes, nose. See how long I could keep you alive, while paring you down to size. But Mariposa, she won't let you off that easy. Ordered me to cut out your tongue and let you go. Like she said, what the hell use is a mouthpiece without a tongue?"

Cash's tongue swelled until it nearly choked him. Dammed the rush of words in his throat.

"In the meantime," Bobby said, "I've got a date with the new girl in town. A *puta* from Big D. Need to break her in before she gets all stretched out."

As if on cue, the whine of rusty bedsprings seeped through the tissue-thin walls. The seesaw sound almost drowned out by the grunts and squeals of rough sex, punctuated by slaps as loud as gunfire.

Voices from the next room screamed out in Spanish. Cash caught every third word but didn't need a translator to get the drift. The pissed-off customer bracketed every command with *puta*. The sobbing woman flung back *pendejo*.

Cash turned toward the lone window to the world, draped by worn curtains. In the distance loomed a velvet mountain range, swaths of dark soil visible where the pines had been stripped away.

A black cloud eclipsed the sun, and the room went dark.

"What's happening?" A hint of panic spiked Cash's voice.

Bobby walked to the window and threw back the curtains. "At least you won't die alone. End of the line for the butterflies too."

"Don't tell me that you've bought into Benanti's butterfly bullshit."

"Don't bad-mouth the butterflies. Every fall, millions of them fly thousands of miles to these mountains to die. They're the biggest tourist attraction in this shithole. Hell, the only tourist attraction, unless you count the country's cheapest whores."

The black cloud passed. "Like the butterflies, you and Eva are doomed to die on the wrong side of the border."

"Take me to her," Cash said.

"You're better off remembering the north-of-the-border bitch. She's been here only a couple of days, but it has taken a toll."

"I'm not asking."

Bobby snickered. "Given your predicament, you best be begging."

"Given my predicament, it's no sweat off your balls to let me see her one last time." Cash stared out the window at the crazy patchwork of pines. Blankets of butterflies coated the mountainside. Everything living on borrowed time.

Bobby pulled a recorder from his shirt pocket. "You can see her after recording your confession to Mister Benanti's murder."

"That's not the deal. Soon as I know Eva's back in the States and safe, I'll cop to killing Benanti, JFK, Epstein, whatever you say."

Bobby leaned in, tequila on his breath. "Here's the new deal. Follow the script or Eva gives her last blow job to my little friend." He kissed the blade of the knife.

Cash slumped. "Give me two minutes alone with her."

"What's the point?" Bobby said. "You can't save her, any more than you were able to save your whore of a mother."

"Never got to say goodbye to my mother." Cash's voice broke. "At least let me say goodbye to Eva."

Bobby left the bedroom and returned with the same two goons who'd jumped Cash in the courthouse parking lot a lifetime ago. Also the same pair who'd flown on the Gulfstream yesterday with Bobby and Cash.

The Manster and Shorty.

Bobby tossed a key to Shorty. "Take the mouthpiece to Eva. If he tries anything, kill them both."

The henchmen led Cash to the last room on the left and locked the door behind him. "This is your two-minute warning," Shorty shouted through the door.

Cash froze at the sight of Eva's bare feet on the bed. Swollen soles crisscrossed with cuts and welts. Marks from a whip or a rod or a clothes hanger. What the hell did it matter? Would make it painful for her to walk, impossible to run.

He inched forward, bracing himself not to react, at least not outwardly. With Eva fully in sight, he choked back a cry of relief. Despite the smothering heat, she lay shivering. A ripped nightie revealed plenty of cleavage and everything from the waist down. Her face, raw from tears, was bruised but uncut.

The only scars were on the soles of her feet. The only visible ones anyway.

She lunged for him, but the chain running from her wrist to the bedpost yanked her back. She cried out.

He rushed to the bed and held her. Her tears soaked through his shirt, burning his chest. "I'm getting you out of here," he whispered.

Her forehead pressed against his sternum. He'd vowed not to ask about the past three days. Nothing he could do about it now. And the more he found out, the greater the risk that rage would cloud his judgment.

Freedom first, revenge later.

To hell with the vow. "Did Bobby rape you?"

She nodded. Cinched it. Regardless of whether he and Eva made it out alive, Bobby wouldn't.

She leaned back and looked into his eyes. "Who'll look after my mother?"

"She's taken care of." He got back on message. "But you're leaving here alive and well."

"You said that already. Trying to convince me or yourself?"

A knock on the door. "Thirty seconds to showtime," Bobby shouted from the hall.

He kissed her forehead. She stared at his forearm. "Since when did you get a tattoo?"

"Since yesterday."

"What's it supposed to be?" she said. "A baseball cap?"

"A net...a butterfly net."

An explosion rocked the whorehouse. Plaster rained from the ceiling, and windows shattered, spraying glass on the buckling floor. Smoke billowed into the room.

The blast echoed across the Sierra Madres, spooking the butterflies into taking flight and blotting out the sun.

# CHAPTER FIFTY-FOUR

Gunfire greeted gunfire. Bursts begat bursts. The cries of the wounded blended into the screams of the dying.

A spray of shots riddled the wall above the headboard, inches from nailing Eva and Cash on the bed. She froze. Cash sprawled atop her. His last and best use, as a shield. Her heart beat faster than the barrage of bullets laying waste to the bedroom.

He yanked on the chain binding her wrist to the bedpost. No give there. If the chain had been longer, he would've shoved her under the bed. Instead, they lay stacked atop the mattress, like teed-up targets.

Any second now, Bobby and his goons would blow through the door and finish them off. Unless...unless....

He hit the floor and belly-crawled to the door, now ventilated by bullet-holes. *Damn.* A baseball-size hole where the lock had been.

He propped a wooden chair against the knob. Wouldn't stop Bobby but might slow him down. Sprinted back to the bed to resume shield duty. Steeled his nerves through a silence more terrifying than gunfire.

A *thump-clang* broke the silence. Followed by another *thump-clang*. The third *thump* sent a canister sailing through the bedroom window. It hit the floor, rolled across the room, and bounced against a wall before spinning to a stop.

The hissing can spewed white smoke, fogging the room in seconds, cutting visibility to inches. Cash vetoed his first instinct to toss the can out the window. It would be too hot to touch.

Besides, his eyes welled with tears, leaving him blind and disoriented. Trying to field the jitterbugging can would be like grabbing a rattler by the tail and doing it blindfolded.

His nostrils and throat burned. Rashes raced across his exposed skin. Bad as his chest ached with every cough, he couldn't stop hacking.

Pinned down by Cash, Eva went wild with fear. Flailing and hysterical, she fought to crawl out from under him. He held her down and pulled a blanket over them, a futile buffer from the tear gas.

Even after the canister stopped hissing and sputtered to a stop, the fog thickened until the room sweat like a sauna. Glistening droplets of moisture dotted billowing clouds of smoke.

As the door took a battering, Cash threw back the cover. He still couldn't see a foot beyond his nose. Couldn't make out the Spanish curses shouted in the hallway.

The door hit the floor with a loud clap. Last line of defense down.

Gas seeped through the walls, ceiling, and floor. Wisps of white ribbons swirled together and parted, like ghosts in a dance of death.

Finally, a spirit morphed into a blur at the foot of the bed, looming more like the dark outline of a body than an actual flesh-and-blood assassin.

Soon a second, then a third spirit took shape. The unholy trinity huddled so tightly they merged into a single, solid unit.

Like a football line.

Or a firing squad.

# CHAPTER FIFTY-FIVE

ash's eyes played tricks on him. Tears blurred his vision. Fear gripped his mind.

"*Quién eres tú?*" a ghostly executioner said.

The fog lifted in stages. The first veil dropped to reveal the barrels of three automatic weapons trained on Cash.

Red dots danced on his torso.

Eva emerged from under the blanket. Head first, then the shoulders and arms. The chain running from her wrist to the bedpost kept her from crawling all the way out.

The dots followed her. The three barrels stayed steadier than she did. In a stare-down with the weapons, she blinked first. Her lips quivered, but no words spilled out.

Cash leaned into the line of fire. Wouldn't save Eva but might spare her from seeing what was coming. Not that he knew what was coming. Whatever, it wouldn't be good.

She clung to his back, tight as a tick on a dog. Moisture soaked through his shirt, sending chills down his spine. Could be her tears, sweat, saliva, all of the above.

He kept his voice flat, calm. "*Soy un Americano y un abogado.*" Realized that one or both admissions might set off the firing squad.

The last vestiges of fog faded from the room, leaving behind the permanent haze from decades of cigarette smoke. Cash coughed up a wad of phlegm, clearing his lungs. His vision crystallized.

The three triggermen were clad in black. Their uniforms, helmets, boots, gloves, gas masks, and even guns, all black. Had to be a hit squad or the Sierra Madre branch of the Darth Vader Fan Club.

The assault weapons commanded Cash's attention. During his sangria-and-salsa days prosecuting drug gangs, he'd seen AK-47s up close. Had even picked up one or two to parade before wide-eyed jurors during closing arguments, in a move calculated to sway even the most defense-friendly holdouts.

But he'd never stared into the business end of a barrel before. Much less, into three of them.

Focused on the weapons, he was slow to notice the words *Policia Federal* stitched in white letters on the uniforms. He breathed easier, but not easy. Sure, the *federales* were law enforcement, more or less. But the south-of-the-border variety could swing both ways.

Just like their cousins to the north.

"Your Spanish," the Alpha Assassin said, "is fucking terrible, man." He turned to his compadres. "These the fools we been told to smoke?" The death sentence sounded all the more ominous for being filtered through the echo chamber of a gas mask.

The sidekicks nodded, as did the barrels.

Still clinging like a boil to Cash's back, Eva tensed. A whimper snuck past her lips.

*Smoke?* If not for the circumstances, Cash would've smiled at the dead giveaway that Alpha had watched way too much

American TV, with its constant loop of gangsters and G-men blasting away at each other between banter.

Cash calculated the odds at less than zero that both he and Eva would survive and slim to none that one of them would see tomorrow.

Time to cut their losses.

"No reason to shoot *la chica*," Cash said. "Missus Benanti wants her alive as long as she's earning more than her upkeep. Kill her now, and Mariposa will have your heads on a platter. If you don't believe me, call her."

No way would the stall work long-term, but it might buy Eva an hour or two. Maybe a day if Mariposa was otherwise engaged.

Alpha led the men in a round of laughter. He stopped laughing first and said, "We are pricking with you, gringo."

Cash remained on edge until an FBI SWAT team stormed the bedroom and fanned out. Testosterone flooded the room, with five agents for every *federale*. Leave it to the Bureau to crash the party late and in overkill numbers.

A woman entered last but became the first to remove her helmet and gas mask. Maggie shook loose her auburn hair. The SWAT gear did a decent job of hiding her curves. Her eyes telegraphed relief over finding Cash alive.

The men followed her lead and took off their helmets and masks. The Mexicans were the last to show their faces.

Alpha turned out to be younger than he sounded. He winked at Eva.

Maggie sent an agent to fetch the key to Eva's cuff and ordered another to video the room. The videographer jumped into action, shooting Eva and Cash from every angle.

Maggie turned to Cash. "Why am I not surprised to find you in a whorehouse?"

"Why am I not surprised that you showed up late?" Cash said. "We could've been killed."

"You can thank me later for saving your sorry ass." Maggie broke eye contact to respond to a text. "And don't worry your pretty little head over what it cost Uncle Sam to persuade the *federales* to play ball. Actually, they proved an easier sale than my guys. When I told HRT that we were going into Mexico to save a criminal defense lawyer, the universal reaction was 'fuck that shit.'"

"Glad you convinced them I was worth saving."

"That didn't happen. But when I showed them Eva's photo, they were good to go."

Eva found her voice. "How did you know we were here?"

Before Maggie could answer, Bobby the bodyguard made a dramatic entrance, landing face first on the floor. Hands cuffed behind his back, he lifted his face to reveal a cut lip and a right eye swollen shut. The smirk survived the fall.

While stepping over Bobby, an agent tossed a key to Maggie, smooth as a second baseman turning a double play. The videographer zoomed in on Eva's raw wrist, now free of the cuff.

Eva pointed to Bobby. "You followed him here, didn't you?"

Maggie shook her head. "What do you think of Cash's new tattoo?"

Eva turned both thumbs down.

"Well, you should love it," Maggie said, "because it saved your life. It covers a tracking device planted in his forearm. We took a page from Benanti's playbook and followed the tracker here."

Eva stood by the bed. "Amazing that you can follow the signal all the way from Dallas to the mountains of Mexico."

"No way," Maggie said. "The signal carries only a hundred or so miles."

Cash did a double take. "Wait a minute. You never said anything about that. That means—"

Maggie cut him off. "We counted on you being right that the bad guys would take Eva to the final resting place of the butterflies."

"And if I'd been wrong about that?" Cash said.

"Then you two would've been sleeping with the butterflies."

Bobby struggled to his knees, then to his feet. "You're all up to your necks in shit, and it's rising fast. When I get back to the States, all hell—"

Maggie side-kicked Bobby's legs out from under him, and he crashed to the floor. "You're not going back to the States," she said. "Part of our deal with the *federales* was to leave you behind. You're checking into a Mexican jail tonight. Good luck with that."

The smirk disappeared. "You can't do that."

She motioned for the Mexicans to take him away. Alpha's buddies grabbed Bobby by the arms and dragged him toward the door.

"Wheels up in five minutes," she said.

"I'm an American citizen," Bobby shouted from the hall. "You have to take me with you."

"The only way you're going back," Maggie shouted, "is as a witness against Mariposa. You've got four minutes to start singing."

"Where is Mariposa?" Cash said to Maggie.

STING LIKE A BUTTERFLY

"Back in Dallas," Maggie said. "She got off the plane before it left Love Field."

Bobby blubbered. "She'll kill me." The Mexicans brought him back to the bedroom.

"Mariposa will be in prison doing life without parole," Maggie said. "No reason to fear her."

"I'm not talking about her." Bobby's voice cracked. "*La Jefa* will kill me."

# CHAPTER FIFTY-SIX

Down but not out described the Black Hawk.

Perched on what passed as a landing pad, the unmarked copter baked in the noon sun. It had touched down at dawn, midway between the mine-town whorehouse and the base of the Sierra Madre—rugged terrain cleared to smuggle dope, weapons, flesh, and cash in and out of Mexico.

A flock of butterflies eclipsed the sun and provided fleeting relief from the heat. As wheels up in five minutes stretched into five hours on the ground, the temperature inside the transport spiked from sauna-like to hellish.

Three passengers sweltered in the belly of a beast that could easily swallow twenty. Cash measured the passage of time not in minutes or hours but in water consumed. He was working on bottle number four and piss number three.

Eva looked flushed. He felt her forehead. No fever but that didn't comfort him. He tried not to imagine who or what had violated her during seventy-two hours of captivity. Glassy-eyed, she seemed a shell of her former self.

He whispered to Maggie, "We have to get her to a doctor. Now."

Maggie's phone pinged. She checked the message, texted a reply, and looked up at Cash. "Soon as we make Dallas, she'll go straight to Parkland, and we're taking off in five minutes."

"You said that two hours ago and again forty-five minutes ago."

"Cut me some slack." She sounded more beat than angry. "My boys are taking down Bobby's statement fast as they can. Who knew he'd punk out so quickly and spill so much? When he's done snitching, we go airborne. But while he's on Mexican soil, we've got leverage over him. Once he's back in the States, he'll develop a sudden case of amnesia."

"You already have more than enough to hang Mariposa," he said.

Maggie handed fresh water bottles to Eva and Cash. "We wrapped her up hours ago. Now we're squeezing Bobby to climb the ladder, and prosecutors in Dallas are putting the finishing touches on an information to be filed under seal as early as this afternoon, first thing tomorrow at the latest. The charges will send Mariposa away for life."

Maggie took a swig. "Last I heard, the body count from Bobby's confession stands at twenty defendants, give or take a couple. A slam dunk that the scum Bobby rolls on today will snitch out others tomorrow. And the beat goes on."

"I get that the Bureau wants to pad its stats, but why do we have to sweat it out in this hot box?"

The agent slapped the hull. "Safest place to be while we're on the ground, or in the air for that matter. This baby's built like a tank. Actually, better than a tank. Bullets bounce off her. Black Hawks have taken hits from anti-aircraft missiles and still managed to land safely."

"What's going to happen to Eva?" He would've preferred to have this conversation outside her presence, but given the stakes, better to hash it out now. His turn to use leverage. "Will she be able to walk away from this?"

"You know the drill. She goes back with us as a material witness. We'll keep her in a safe house and get her ready to take the stand."

*Nice try, Maggie.*

"I was born at night," he said, "but not last night. What happens to her after she testifies at trial...after you're done with her?"

The agent waited a beat too long to answer. "That'll be up to the U.S. Attorney."

"Not good enough," Cash said. "She won't testify until she becomes an American citizen, and don't waste your breath telling me it can't be done. If you want Mariposa and her crew bad enough, it'll get done."

Maggie's jaw tensed. "For someone banned by the court from practicing law, you sound a lot like a lawyer."

Cash took that as a compliment. And a warning.

Eva leaned forward. "What's going to happen to Cash?"

This time the agent didn't hesitate. "Depends on whether your boss plays it smart or suicidal. If he's smart, he enters the witness protection program and gets the fresh start he desperately needs. New name, new city, new occupation, new life."

Eva sighed. "He's not all that smart."

Maggie ignored her pinging phone. "It would be suicide for him to stay in Dallas."

"Since it's my life you two are laying out," Cash said, "I may want to weigh in here. For starters, I'm not leaving Dallas, nor the bar. As a reward for my invaluable assistance bringing down a crime family, I get my license back. Then before you can say *not guilty on all counts*, I'll be kicking the Bureau's ass in court-houses all across the country. Just like old times."

Gunfire aborted the debate over Cash's future. The echo of the exchange faded into silence. Shouts and screams in a mash-up of English and Spanish broke the calm. A big bang shook the Black Hawk.

The copter shuddered and rocked under fire, as it got pounded like a drum.

Bad time for piss number four.

# CHAPTER FIFTY-SEVEN

The first spray of bullets sent the passengers diving to the floor of the Black Hawk. Maggie, Eva, and Cash scrambled away from the open door and crouched behind the last row of seats.

The chopper took fire from all sides. Bullets pinged off its hard shell, but a volley found the open door, shredding the front row of seats.

During a lull more terrifying than an all-out assault, Eva went catatonic, her body stiff as rigor mortis. Maggie slapped her hard, snapping her from a state of stillness to a frenzy of sobbing and shaking.

Cash took charge of comforting the hysteric. Not Maggie's department. He held Eva tightly, his chest muffling her sobs. "Hang on. Cavalry's on the way." The lie sounded hollow, even to him. Not that it mattered. No way could he be heard over a fresh burst of gunfire.

Maggie unlocked a metal box and grabbed two grenades, one in each palm. "You two stay here and keep low." She belly-crawled forward. Near the open door, she sat up. Pressed her back to the hull. Bent her legs. Ready to spring.

She closed her eyes and crossed herself before pulling the pin and tossing a grenade outside. Waited five beats, then threw the other.

Twin explosions rocked the copter, as if the whole world had been jolted off axis. Black smoke clouded Cash's vision and set off a coughing jag. The ringing in his ears drowned out all other sounds, but only for a brief respite. As the din from the outside slowly seeped in, the cries of the damned pierced the fog.

When the smoke cleared, Maggie was gone.

Bullets raked the Black Hawk. Screaming, Eva broke free and bolted for the exit, following Maggie to certain slaughter.

Cash tackled her from behind, only inches before she would've been blasted to oblivion. He dragged her back to the tail section. She struggled to slip away, but he held her down. Her breaths were hot and heaving. Her eyes, wild with fear.

He weathered slaps to the face. Buckled as her knee hit groin, but refused to let go.

Pinned on her back, she pummeled him but not as violently as before. The war of wills prolonged more by inertia than energy. Her slaps lost their sting. Her heels skidded piston-like against a floor slick with sweat and blood.

"We're safer here than outside," he said.

She stopped struggling, but her eyes said she wasn't buying it. "They're coming for us." A full-body tremor rattled her voice. "We have to get out of here."

"We stay put. Maggie will be back with her team, and then we'll take off."

He looked around for a weapon. *Nada.* Checked inside the metal box where Maggie had found the grenades. Empty except for a toolbox and a tire iron. He grabbed the tire iron. Not that it would be much good against assault weapons, but best he could do.

From behind the last row of seats, Cash couldn't see the opening but sensed that the chopper was taking on troops, a hunch confirmed by the shuffle of approaching boots. A clear sign the end was near.

Both hands gripped the tire iron. With a few good swings and a little luck, he might fell one or two of the enemy before going down. If he had a gun with a single bullet, he'd use it on Eva now. Take her out quickly and cleanly.

Not an option with a tire iron.

The drumbeat of boots echoed inside the Black Hawk and rumbled like an advancing army. The tip of a black barrel nosed into view. Cash sprang from his crouch, tire iron cocked for a home run swing.

A dozen automatic weapons smelled blood and clicked for the kill. All aimed at his chest. None opened fire.

Cash checked his swing in time to keep an FBI agent from suffering a concussion or worse. Also in time to stop a thousand rounds from reducing him to bacon bits, not only saving his ass but also sparing the HRT commander the headache of filling out reams of paperwork to explain the loss of one, maybe two witnesses against Mariposa.

Cash loosened his grip, and the iron bar clanged to the floor.

"Shoot the bastard," Bobby said. "I'll back you up that it was self-defense."

"Shut the fuck up, snitch," the black HRT commander said before turning to Cash. "Where's Maggie?"

"She left five minutes ago," Cash said. "Went to get you guys."

The commander mouthed *damn*. "She should've stayed put."

Gunfire pelted the copter and gave Bobby a bad case of the shakes. "Hey, fellas, we've got to haul ass out of here. Those bangers want me dead."

Cash got in Bobby's face. "And that's a bad thing because...?"

The commander separated them. "We need him to make about a hundred cases against Benanti and her organization." He turned to Bobby. "But FYI, snitch, HRT does not leave a man behind."

"No problem," Bobby said, "cause we're leaving a bitch behind. *Vámanos.*"

"One more word, asshole, and I'll throw you to the wolves." Disgust laced the commander's voice.

A stubby agent stationed by the door signaled for the commander to come over. When he took in the scene outside, he mouthed another *damn*. "How many out there?"

"A dozen or so," Stubby said, "but the number grows by the minute."

Uninvited, Cash sidled over for a look. Blindfolded and gagged, Maggie teetered atop a wooden box. Her ankles lashed together, knees too. Hands bound behind her back. The rope around her neck tied to the limb of a tree, so taut that it forced her onto tiptoes.

A crescent of dried blood ran from the corner of her mouth to her chin. A rip in her shirt bared the right shoulder, revealing cigarette burns on her breast.

Two gunmen flanked her, each bearing an AK-47. The one on the left nudged the box with his boot. She lost her balance and let out a squeal before regaining her footing. Lefty laughed like a madman.

The one to her right shouted, "You have what we want, and we have what you want. We trade your *puta* for our *pendejo.*"

Stubby pulled a Glock. "I can drop both bastards before they get off a shot."

The commander shook his head. "No telling how many men they have stationed out of sight. If we open fire, Maggie's dead."

"Then let's do the deal," Stubby said. "We can still make our cases without the scumbag."

Bobby's eyes ballooned. "Hey, I haven't even started naming names." Panic pushed his voice higher. "I can give you more cases...whoever you want...whatever you need."

The commander glared at Bobby. "We need him to take out the ones above Mariposa."

"We have to do something quick." Stubby looked outside. "We're on their home turf, and our odds get worse the longer we wait."

Cash pointed to Bobby. "He and I, we're roughly the same size."

"Meaning?" The commander's tone conveyed that he knew exactly what Cash meant.

"Bobby and I swap clothes. Then you trade me for Maggie. Before the bad guys catch on, you're in the air, all agents aboard and cases intact."

The commander walked over to Cash. "You know how this will end."

Eva held Cash like she'd never let go. "You can't do this." Her forehead butted his chest. "You can't leave me. I won't let you."

Cash pried her loose and held her at arm's length. "Hey, don't think I'm doing this for you. This is strictly for me. Instead of getting shot at like a sitting duck, I'm giving myself a chance to talk my way out of a jam." He forced a smile. "That's what I do for a living."

The commander pulled Eva away and held onto her. "All I can say, mouthpiece, is you'd better be damn good at it."

"The best." While unbuttoning his shirt, Cash turned to Eva. "Remember, you don't testify to squat until you become a citizen. Goldberg will draw up the papers."

He tossed his shirt to Bobby and said, "I'll want this back."

# CHAPTER FIFTY-EIGHT

*Ten days later*

Cash had hoped for a better turnout for his sendoff into the great unknown. Alone in an office at the funeral home, he viewed the chapel through closed circuit TV. A state-of-the-depart sound system picked up every sniffle, sigh, and ill word uttered of the dead.

He counted the mourners in attendance. Six. Pathetic. Too few to make a jury. Wilting floral arrangements surrounded a framed photograph of a smiling Cash, mounted on an easel. No body to bury. Hence, no casket.

Crying jags had left Eva's eyes bloodshot. Black eye-liner had run into her sunken cheeks. She leaned against Paula's shoulder. Though Paula's makeup was still in place, she had a glazed look. Cash had to admit that the couple fit together and might have a future.

To Eva's left slumped Goldberg, frozen in a faraway stare. A half-step from death himself. In shock at having outlived his surrogate son.

Cash almost fell from his chair when Judge Anna Tapia showed up. In a black dress instead of her customary robe, she still managed to own the room. All eyes turned to her.

At the judge's entrance, Goldberg instinctively rose but stopped mid-crouch. His knees double-popped on the way up and down. As a reward or punishment for the half-hearted show of deference, Tapia sat next to him on the pew.

The sound system crackled to life with Springsteen's *Land of Hope and Dreams*:

*This train carries saints and sinners.*
*This train carries losers and winners.*
*This train carries whores and gamblers.*
*This train carries lost souls.*

"You choose the music?" Tapia said to Goldberg.

"I took the songs from Cash's playlist in the pen," Goldberg said, "so you might say they're dedicated to you. Brace yourself for big doses of the Boss, with a few gems from Merle and Johnny tossed into the mix."

"Fine by me." She surveyed the room. "Not much of a turnout for a standup guy."

Goldberg grunted. "You have a keen sense of the obvious." That crack would cost him the next time he had the misfortune of landing in her court.

"I thought the criminal defense bar stuck together," she said.

"Great white sharks don't swim in schools."

Cash smiled. Not the first time Goldberg had used that line.

"I see the FBI has turned out in force." Tapia nodded to Maggie Burns across the aisle.

Maggie nodded back. The lone fed had a pew to herself and the bloodiest of bloodshot eyes. Her outfit screamed Bureau, down to the shiny brass buttons, Navy blue blazer, and knee-length skirt, regulation cut and color. A white shirt starched to within an inch of its life. Red eyes, the only splash of bright color.

Tapia leaned closer to Goldberg. "I understand that Burns went down to Mexico on her own nickel to search for Cash."

Goldberg nodded. "Blind luck she didn't end up buried in the desert beside him."

The judge's iPhone buzzed. She checked the message and fired back a reply. "Surprised our esteemed U.S. Attorney hasn't made her grand entrance."

"No TV cameras here." Goldberg sounded bitter.

"With the takedown of the Benanti crew," Tapia said, "hasn't Jenna hit the saturation point on publicity?"

"Too much is never enough for the likes of her," Goldberg said. "Frankly, I'm more surprised by your presence than by her absence. Thought you didn't like my boy."

"Surprised myself by showing up." She stared at Cash's photo on display. "My mother was a grade school teacher in Post, Texas. Logged four decades in the classroom. Years after her last class, she told me that two types of students stuck in her memory: the angels and the devils." She smiled. "Your friend Cash, he was a little of both."

"Actually," Goldberg said, "he was a lot of both."

"The courthouse will be a duller place without him."

Goldberg nodded. "Good line. That one's going on his tombstone."

New song, same great E Street Band. The opening strains of *The Rising* rocked the room.

Cash couldn't contain himself any longer. He strode into the chapel and stood next to his photo. He looked like a beach bum. Shaggy hair, sandals, khaki shorts, Tommy Bahama shirt, end-of-summer tan.

"Goldberg," he said over the music, "you always said I'd be late for my own funeral." Sounding surprisingly chipper for a dead man.

The Boss filled a silence that seemed to stretch forever. Finally, Goldberg found his voice. "And underdressed to boot."

# CHAPTER FIFTY-NINE

*One month later*

Cash stood before the jury box in Tapia's courtroom, both palms on the railing. A kaleidoscope of faces flitted in and out of focus, in and out of his mind. Ghost jurors from past trials. Forepersons, free thinkers, followers, and filler.

"Ladies and gentlemen of the jury." Cash's words echoed in the empty courtroom. Jazzed by the rush of a trial, even a fantasy one, he found his mojo. Like a slugger at the plate, he was home.

A creaking door interrupted the opening statement. Shafer paused at the threshold, shit-eating grin in place. "Don't get ahead of yourself, McCahill. You don't have your license back yet."

The phantom jurors vanished, and Cash turned toward the agent. "What are you doing here? Eva sure as hell didn't invite you to the ceremony."

"Last time I checked, courtrooms were open to the public." Shafer approached him. "Besides, I'm here on official business.

Got a document to serve on you." He waved the papers in his right hand.

"Jesus H. Christ, not a goddam arrest warrant." Cash sounded more annoyed than angry. "What's it for this time? Spitting on the sidewalk? Crossing against the light? Singing too loud in the choir?"

"Yeah, like you'd darken the doors of a church." The agent handed the document to Cash. "Much as I wish it was an arrest warrant, it's a subpoena for you to testify at Mariposa's trial next month." Shafer shook his head. "Don't know whether to laugh or cry at the prospect of calling you as a witness for the government."

Shafer pulled a second subpoena from his pocket. "Got one for your lovely and almost legal secretary too."

Cash hit eleven on an anger scale that topped out at ten. "And you thought it was a good idea to serve it on her today? What a dick move!"

Shafer took a step back. "Settle down, shyster. This subpoena is the best thing that's ever happened to Eva. We get her testimony, and she gets citizenship. You brokered the deal. Happy ending for her."

"Happy ending for you too," Cash said. "After a decade of hitting dry holes and dead-ends, you can finally close the book on the Benanti organization."

Shafer frowned. "Bit of a tragic ending as well. Looks like you'll get your license to lie back."

Eva entered the courtroom, with Paula and Goldberg on each arm. Eva looked stunning. Charcoal eyes aglow, she broke into a smile that showcased dual dimples. The smile must've been contagious. Even Paula seemed halfway happy to see Cash.

Goldberg, well, he looked as if he'd been ridden hard, then ridden some more. His rumpled suit screamed buy-one-get-one-free. Tie didn't match the suit. Cash made a mental note to put Eva in charge of the old man's wardrobe.

Cash snatched the subpoena from Shafer. "I'll accept service for her."

"You authorized to do that?" the agent said.

"Yeah, I'm her designated spear catcher." Cash tucked both subpoenas in his coat pocket and rushed to Eva. "Ready for this rodeo?"

"My heart's beating a mile a minute." She sounded almost giddy.

"Relax," Cash said. "This is one of the few days when everyone goes home from court happy."

Eva waved to Shafer. "He doesn't look so happy."

Cash laughed. "Oh, that's his happy face."

Eva took several deep breaths. "We made the right choice, didn't we?"

"Trading your testimony for citizenship? No-brainer."

"Not about that," she said, "but turning down witness protection."

"We're good."

"I don't know." Her voice wavered. "Just 'cause you dodged death in Mexico doesn't mean you'll luck out a second time."

"Luck had nothing to do with it."

"I know you think you can talk your way out of any jam, but—"

Cash cut her off. "Trust me, we're safe." *For the time being.*

"Well, promise me one thing," she said. "We take no more drug cases and no more cartel work, period. From now on, we're strictly white collar."

Cash winced. "Afraid I can't do that. To keep from being spit-roasted over an open fire, I offered *La Jefa* a freebie the next time one of her soldiers got pinched north of the border. I have to take the case of her choice, and I have to win it."

Eva's mouth fell open, but no words spilled out. She finally found her tongue. "Out of the fire...."

The bailiff called the court to order. Tapia took the bench and motioned for everyone to sit. Her face, a mask of utter indifference to the proceedings. Or maybe she'd had a recent Botox fix. "Miss Martinez, are you ready to become an American citizen?"

Eva stood. "Yes, your honor."

Shafer started to slip out, but Cash grabbed his arm. "Stick around, flatfoot. After Eva learns the secret handshake, I've got one more defendant to add to the body count."

"Who?" The agent sounded skeptical.

"The courthouse mole."

# CHAPTER SIXTY

Two steps inside Sandy Robinson's office and Cash noticed what was missing. Besides Sandy, that is.

"The noose is gone." Said more to himself than Shafer.

The IRS agent hung back in the hallway, though it was his badge that had gotten them this far. "What are we doing here?"

"Robinson was Benanti's mole in the federal courthouse."

Shafer moved to the threshold. "That's crazy. I've known Sandy for decades. She's practically family."

"Exactly." Cash spread out the papers on her desk. "She's courthouse family, which is what made her so valuable to the Benantis."

"Even assuming they had an informant in the courthouse—"

Cash cut him off. "Safe assumption."

"Even so," Shafer said, "what makes you suspect Sandy? A thousand people work in this building."

Cash sat behind the desk and rifled through the drawers. "For starters, it has to be a woman."

"I don't see how you can—"

Cash cut him off again. "The night you busted me at the Ritz, someone passed ten thousand dollars to Yvonne Strauss in the bathroom. Only a woman could've slipped in and out of that restroom without attracting attention. At first I suspected Tapia, but she's too well-known. Someone would've recognized her."

"Ruling out the men," the agent said, "still leaves five hundred or so female workers in this building."

"We can narrow it down further. The informant had to be in the court's circle of trust. Someone close enough to gain access to confidential juror information. Names, contact info, occupation, work history, financial problems, brushes with the law. Data that was used to target a vulnerable juror, one who could be bought or bullied into delivering an acquittal, or at worst a hung jury."

Shafer started to speak but stopped. His brow furrowed.

Cash had seen that look before, when jurors were about to flip sides. "Info like that is limited to judges, their law clerks, bailiffs, and probation officers."

Shafer perked up. "Now we're down to a handful of people. A small enough number that I can subpoena their bank records to see who's come into a recent windfall. Pull credit card data to flag large purchases."

"That won't be necessary," Cash said. "The answer has been in front of me the whole time. I should've known something was wrong when Sandy paid a visit to the Benanti mansion hours before my arrest. Since when do probation officers make house calls at night? She was there to pick up the cash. The ten thousand dollars to pass to the juror at the Ritz."

Cash went on. "And every week I checked in with Sandy, she looked different. Not just different but better."

"Lots of women undergo midlife makeovers," Shafer said.

"It was more than a makeover. It was a transformation. That's what Benanti did to the women he owned."

"I'm still not completely sold," Shafer said, "but I'll round up another agent, and we'll tag-team interview Sandy this afternoon."

Cash stared at the empty coat rack. "Too late. She left work early and took the noose home for a reason."

* * *

"Sandy Robinson hung herself," Cash said in the safety of Goldberg's office. "The agents found her body an hour ago."

Eva gasped.

Goldy leaned back in his chair, fingers clasped behind his head, boots on the desk. "Dollars to donuts, she wasn't the only mole in the courthouse."

Eva clutched a large envelope to her breast. "While we're on the subject of hangings." She opened the envelope and arrayed on the desk six full-color photos of a nude Martin Biddle hanging in the prison chapel.

"What the hell?" Cash said. "How did you get these?"

"I filed a request under the Freedom of Information Act," she said. "Once the feds closed the investigation into Biddle's death, they had to turn over the coroner's report to me."

Cash shook his head. "Eva, I couldn't have made it clearer that—"

She cut him off. "Take a closer look."

He picked up a photo without trying to hide his annoyance. The longer he stared at it, the quieter the room got.

"What do you see?" she said.

He pulled the photo closer to his eyes. "It's what I don't see."

"Exactly." Her voice had the ring of I-told-you-so triumph. "There's nothing on the floor beneath Biddle. No piss, no shit, nothing."

Goldy grabbed a photo. "Well I'll be damned. The boy was killed somewhere else and then hung in the chapel."

Eva spelled it out. "Staged to look like a suicide."

Cash silently conceded her point.

Eva collected five of the photos and slipped them into the envelope. Cash offered her the sixth.

"Keep it," she said, "as a reminder that two little girls will grow up thinking their father killed himself."

Cash retreated behind his last line of defense. "What difference will it make to those girls if their father killed himself or was murdered? Either way, he's gone."

"What difference would it make to you," Eva fired back, "if your mother abandoned you or was kidnapped?"

Leave it to Eva to kick him while he was down.

# CHAPTER SIXTY-ONE

*One month later*

Warden Stockman blocked the entrance to the visiting room at Seagoville, F.C.I.

"Bet you thought you'd never see me again," Cash said.

"Wrong." The granite face of a mountain had more warmth. "Hoped I'd never see you again, but always pegged you for a repeat offender."

"Miss me?" Cash asked.

The warden grunted.

"I'll take that as a yes." Cash's smile didn't prove infectious. "Sorry to break your heart, but I'm here for a visit."

"It's not visiting day." Stockman's deadpan delivery betrayed only a hint of the pleasure he derived from bearing bad news. "Come back Saturday, and we might be able to squeeze you in."

Cash flashed his newly minted bar card. Gold with black letters, it looked more like an American Express credit card than professional credentials. "This baby admits me into any institution any day of the week for an official *attorney* visit. Don't leave home without it."

The warden finally managed a full-on expression. Disgust. "That the bar took you back would've destroyed my faith in the legal system, if I'd had any to begin with."

"Thanks for greeting me at the door," Cash said, "but I'd better get on with my visit."

"Sure you want to face Big Black? You two didn't part on the best of terms."

"We'll be fine," Cash said, "but I'm touched by your concern."

Stockman's expression hardened from disgust to pure disgust. "My only concern is the paperwork I'll have to fill out if Big Black does the world a favor by tearing you limb from limb."

After the warden left, two guards escorted Big Black into the room. Hannibal Lecter style. Cuffed and shackled, with chains running wrist to wrist, ankle to ankle, and wrist to ankle.

Big Black hobbled to a chair and landed hard. The chair groaned.

Cash sat next to him. "Big guy, I brought you a peace offering." He placed a hardback copy of *Great Expectations* on the prisoner's lap. "Try not to destroy this one."

Big Black fumbled for words before finding the wrong ones. "You're the Uncle Joe to my Pip."

Cash let pass the off-the-wall literary allusion. "What would you say if I donated the complete works of Charles Dickens to the prison library in your honor? After finishing *Great Expectations*, we can start on *David Copperfield*."

The prisoner teared up. "Then can we read *Oliver Twist*?"

Cash nodded. "Sure, but first we need to talk about Martin Biddle."

Big Black recoiled, his eyes growing wide. He shut off the waterworks and turned down the donation.

# CHAPTER SIXTY-TWO

ash pulled into the circular drive at the Benanti mansion to find Maggie Burns leaning against her G-car, a tan Ford with all the pizzazz of a cardboard box. The clunker shouldn't be allowed in the same time zone as his silver-and-black Carrera, fresh off the dealer's lot, still sporting paper plates.

Maggie looked better than ever. Her skinny jeans and tight T-shirt signaled a day off from the government grind. The Bureau had relaxed the dress code since Hoover's reign of terror, but not this much.

Though the owners had been gone only months, the mansion already showed signs of neglect. The grass needed mowing; the flower beds, weeding. An outdoor fountain had the dry heaves.

That's what happens when the feds gift-wrap a place with crime tape as the first step in forfeiture proceedings. There goes the neighborhood.

Judge Tapia had locked up Mariposa pending trial. Too many overseas accounts and missing assets to risk letting her run loose. A toss-up whether she'd live longer inside or out. No line on whether she'd survive to the trial date.

"Did you bring the keys?" Cash said.

Her look straddled concern and curiosity. "First, tell me why you want to go inside."

"I'm on a humanitarian mission."

Her expression changed. The new one said *not bloody likely.* "If you plan to remove something incriminating from the house, you're too late. Twenty of our finest executed a search here last month. You'll be lucky to find a dust bunny inside."

"I'm not here to help Mariposa beat the rap," he said.

"If the goal is to plant incriminating evidence, again too late."

"Just unlock the door," he said. "I won't be five minutes."

She looked over her shoulder. The street was quiet, except for the coughing of the fountain.

He touched her arm. "Big brother's not watching."

She moved toward the front door. "Ok, but I'm going in with you." Her tone nipped any debate.

"Fine by me." Once they were inside, he pointed right. "Head that way and open all the windows on the ground floor. I'll go left and do the same." They reunited at the back door. "Now hustle out the front door. I'll be right behind you."

Not exactly right behind her. More like thirty seconds later, he joined her on the lawn.

She looked puzzled. "I still don't see—"

He cut her off. "You will." He took her hand. She tensed but quickly relaxed and rested her head on his shoulder.

Flocks of butterflies flowed through the open windows. Rising like ribbons into the sky. Merging into a dark cloud that drifted south.

When the butterflies were out of sight, Cash and Maggie got into the Carrera. His hand froze short of the gear-stick, inches from the black butterfly perched there.

His foot pumped the pedal. The engine roared, purred, roared again.

The butterfly escaped through the open roof. A speck against the sky that quickly vanished.

Maggie fastened her seat belt. "Where to now?"

"We're going to get my soul back."

She laughed. "Where would we even start?"

He shifted into drive. "First stop, the home of the widow Biddle. Then I have some unfinished business at Seagoville."


THE END

# ACKNOWLEDGMENTS

At the head of a long line of people to thank are my parents, from whom I inherited a precious gift: a love of reading and writing. I am blessed to have in my life a wife, Regina, and daughter, Jessica, both writers themselves, who are infinitely patient and supportive.

I am eternally grateful to super-agents Jan Miller, Austin Miller and Nena Oshman at Dupree Miller & Associates. Jan is more than an agent to my family and me. She is a longtime friend, a confidant, and most importantly, the godmother of our only child.

It also takes a village to produce a book, and I had a great team at Savio Republic and Post Hill Press, including the dynamic duo of Debra Englander and Heather King.

I have the good fortune of being a small cog in a group of talented writers who break bread on Wednesdays and critique each other's works. The "Wednesday Night Writers' Conspiracy" includes: Jan Blankenship, Victoria Calder, Will Clarke, Peggy Fleming, Harry Hunsicker, Brent Jones, Fanchon Knott, Brooke Malouf, Julie Mitchell, Clif Nixon, David Norman, Glenna Whitley and Max Wright.

Finally, my belated and wholly inadequate thanks to lawyer and friend, Jim Blume, and my Austin angel, Erin Brown, both of whom love mysteries as much as I do and who have read every word I have written. My trusty sidekick, Veronica Long, who is my Della Street, makes working at a law firm fun.

# ABOUT THE AUTHOR

Paul Coggins is a nationally prominent criminal defense attorney, whose clients have included high-ranking politicians, Fortune 500 executives, professional athletes, nonprofit organizations, and government bodies. He is a former United States Attorney for the Northern District of Texas and is currently the president of the National Association of Former U.S. Attorneys.

He is a Rhodes Scholar, a former host of a popular radio call-in show, a frequent commentator for the media, and a contributor of articles for newspapers and magazines.

The Texas Attorney General has tapped him twice to represent the State of Texas, and the United States Court of Appeals for the Fifth Circuit recently appointed him to investigate allegations of wrongdoing involving federal court personnel.